A LADY'S REQUEST

Conor drew a lazy finger along the line of her jaw, then caught her chin in his hand and brushed his lips across hers.

Gus had closed her eyes in anticipation. Now she opened them to scowl. "Not that sort of kiss. I want you to kiss me like you once did. Even better, kiss me as if I were that dollymop who wished to dance with you. And I doubt very much that was all she wished to do!"

Gus was jealous. Why, Conor couldn't imagine, since he had his own suspicions about her reasons for wishing to be kissed. However, it was not his habit to argue with ladies who wanted kissing, especially since he felt very much like properly kissing Gus. He laid his hand against her cheek. She turned her face into it. The gesture moved him strangely. "Are you certain, Gus?"

Gus had never been more certain of anything. "If you refuse to kiss me properly, then who will? I don't wish to die without ever having had a proper kiss."

Conor slid his hand from her smooth cheek, along her graceful neck, and rested it on her nape. Her skin was the softest he had ever touched. With his other hand, Conor clasped her slender waist and drew her closer to him. "Are you planning to die soon?" he murmured, as he rained lazy kisses from her temple to the fine line of her jaw.

Faithless, wicked, irresistible as sin . . . His thumb traced lazy circles on her skin as his lips moved closer to hers . . .

Books by Maggie MacKeever

CUPID'S DART

LOVE MATCH

LOVER'S KNOT

Published by Zebra Books

LOVER'S KNOT

MAGGIE MACKEEVER

ZEBRA BOOKS
Kensington Publishing Corp.
http://www.zebrabooks.com

ZEBRA BOOKS are published by

Kensington Publishing Corp.
850 Third Avenue
New York, NY 10022

All Kensington titles, imprints and distributed lines are available at special quantity discounts for bulk purchases for sales promotion, premiums, fund-raising, educational or institutional use.

Special book excerpts or customized printings can also be created to fit specific needs. For details, write or phone the office of the Kensington Special Sales Manager: Kensington Publishing Corp., 850 Third Avenue, New York, NY 10022. Attn. Special Sales Department. Phone: 1-800-221-2647.

Zebra and the Z logo Reg. U.S. Pat. & TM Off.

First Printing: June 2004
10 9 8 7 6 5 4 3 2

Printed in the United States of America

ONE

Conor Melchers regarded the early morning sunlight with an unappreciative dark eye. Conor was not a fan of early morning in general; and the sunlight had only caught up with him this day because he hadn't yet been to bed. It was an especially fine, bright sun, burning through London's customary pall of sea-coal smoke and haze to glint and shimmer and sparkle and dance until it damned near gave a man a headache. Conor wondered why the devil some people fancied this ungodly hour.

Ah well, since he was up, he might as well make the best of it. He had an excellent reason for being awake, having spent the past several hours in the pleasant company of one of his favorite highflyers, a little opera dancer whose most impressive talents were demonstrated off the stage. The lady, having been especially inventive in her appreciation of his person, from the crown of his head right down to his toes, was the reason why Conor was whistling as he walked into the hustle and bustle of the Covent Garden market. More than one pedestrian turned to watch his progress, for Conor was a striking man, with a swarthy complexion, unruly silver-threaded dark hair, and strong white teeth that flashed when he smiled, his tall muscular person

set off nicely by a midnight blue coat, breeches, and
tall boots. Because the evening had been chill, he wore
a long topcoat.

Covent Garden was crowded with hawkers and vendors of everything from crockery and poultry to
birdcages and old iron, herbs and vegetables and fruit.
Wagons and carts had been arriving there ever since
daybreak, porters busily transferring merchandise to
the various stalls while the sky was still dark. Vegetables and fruits were to be found in one section of the
piazza, which was bounded on the north and east by
Inigo Jones's arcaded portico houses; potatoes and
coarser products were assigned a distinct quarter
nearer the Tuscan portico of St. Paul's Church; potted
flowers and plants bloomed on the west side of the
square. The center of the piazza was crowded with
sheds and stalls thrown up all higgedly-piggedly in a
great unruly, unorganized sprawl.

The air was filled with the shouts of vendors, the
clatter of donkeys and horses, the rattle of wagon
wheels on stone. Conor winked at a little lavender girl,
tossed a pieman and won, and stepped aside to avoid
colliding with a higgler who carried dead rabbits dangling from a pole. Fashionable Londoners rubbed
shoulders here with farmers and costermongers and
sellers of everything imaginable. Not that Conor expected to encounter any of his friends at this
uncivilized hour. He contemplated a ripe pineapple,
disdained a bunch of carrots, and paused by a display
of herbs and live hedgehogs.

"How 'bout a nice 'edge 'og, gov? Keep you clear of
bugs and earthworms and the such. 'Specially partial
to beetles, 'ogs are. See, 'ere's a fine little nipperkin."
The seedsman, a squat amiable-looking individual in

gray furze breeches and jacket and a battered felt hat, scooped up a hoglet in his hand. "Teeth good and strong for crunching," he added, as the hedgehog displayed a fine set. "Notice the fine color of the quills. Ears nicely rounded. Well shaped little tail. Proper number of toes—five on the front feet, and four on the back. Bright clear eyes."

Conor wondered if he had the appearance of being plagued by either beetles or earthworms. The hedgehog looked like an upside down quill-covered bowl, a sharp narrow face sticking out at one end. Amused, Conor held out his hand.

"Careful!" warned the seedsman. "'E might be feeling a bit peckish and mistake your finger for a bug. 'edge 'ogs don't see partic'ly well. If 'e *should* decide you'd be a tasty bite, don't pull away. 'E'll munch down all the 'arder if you're wiggling."

Conor was far too experienced to squeeze when he should stroke, or to wiggle when he should hold still. Gently he cupped the hedgehog in his palm. Soft fur covered its face and belly. The hedgehog felt like a bristly brush. An inquisitive bristly brush: it huffed and snuffled and inspected his hand thoroughly with a busy black little nose. Rather like a certain opera dancer not too long ago.

Conor judged the creature familiar enough with him to perhaps welcome a gentle scratch. He stroked a finger lightly over the quills that covered its rump. Bright black eyes looked up at him. Conor dared to stroke its forehead. The hedgehog seemed to consider this, then grunted, curled up in a ball, and purred.

Damned if the gent wasn't a knowing one, marveled the seedsman; 'e'd cast his winkers over the wares and unerringly picked out the cream of the 'oglet crop, for this young 'un was a prime goer, pretty behaved as could be until 'e 'eard a bug, and then off 'e'd go like a shot and gobble that little bugger right down. A 'og did fancy 'is bit o' crunch. So keen a sense of 'earing 'ad the nipperkin that 'e could track an earthworm by putting 'is ear to the ground. And agile—Strike the seedsman dead on the spot if 'e 'adn't seen this little 'og jump straight up and snatch a moth right out of the air. Quite a way the gent 'ad with a 'edge 'og, if 'e didn't mind one saying so as should know.

Conor didn't mind. He contemplated the round little body curled in the palm of his hand. The hedgehog twitched and snorted in its sleep.

Mr. Melchers was not without his own code of honor—he didn't seduce any lady who didn't wish to be seduced, for example; and young misses were (in general) safe from him. Although undeniably a rake-hell, a rascal, and the black sheep of his family, Conor was in his own way kind, and not a man to abuse any creature's trust. Since this creature clearly trusted him, it looked like he would be spending some time with a ball of quills. Or someone would.

Who among his acquaintance might fancy a hedgehog? The answer was not long presenting itself. Conor smiled. Even the seedsman blinked at that lazy, mocking, wicked smile, which had caused many a female to toss prudence to the winds and discover for herself just what this impenitent rascal could teach her about sin.

A round of bargaining commenced, at the end of which the seller pursed his lips and allowed that 'e'd known as soon as 'e clapped glaziers on the gent that 'e be'eld a 'ard bargainer, a cove with no flies on him, so to speak; and therefore 'e shouldn't be surprised that the gent 'ad made 'isself a very tol'able deal. Very tol'able indeed. Many more such shrewd bargainers and the seedsman would 'ave to find 'imself another line of business, so little profit 'ad 'e made.

Expectantly, he paused. Conor raised an eyebrow. A right knowing one, conceded the seedsman; and the nipperkin would fancy a bite of banana every now and then. Conor slipped the sleeping hedgehog gently into the pocket of his topcoat, and went on his way.

The piazza had grown increasingly crowded as the morning wore on. Carts creaked, horses neighed, donkeys brayed, vendors and shoppers haggled over wares. Beneath Conor's feet, the pavement was strewn with decaying vegetables and other refuse. The fragrant aroma of the flower girl's sweetbrier mingled with the stench of unwashed bodies and horse manure.

An uproar broke out in a nearby part of the market, where carts and wagons heavily laden with vegetables were drawn up double ranks deep. Conor strolled in that direction. Ordinarily, he might not have been drawn to investigate a commotion, but he had just pleasured a ladybird, and purchased a hedgehog, and was in an adventurous frame of mind. Onions from the Bedfordshire sands of Deptford, cabbages from Battersea, celery from Chelsea, asparagus from Mortlake—"Oh, curses!" shrilled a woman's voice, over the loud squealings of a pig. Conor stepped around a porter carrying a load of green peas and gooseberries.

It didn't surprise Conor in the slightest to find a female in the center of an uproar; in Conor's experience most uproars *did* involve females, which was one of the many things that made the fairer sex so endlessly interesting. This female, however, was not the sort generally found wandering around Covent Garden, neither market woman nor wench from the Turkish baths, brothels, gin houses, and gambling dens that thrived in the surrounding streets. If not Quality, the female looked respectable, dressed as she was in dreary black from the tips of her scuffed boots to the bonnet on her head. In one hand she clutched a shabby valise, and in the other a stout rope attached to a pig's red leather harness that was considerably more stylish than the young woman's dress. The pig himself was a handsome sparkling white, with dainty black split hooves, short little legs, bright black eyes, long drooping floppy ears, a pretty pink snout, and a curly tail; a splendid sort of pig that belied the old adage that one couldn't fashion a silk purse out of a porcine ear. Fully grown, this gentleman would have no problem whatsoever servicing two sows a day for several days in succession, would probably even demand a harem of his own.

Just now, however, it wasn't female pigflesh that the porker fancied. His head swung from side to side as he oinked and squealed and jerked at his makeshift leash, as might only be expected from a hungry fellow set down in the midst of twenty square yards covered with beautiful vegetables.

"Pontius!" The pig's owner tugged hard on his rope. "Behave yourself! Oh do hush, you wretched swine!"

He thought about it, truly he did; but food makes a pig happy, and whereas this pig would eat anything— as evidenced by the fine size of him—he especially fancied a fine turnip, and not far from his twitching nose and eager trotters was an entire wagonload of those vegetables. A nice fresh turnip, followed maybe by a juicy bunch of radishes, or some good green asparagus—

The pig heaved. His mistress hauled back on the

rope. He strained all the harder. She resisted all the more, and uttered a word or two that should not have graced a lady's lips.

Conor pushed through the milling crowd. He was not alone in enjoying the spectacle, but while Conor was observing merely with amusement, other spectators' intentions were less innocent. Some bystanders were covetous of the pig, which even at its young age would make a dandy meal or seven, for he already weighed upward of eight stone; while others had an eye on the young lady's valise. Covent Garden was a dangerous place for a respectable young woman without a chaperone, and the greedy pig could hardly qualify as such. Young the woman was, if past her first youth, with curly sandy hair, brown eyes, and a freckled snub nose in a nicely rounded face.

The inevitable happened, as frequently it does, when a determined-to-move object tussles with equally stubborn resistant force: the pig tugged, the young woman dug in her heels, and the rope broke. The pig barreled forward like a fresh-shot cannonball, while the young lady tumbled backward smack into a costermonger's cart. The cart collapsed, burying her beneath a pile of broken boards and cauliflower.

The pig paused, torn between the demands of his belly and his loyalty to the lady who generally saw to that belly being filled. It was a terrible temptation—turnips and radishes and cabbages and asparagus—but loyalty won out. The pig returned to paw and root and chew his way through the scattered cauliflower in search of his mistress, pausing between mouthfuls to squeal piercingly.

No longer amused, Conor chased off a number of people who were trying to grab hold of the pig and the valise; shoved aside the costermonger, who wanted to know who was going to pay for the damage to his cart and wares. "Quiet!" he said to the pig, which paused in midsqueal to blink at his stern tone; and to the costermonger said, "Help me get this garbage off the young lady, you dolt." Whereas the costermonger didn't care to hear his cauliflower spoken of in such a manner, not to mention himself, this was clearly a gentleman sufficiently well breeched to purchase any number of cauliflower carts. Too, the young lady *was* lying very still. It wouldn't be good for business were it to become common knowledge that his cauliflower had killed a gentry mort. He pulled a broken wooden plank off the girl, and heaved a sigh of relief when he saw her breast rise and fall.

As did Conor, and for once his practiced eye didn't linger to assess the breadth, and weight, and possible texture of that breast, but moved quickly to her face, so pale that her freckles stood out like inkblots. The ugly bonnet had been lost somewhere in the scuffle. Conor slipped his hand beneath her head. His fingers slipped in hot, sticky blood. "Gorblimey!" gasped the costermonger, as Conor lifted the bleeding woman into his arms.

TWO

Morning sunlight poured through the tall windows of an elegant establishment in Grosvenor Square, one of several residences belonging to the Countess of Witcham, a grand structure in the Palladian style that possessed not only its own garden but also a water closet with a valve at the bottom of the bowl that worked on a hinge. Lady Ysabella's houseguests, having already inspected this marvel and having oohed and aahed appropriately, were now seated around an oval table in the breakfast room. The table was made of wood brought from Honduras, reddish in color, of a fine close grain. The walls of the room were painted white; the floor was of polished oak; the coved ceiling had a cornice enriched with classical ornament, and an oval centerpiece embellished with leaves and fruit and swags. More decorative carving framed the windows and doorway.

The youngest member of the party, Miss Annette Slyte, sat a little apart from the others, her nose stuck in a magazine. Sunlight streaming through the window caressed her sprig muslin gown, making a gilded halo of her hair. Just turned seventeen, Miss Annette was surely the most ravishing damsel ever set down upon the earth. While she bore a strong resemblance to her brother and her aunt, who were also seated at the table, Annette's glorious curls were so dazzlingly golden as to make theirs seem a paltry yellow; her eyes a brilliant bewitching blue while theirs were only bright; her pale cheeks colored naturally with the softest rose; her petite person pure perfection from her dainty ankles to her retroussé little nose. If the young lady had a flaw at all, which was debatable, it was the tiny space between her upper two front teeth, which drew attention to lips that were as plump and kissable as any ever seen.

Just now, those lips were forming silent words as one dainty little finger followed along a line of print. Having looked at all the pictures, Annette was now picking through "Hints for the conduct of females who have by accident taken fire," which contained a great number of words that she didn't understand. Nor did she understand why the other members of the party were playing cards at the breakfast table, but then she wasn't accustomed to town ways.

On the table sat the remnants of a light repast. The ladies had refreshed themselves with tea and muffins, while the gentleman had regaled himself with beefsteak and a couple eggs. Also on the table, along with teapot and milk pot and sugar dish, was a large pile of buttons of every conceivable style. Silver buttons, gold and brass; carved buttons, inlaid and stamped; buttons with exquisite scenes painted on ivory glass; engraved buttons, bone buttons, buttons wound around with intricate metal thread. Lady Ysabella—who wore a pale blue gown trimmed with lace, and looked nowhere near her seven-and-forty years, despite the wire-rimmed spectacles perched upon her elegant nose—scooped up all the buttons. "I win. Again."

"It's enough to put anyone off his breakfast," said

her nephew, who was *en déshabillé* in shirtsleeves, breeches, and boots. "If you wasn't my aunt, I'd think you fuzzed the cards."

"Calumny," retorted the countess without rancor, and reached for the teapot. The third card player said nothing, but gazed wistfully at the button pile. A woman in her early thirties, Lady Augusta had chestnut hair drawn back in ringlets, gray eyes beneath sharply defined brows, and elegant features marred with discontent. This morning she wore a long-sleeved gown fashioned from green chintz.

The gentleman toyed with the sugar dish. "Aunt Syb has the luck of the devil. While our Gus has no luck at all."

That lady's aristocratic nose twitched with irritation. "Go to blazes, Nigel. And I'm not your Gus."

"No," Nigel said cheerfully. "You're nobody's Gus. Nor are you like to be with that Friday face. Is it so bad that Aunt Syb dragged you to London? Even you must admit that things could be in a worse case."

Lady Augusta looked at the fourth member of the party, who having not been invited to join in the card game, was reading—or attempting to—the latest issue of *The Lady's Magazine*. "And probably will be," she remarked.

Mr. Slyte followed her glance. Lady Ysabella also regarded the reader with a distinct lack of enthusiasm, and sighed.

Belatedly aware of the silence in the room, Annette looked up from her page. "Is it improper of me to be reading while you are talking? I did not mean to be rude. Did you lose again, Lady Augusta?"

Nigel snickered. Lady Augusta's nose twitched.

"*Why* do you play when you never win?" Annette added. "I don't understand."

No one at the table was sufficiently unkind as to point out that there were many things the young lady didn't understand. "Gus plays because she cannot help it," said Nigel. "As you cannot being so beautiful that all the young bucks look at you as if they could eat you without salt."

"*Eat* me?" Annette wrinkled her pretty brow. "Why would they want to do that?"

Gus reached for a muffin and slathered it with butter. Lady Ysabella poured more tea into her cup. There was good reason why Nigel, who nicknamed everyone, called this particular sister Nit. "Lord help us." He sighed. "I mean that you'll be all the crack."

Annette wondered what the Creator had to do with her London Season. As the acknowledged beauty of her large family, it was her responsibility to marry well. Nit looked forward to having her own household, where she could do anything she wished, or *not* do it, which was more likely; and drink chocolate at any hour of the night or day; and no one would dare tell her that she was foolish except her husband, and *he* wouldn't mind if she was foolish because he'd be too busy worshipping the ground beneath her feet. Even though it was not fashionable, Nit intended to be loved. To that end, she would not bite her nails, or yawn, or drum her feet upon the floor; she would not fidget or cross her legs or laugh immoderately loud; she would not express forcible opinions, no difficult task, because if Nit had any opinions—and she didn't think she did—they would surely not be *forcible*; and she had practiced her curtsy until she could genuflect to the Queen without sending her petticoats flying over her head. Now it only remained to select the gentleman who would best appreciate the paragon she'd become.

Thoughtfully, she chewed her lower lip. "I must have a duke, I think. Or at the very least an earl. He will fall in love with me at first sight, and sing serenades beneath my window, and send me billets doux."

Lady Syb picked up the cards and began shuffling them. "No billets doux, I beg you. No rapprochements, no tête-à -tetes."

Nit hoped she wasn't being denied something splendid. "What's a rapprochement?" she asked.

"A nasty thing," said Nigel, quickly. "You don't wish to know."

Did she not? Nit gave her brother a searching glance. Still, he was older, and a gentleman, and must know what was best.

Even if she could not have billets-doux, or rapprochements, whatever they were, Nit was eager to get about the business of finding herself a doting husband so she could start having babies, although she was uncertain how one went about the business, and had the vague notion that it had something to do with a cabbage patch. Meanwhile she must make the best of her opportunities, and not give Lady Syb a disgust, so that the countess might be inclined to repeat her generosity when the next Slyte damsel came of age.

And Lady Syb *was* generous. Already Nit had visited milliners and modistes and mantua makers, had gone with her aunt to Ackerman's—this despite her brother's comment that it was hardly worth the effort since she could barely read, which was most unfair because Nit could read very well so long as the words didn't have an unnatural number of syllables, not that she took her brother's words to heart, because she knew Nigel doted on her, no matter what he said —had been talked out of a pair of scarlet stockings; and enjoyed an ice at Gunther's in Berkeley Square. She had been displayed in her aunt's dashing curricle in Hyde Park; had been seen at the Opera House; and had taken part in a small musical evening at Lady Webster's, where she had conducted herself quite nicely, and forgotten not a single word.

Lady Augusta had gone shopping with them also, though she said she didn't wish to, and had been gifted with new clothes of her own, which she didn't appear to appreciate in the least. Through lowered lashes— thick, of course, and astonishingly dark for a damsel so fair—Nit watched Gus follow Aunt Syb's fingers on the cards. Poor Lady Augusta would never get married and have babies, which was probably a good thing for the babies, because she was so very cross. "Why do you play for buttons?" Nit asked.

Nigel watched his aunt demonstrate a perfect pasteboard waterfall. "We're playing for buttons because Aunt Syb has cleaned us out. Gus is in the basket, and I haven't a feather to fly with myself. Or a button to hold up my breeches! When I stand up, they'll fall down around my ankles. 'Twill be a shocking sight."

"Speaking of enough to put anyone off his breakfast," remarked Gus. "Don't look so stricken, Annette! Your brother is bamming you again."

Nit frowned at Nigel, an expression that sat on her perfect features as gloriously as did any other. "He must be as forgetful as I am. Because if he *wasn't*, he'd remember that I'm a ninnyhammer, and wouldn't try and bamboozle me, because I sometimes take him seriously when I should not."

Nigel had the grace to look ashamed of himself. "A facer," murmured Gus. Lady Ysabella abandoned the cards and began to sort through the post. Gus picked up the deck.

Annette watched her riffle the cards. "Why does Lady Augusta keep playing when she never wins?" she repeated.

"Speaking of facers," murmured Lady Syb.

Gus studied her cards. "I play because I must, as Nigel has already told you. May we talk about something else?"

"I'm sorry!" Nit clapped her hands to her mouth. "I forgot. Your brother—"

"Aunt Syb is going to open a button-selling shop," Nigel interrupted, and Lady Syb looked up from the post to frown at her niece. "Gus will manage it for her. Believe that clanker and I'll tell you another, sis! You must get over this habit of literal-mindedness, because if you take everyone you meet in London at his word, you're bound to get into a scrape."

Annette promptly forgot about Lady Augusta's shameless brother, who'd gambled away the family fortune and then fled the country, leaving his sister to try and pick up the pieces of her life. "You think I'm going to make a cake of myself!" she wailed.

"No, he doesn't. Your brother knows you'll do just as Lady Syb says you should." Under cover of the table, Gus kicked him. "*Don't* you, Nigel?"

Nigel knew that his sister hadn't far to go before reaching her wit's end. "You'll be all the crack! Said it before, didn't I? Bound to cast all the other hopefuls in the shade. Make all the matchmaking mamas wish to slit their wrists in utter despair."

Nit giggled, all her gloom forgotten. "What a hand you are! Mama would say you've taken a maggot into your brain."

Lady Syb roused from the missive she'd been reading. "Gentlemen don't have maggots," she said, sternly. "And we have received vouchers for Almack's, Annette."

"Almack's!" Nit clapped her hands together and bounced in her chair. "Jupiter! I don't think I have ever been more pleased with anything in all my life, Aunt Syb!"

And so she should have been pleased, for those fortunate young ladies making their come-out at an Almack's ball had their dancing partners personally chosen for them, by one of the lady patronesses, from the cream of London society. Nigel wondered which of those forbidding ladies his aunt had blackmailed. "That's the same thing you said yesterday when I took you to Astley's," he pointed out.

"Yes, but I *mean* it now!" cried Nit, then frowned. "Although I also meant it then."

"Nor do ladies say 'Jupiter.'" Lady Syb folded the spectacles, which she used only for close work, and sometimes not even then, depending on the vanity of the moment, and tucked them away. "You must promise me that you won't dance until you are given permission, Annette."

"I promise that I shall do exactly as you tell me!" So excited was Nit that she practically danced on her wooden chair.

"Providing she remembers it," murmured Nigel. "Which we *can't* count on." Gus said nothing, but laid out a hand of patience and studied her cards.

Nit could have hugged herself, she was so excited. Matrimony and babies lay just around the corner, and meanwhile she was to make her appearance in Almack's Assembly Rooms in King's Street, St. James's, where three-quarters of the nobility were not privileged to set foot. "Have you been to Almack's, Lady Augusta?" she asked, then answered herself without pausing for breath. "How silly I am. Of course you have. Do you remember what it was like?"

Lady Augusta wasn't long on forbearance. "Of course I remember. I'm not in my dotage yet."

Nigel tsk'd. "Shame on you, Nit. It's not nice to remind poor Gus that she's on the shelf."

"You've done nothing wrong, Annette!" Lady Syb said quickly, in response to that young lady's quivering chin. "Your brother was teasing you again. You will stop it at once, Nigel. And you will apologize to Gus."

"No, he won't," said Lady Augusta. "I wouldn't wish him to compromise his principles. Yes, I remember Almack's. I liked it very much."

"No, you didn't," murmured the irrepressible Mr. Slyte. "Weak tea and tepid lemonade. Good of you not to wish to spoil Nit's pleasure, though I doubt you could. She's a happy creature. Her totty-headedness makes it easy to forget the things that make her sad." He paused. "Which now I think on it, ain't a bad way to be."

Gus glared at him. "If you dare suggest I try it myself, I swear I won't be responsible for what I do."

Nit felt sorry for Lady Augusta. It must be very hard to be a poor relation like she was. Although she wasn't all *that* poor because her cousin the duke had restored her dowry, even though she couldn't act as his hostess anymore because he'd taken himself a wife. Still, even with her dowry, what gentleman would wish to wed such a gloomy Gus, even if she wasn't so long in the tooth as to be leading apes in hell? *Not* that a young lady on the verge of making her come-out should use such a phrase. Annette giggled at herself.

Lady Syb unwittingly brought her niece back to the

present. "But that's a horse of a different color," she remarked.

Nit perked up. Horses were her passion. She knew the difference between an Andalusan and a Traeker and a Dutch Warmblood, although her personal favorite was a Hanoveran; and she was familiar with all the different paces from the common trot, canter, and gallop through the asymmetrical to the *paso fino* and the rack. Her own sweet little mare, Fancy, had been left reluctantly at home, for fear Nit would forget herself and gallop in Hyde Park.

She looked around the breakfast room. "Horse? Where?" Nit asked.

Lady Syb, who had been talking not about horseflesh but about the latest development in the ongoing hostilities between the Prince of Wales and his princess, dropped her head into her hands. "Oh!" said Nit, with sympathy. "Have you the headache again? Perhaps you should go to bed and I will pour some lavender water on your brow."

Gus swallowed a laugh. "One doesn't *pour* lavender water, Annette. One massages it into one's temples, or dampens a cloth."

Nit scrunched up her lovely face as she considered this. "I knew I must have got it wrong!"

Nigel looked up as the tall, cadaverous, white-haired butler scratched at the door, then stepped into the room. "Come to join us for breakfast, have you, Mortimer?"

The butler—whose name, in fact, *wasn't* Mortimer, but something deemed not sufficiently butlerlike by the irreverent Nigel so many years ago that not even Mortimer now remembered his real name—didn't acknowledge this sally by so much as a muscle twitch.

"Mr. Melchers wishes a word with you, milady. On a matter of some urgency."

Nit sat up even straighter. "Oh! A gentleman!"

"*Not* a gentleman," said Nigel sternly, as Lady Syb rose to precede her butler into the hallway. "A rakehell. You will have nothing to do with him, or I will have to challenge him to a duel, in which case he will shoot me, because he is better with firearms than I am. You wouldn't like to see your favorite brother shot dead."

Nit frowned enchantingly as she considered this. "No. Although I think my favorite brother is Luke, but perhaps I think that only because he isn't here!" She giggled at her cleverness. "What is a rakehell?"

"A gentleman who females fuss over," explained Gus, as Nigel rolled his eyes heavenward. She lowered her voice. "Oh, to be that young."

"You *were* that young once," said Nigel. "I remember it. For that matter, so was I."

Gus watched Nit pick up her magazine and begin to struggle through a description of Brighthelmstone. "I was never that beautiful."

"No one was ever that beautiful. *Or* that empty-headed, including you," Nigel retorted, irritably. Gus gave him an astonished look.

Whether Mr. Slyte did or didn't mean to compliment his companion—most likely he didn't, since they had been for years at daggers drawn—remained unclear. Lady Syb returned to the room with Conor Melchers in tow. Lady Augusta glanced up at him and scowled. "Prunes!" snapped Lady Syb. Gus sighed and smoothed her brow.

Conor raised an inquiring eyebrow. "Aunt Syb is trying to teach Gus not to frown," Nigel explained. "She ain't having a great deal of success."

Nit dropped her magazine to study the newcomer. "Is this the rakehell? You didn't tell me he was *old*."

Conor looked startled, Nigel grinned, and Lady Syb tsk'd. Gus burst out laughing, which transformed her into someone younger, prettier, and considerably more approachable.

Nit flushed guiltily. "I didn't mean to hurt your feelings. Despite your age, you are still very comely, sir!"

Gus doubled over with merriment. Nigel pounded her on the back. "Thank you," Conor said gravely. "I promise you, my feelings are not hurt."

Annette regarded him, head tilted to one side. "*Do* females fuss over you, like Lady Augusta said? Perhaps it is because you have so very nice a smile."

"Enough!" Lady Syb put her hands to her temples and gave them a brisk rub. "Augusta, I need you. Nigel, stay here and keep your sister entertained."

That something was in the wind was obvious to everyone but Nit, who was delighted to have an opportunity to have her brother to herself, an event that Nigel tried hard to avoid, for fear he'd throttle her. "Oh, will you play cards with me, Nigel?" she begged. "I especially wish to learn to play piquet!"

At the notion of teaching—or trying to teach—the intricacies of piquet to his sister, all Nigel's mirth fled. "Point, sequence and set," murmured Gus, as she crossed the room to where Conor waited with Lady Syb.

Mortimer hovered in the doorway. In all his years with Lady Ysabella, this was her queerest start yet. And now, if he read the signs aright, she was going to sweep right past him without so much as a word.

The butler cleared his throat. "Milady," he said emotionlessly. "You have not said what you wish us to do about the pig."

THREE

While Mr. Slyte attempted to explain to his sister the difference between pique and repique, and what made up a *parti,* and Mortimer struggled with the matter of the pig, the remaining members of the household— save, of course, the innumerable servants—gathered in the blue bedroom, so called due to the color of the damask bed and window hangings, and the silk upon the walls, and watched as the physician examined the young woman who lay unconscious in the domed tester bed. The countess and Augusta, with the aid of Lady Syb's long-suffering abigail Throckmorton, had managed to wrestle the strange young woman out of her dreary black dress and into a crisp nightgown, Lady Syb overriding all objections with her firm opinion that one's spirits were always elevated by clean clothes, even when in a state of senselessness. At the foot of the bed stood Conor Melchers, who had not been present for these efforts, although he probably had as much experience in dressing and undressing females as the three women, if not more.

The physician, Sir Edmond Jessop, was a no-nonsense sort of gentleman, brisk and efficient and close to Lady Ysabella's age, who had received his knighthood for certain delicate undertakings performed on behalf of the Crown. His expression was somber as he inspected the young woman's injured head with deft and gentle hands. "Has she vomited?" he asked. Lady Syb looked inquiringly at Conor, who shook his head.

Sir Edmond was long acquainted with Lady Ysabella—who was prone to threaten to turn up her toes when she was feeling bored, or irritable, or both—and her circle of friends, including Conor Melchers, that notorious connoisseur of females. This particular female Sir Edmond judged to be in her midtwenties, sturdily formed but not overly well-fleshed; not a pretty woman but one whose features might be pleasant enough were they not so waxen, and were her sandy curls not matted with blood. He reached for the basin of hot water that a maidservant had placed upon a nearby table, and carefully washed away dried matter from around the wound. "You have no idea who she is?"

Lady Syb hovered at his elbow. "We know nothing more about her than that Conor brought her here. There was an accident—something to do with a wagonful of cauliflowers and a pig. You needn't look so skeptical, Edmond. I have met the pig. And you must admit that this young woman is hardly in Conor's style."

"It was obvious to me that she was respectable," offered Conor. "So I brought her to Lady Syb."

Gus cast a disapproving glance at Mr. Melchers' evening coat. Who better to know whether a female was respectable or not? "Considerate of you," she muttered. "Since taking her to *your* home would surely have meant her ruin."

Conor quirked an eyebrow. "Have I neglected you, sweeting? Pray consider yourself welcome in my home at any time."

Gus bit her lip against a rude remark. Conor Melchers was nigh irresistible, and she wasn't about to succumb to such practiced charm, much as she might like to, which didn't say a great deal for her common sense. There was some consolation, she supposed, in that every female who crossed the wretch's path experienced the same mizzy-mindedness. Except for Nit, who was mizzy-minded to begin with, and perhaps therefore immune.

Conor wondered why Gus was smiling. A private amusement at his expense, no doubt. He didn't begrudge it to her. Lady Augusta found little enough to smile about.

Sir Edmond removed a pretty porcelain container from his bag. "She'll have to be bled." Lady Syb, who was accustomed to having leeches administered for her headaches—although she also swore by the efficacy of an infusion of lemon water and orange flowers, along with a nice foot bath—didn't blink an eyelash. Gus, who loathed the slimy creatures, backed away.

Conor didn't care for leeches himself, though the sight of them didn't cause him to turn green. He studied Gus. A slender woman, fine-boned as a thoroughbred, and as skittish; thick chestnut hair, strongly marked dark brows, patrician features, fine fair skin, very pretty lips when they weren't being primmed—and stormy gray eyes, which were glaring at him. A queasy-looking woman who was in sore need of distraction. Conor was excellent at providing distraction. "Prunes?" he said.

Gus looked no less irritated. "You know that Lady Syb must have a project. Although I have been in large part supplanted by Nigel's sister, thank God. I'm not sure Lady Syb hasn't taken on more than even she can handle this time. She's already threatened to cut Nigel out of her will twice this week."

Lady Ysabella was as irresistible as a force of nature, as a number of people had already learned, including the Prince of Wales and several elder statesmen, not to mention one of the lady patronesses of Almack's. "Why did you tell that feather-headed child that females fuss over me?" Conor asked.

Gus's scowl relaxed, marginally. "Nit wanted to know what a rakehell was. Don't look so disapproving. It was Nigel who named you that and unfortunately it fits."

Disapproval was not an emotion that figured large in Conor's repertoire. More often he was amused by the foibles of his fellow man. Or woman, in this case. Lady Augusta made no secret of her dislike of him, and it amused him to set up her back. "You are full of surprises. I didn't realize you were an authority on rakehells."

How was it that in every conversation with this man she found herself at a disadvantage? "Don't try and charm *me*!" Gus snapped.

'Twas an unfair accusation. Conor never had to *try* and charm a lady. "You wound me. Again. Dearest Gus, how fortunate that I can always trust you to prevent me from having too high an opinion of myself."

Gus was no one's dearest. Nor did she wish to be. And even *did* she wish to be, it was a great deal too late for that, for she had turned into a cross-grained contrary female with neither fortune to recommend her, nor beauty or youth. "I'm a shrew. I admit it. I wish you would go away."

Conor didn't doubt she meant it. "You forget that I have been a Good Samaritan. You must allow me to

savor the moment. Virtue being so foreign to a nature
so depraved as mine, as you are fond of pointing out."

Gus was not so green as to be drawn into a discussion about virtue, or the lack thereof, with Conor
Melchers. She shot him a scathing look, then returned
her attention to the still figure on the bed.

Sir Edmond had placed six leeches around the
wound, and now was conferring with Throckmorton
and Lady Syb. "It's encouraging that she hasn't vomited, but her pupils are contracted, and her pulse is
small and weak. There is little question but that she has
a concussion of the brain."

Not the squeamish sort, the countess watched the
once-skinny leeches swelling up with blood. Less stalwart than her mistress, Throckmorton fixed her gaze
on a curved bedpost. "What can be done for her?"
asked Lady Syb.

"Little enough." One of the leeches having drunk its
fill, Sir Edmond placed it back in the jar. "Above all,
she must not be moved. Keep her warm, especially her
feet; and cool her head with ice. Her diet must be reg-
ulated to the lowest ebb, though she may be given
barley water if she will drink. The stupor may continue
for a shorter or longer period, according to the violence
of the shock. We have found that the chief danger after
a concussion of the brain is inflammation affecting either the organ itself or its covering membranes."

Physicians, even the best of them, which Sir Edmond was, were overly fond of hearing themselves
speak. "Which means what, in ordinary terms?" demanded Lady Syb.

"It means that it's too soon to assess the extent of the
damage, and that someone must be with her at all
times." Sir Edmond returned another bloated leech to

its porcelain cage. "The violence of the injury may go beyond simple concussion. There may be a rupture of the substance of the brain, or of a single vessel, causing an effusion of blood. In such a case, the individual may never rally from the first condition of unconsciousness, or may rally only partially."

"In other words," said Lady Syb, with the callousness of a woman who had outlived several husbands, "the girl may die."

Sir Edmond did not care to hear it put so bluntly. "I do not think the injury is so serious as that. If the case *should* run on to a fatal termination, there is generally apoplectic stupor, paralysis, convulsions, one or all of them. You must be on the alert. It is very good of you to take in a stranger, Lady Ysabella."

"Pish tush!" said Lady Syb, who enjoyed a challenge, and was even then fancying herself engaged with the Grim Reaper in a wrestling match, a tussle which would probably prove less strenuous than seeing Nit through a London Season without mishap. She laid her fingers lightly on the young woman's cool cheek. "Surely the poor child has a family. If only Conor hadn't lost her valise!"

"So much for being a Good Samaritan," murmured Gus.

"Ah," countered Conor. "But I didn't lose the pig."

"A pig, of all things," mused Sir Edmond as he prepared a dressing.

"Am I supposed to be grateful?" asked Lady Syb.

"Yes," retorted Conor. "Because I didn't also bring you a wagonload of mangled cauliflowers, which I might well have done, since I paid for them. In all the confusion, someone must have made off with her bag.

I doubt there was much of value in it, for it was a shabby thing, but it might have told us more about her."

Lady Syb looked at the young woman's freckled face and capable hands. "She has spent some time outdoors. And there are no calluses on her palms."

Conor lifted his hands. "Say no more. I'm off to Covent Gardens in search of a missing valise."

Lady Syb glanced at Augusta, whose skin was still tinged green. Her plans didn't include tending to a second invalid. "Take Gus with you. The fresh air will do her good."

Gus didn't know how fresh London's air could be said to be, but it was preferable to leeches, four of which were still stuck, fat and bloated, to the woman on the bed. She followed Conor into the hallway.

He smiled down at her. "Odd to find me the lesser of two evils, isn't it? Fetch your cloak. It's still cool outside."

Gus disliked to be given orders. She opened her mouth to tell Mr. Melchers that she had changed her mind, because he wasn't the lesser of any evils, and furthermore she would rather have leeches applied to her own body than go anywhere with him, none of which was true, but it would have been an excellent venting of her spleen. The expression on his face stopped her. Conor seldom frowned.

Even less often did he feel chagrined. Conor had forgotten about his purchase. He hoped it hadn't suffocated in the pocket of his coat. Gently he scooped up the hoglet and brought it carefully out into the light. None the worse for its adventure, the hedgehog blinked, uncurled itself, stretched, and gave a huge yawn. Gus stared in astonishment.

Conor held out his hand. "It reminded me of you."

The hedgehog resembled a stack of finely packed needles. Gus supposed she should take offense. "Consider this little one a peace offering," Conor added. "You have been angry with me so long that I have forgot precisely why. Hold out your hand."

Gus remembered precisely why she was angry with Conor. She did not care to enlighten him. She frowned at the small creature in his hand.

Irritation struggled with curiosity, and curiosity won out. Gingerly, Gus took the hedgehog on her palm. The little black nose twitched, the little mouth opened slightly, and the upper lip curled; the hedgehog huffed at her.

Gus didn't know if she should huff back or drop the creature. "It likes to be stroked," Conor suggested.

Anything would like being stroked by Conor, thought Gus; being stroked by her was quite something else. Gingerly, she touched her finger to the hedgehog's back. When the creature didn't hiss or bite, she relaxed a little bit, and dared tickle one soft ear.

Conor remained silent. To glimpse Lady Augusta in an unguarded moment was rare indeed. She held her breath as the hedgehog began to explore her hand and wrist. With soft snuffling sounds, it crawled up her arm, and Gus smiled with delight.

Conor scooped up the hedgehog before it could get tangled in her hair, and settled it on her forearm. "You're welcome," he said gently. "Now fetch your cloak. I'll wait for you downstairs."

Gus opened her mouth, then closed it, and turned hastily away, because for the life of her she could think of nothing to say. Conor was no more to be trusted in this moment of generosity than in any other. The man could charm birds out of their trees, or ladybirds out of their corsets, if ladybirds *wore* corsets, a subject about which he would know a great deal more than she. Cradling her hedgehog, Gus strode briskly down the hall.

FOUR

Abby awoke from a confused dream of bell ringers and brewing ale to find herself tucked up in a very comfortable domed bed in a strange blue bedroom, wearing a nightgown she'd never seen before, and nursing a throbbing head. More blue hung at the sunny windows, and a patterned carpet lay upon the floor.

Gingerly, she turned her head on the pillow. Serpentine-fronted bureau dressing table with asymmetrical handles and brass work, tallboy chest of drawers; open-fronted corner basin stand—and a long-legged angel sprawled in an elegant upholstered chair. An angel in snug breeches and snowy linen, with a face that might have fairly been called beautiful if it were not so masculine, guinea gold hair styled *à la Brutus*, and elegant sideburns extending down toward his chin.

For a startled moment, Abby thought she'd died and gone to heaven. Then she saw the hedgehog snoozing on the vision's knee. Were hedgehogs allowed in heaven? "Pontius," she whispered.

The angel, who'd been napping, opened bright blue eyes. "As in Pilate? I am not so infamous as all that. At least *I* don't think I am, but my family might not agree. Fortunately, none of them are with us at the moment. My name is Nigel."

She had not died, decided Abby. No angel ever had such a mischievous look. She tried hard to focus her attention. "Not you. My pig."

The young woman was well-spoken, mused Nigel. And she didn't look the least bit like his sisters, thank God. Or like Gus. Nigel suspected this young woman would be more likely to smile than frown, though he didn't know why he thought that, for she wasn't smiling at the moment, but was looking perplexed. "Of course. Pontius the pig. It makes perfect sense. Cook has taken your Pontius in hand. No, don't look so stricken! He ain't been turned into a roast. We rather thought he was a pet from the way he made himself at home. Cook says he is a very friendly and well-mannered fellow, and has made him up a bed by the kitchen hearth. I'm sure you would like him with you, but Aunt Syb balks at having a pig abovestairs."

Pontius was safe. Abby sagged with relief. Then she wondered why she had thought he might not be. She also wondered where she was, and why her head ached so abominably. Gingerly she raised her hand to touch it, and found a bandage there.

"I'm afraid some of your hair had to be cut off," said Nigel. "Do you know anything about hedgehogs? It's not *my* hedgehog; Conor gave it to Gus, which makes perfect sense, because Gus is a bit of a hedgehog herself. But Aunt Syb sent them off on an errand, and Gus gave me the creature to tend." He looked at the snoozing creature doubtfully. "However one tends a hedgehog. At least it ain't bit me yet."

Was she acquainted with hedgehogs? Abby was uncertain. This hedgehog looked considerably more comfortable on the gentleman's knee than the gentleman looked having it there. "Give it here," she said.

Gingerly, Nigel scooped up the hedgehog and deposited it in her lap. Unaccustomed to as much excitement as it had already experienced this day, the hoglet blinked at this new stranger, gave a token huff, then curled up in the crook of her elbow and went back to sleep. Abby touched its bristles. "What a very nice hedgehog."

This, decided Nigel, was a very nice young woman. Aunt Syb would be pleased. Whether the young woman would be pleased by Aunt Syb remained to be seen.

"You will be wondering where you are," he said comfortably. "We've been wondering *who* you are. I'll go first, shall I? You're in my aunt's home in Grosvenor Square. Aunt Syb will be very sorry that she wasn't here when you woke up, but she's overseeing my sister Nit's come-out. I told her she'd regret it, and she already has, not that she'll admit it, because she's as stubborn a female as ever drew breath. Gus and Conor are out making inquiries, so you're stuck with me. How are you feeling? None the better for my asking, I make no doubt."

Abby was dazed and confused. Still, there was something soothing about the golden gentleman's nonsense. "Nit?" she asked.

"Annette," explained Nigel. "My sister, or one of them. You're not up to meeting Nit yet; she'd give you a fever of the brain. Stands to reason: She gives the rest of us a fever of the brain, and *we* ain't been hit on the head. In case you don't know it, you've had a wagonful of cauliflowers collapse on you. I ain't clear exactly on how it happened, but it had to do with your pig."

Cauliflowers? Grosvenor Square? "I'm in London?" Abby said slowly. "I don't understand."

Neither did Nigel. Why, for example, should someone name a pig Pontius? For that matter, why should one name a pig anything at all? "You were in Covent Garden. There was an accident. Perhaps you might recall what business you had there."

Abby clutched the coverlet. Her hands looked foreign to her, capable and short-nailed and altogether strange. The hedgehog snuffled, and she stroked it absently. Why had she gone to Covent Garden? For that matter, why was she in London? She whispered, "I don't know."

For all his prattle, Nigel was shrewd, and this strange young woman was much too tense and pale. "Never mind! Your poor head probably still hurts. I daresay you're thirsty, but I'm not allowed to offer you alcoholic stimulant, though if I was you I'd want some, waking up to find someone nattering away at you like this." He poured some barley water into a glass and helped her sit up to drink.

His arm was warm against her back. He smelled of leather, and clean linen, and the pomade he'd put on his hair. Abby didn't think she'd ever seen a more handsome man. Not that she could remember any other men at all, which was a puzzle in itself. Cautiously, careful not to further disturb the snoozing hedgehog, she drank.

Nigel was not so odd a choice for a nursemaid as might at first appear. Due to the earliness of the hour, it was not yet time to go visit the clubs or do any of the other things so beloved of gentlemen of fashion, all of which secretly bored him half to death; and due to his numerous active siblings, Nigel was not unacquainted with injuries. He laid his hand against the young woman's cool forehead, then peered into her eyes, which were a very pretty honey brown. They were also, at the moment, puzzled. Since she didn't appear on the verge of paralysis or convulsions or apoplexy, he adjusted the pillows behind her head. "We'll start with the simple things. Tell me your name."

Abby winced as she settled back against the pillows. "Abby," she said, then paused, and turned paler still.

Nigel set the glass back down on the table. "Abby is a very nice name," he said, encouragingly. "And your last name is—"

Abby stared at him. "I don't know."

She looked very frightened. Nigel perched carefully on the edge of the bed. "You ain't an unfortunate female, are you? Aunt Syb might not like that. Although Conor wouldn't mind. Probably Aunt Syb wouldn't mind either, now that I think on it, but she'd probably set about reforming you, and you might not like that."

Abby's poor head might be stuffed with such queer snippets as a collection of spiders and stuffed birds and homemade soup, but she recognized that her not-angelic companion was trying to be kind. "Has she reformed *you?*" she inquired.

Nigel grinned at this sign of spirit. "No, but she ain't given up yet. You'll distract her with not knowing who you are. Damned if I'm not in your debt."

"What you are," said Abby, "is a humbug. And on purpose, I think. Whoever I am, I can't be a burden to you and your aunt."

"Yes, you can," Nigel said, and placed a restraining hand on her shoulder. "Aunt Syb will disinherit me again if I let you out of that bed. Besides, where do you plan to go, since you don't know who you are? And who do you think will feed that handsome pig of yours, or prevent him from ending up on someone's dinner table with an apple stuck in his mouth? Even if it ain't what you're used to, you're much better off with us."

Abby's brief attempt at rising convinced her of the wisdom of his words. The room swam around her, and she sank back against the pillows. "Cool cloths," said Nigel, and plopped one on her brow. "If I leave you alone, do you think that you might rest?"

"No." Abby clutched his arm. Whether she rested or not, she didn't wish to be left alone. "Please don't go. Tell me about your other sisters. Are they all like Annette?"

Nigel looked at the hand clutching his jacket. He wouldn't be the one to tell Abby that she appeared to be in mourning, judging from her dreary black gown. Not that he'd seen the garment himself, but his valet Bees—short for Beeson, because the man was so infernally busy—had been horrified. Himself, Nigel preferred a bit of color. Quite a lot of color, actually, although to date Bees had prevented him from mixing clocks and stripes. 'Twas only a matter of time, however. Nigel planned just such an ensemble for the next time Lady Syb appeared to be growing bored, a time that had receded some distance into the future, between Gus and Nit and now this stranger in the house. In Abby's honor he had put on a dark green jacket suitable for lounging in a sickroom, enlivened by a bright yellow waistcoat and a spotted cravat. He wondered if she appreciated the effort that he'd made.

Gently, he disentangled her fingers from his sleeve, and clasped her hand between his own. "There's no one else like Nit," he said. "Thank God. My eldest sister Beatrice married a title, and is off in Somerset popping out heirs. Cyn, the next oldest, is in Scotland with her laird. Then comes Nit, and the twins, and the baby, all of them from my father's second wife, who isn't the brightest candle in the chandelier, alas, though as good-hearted as she can be. That's why Aunt Syb is seeing to Nit's come-out. The mind boggles at the notion of both Maria and Nit set loose on the town."

Abby was not overwhelmed by this spate of information, and its deliverer, as many people were. The sound of his voice was oddly comforting. "Go on," she whispered. "Please."

Thoughtfully, Nigel studied her. No gentleman who'd grown up so surrounded by female beauty could be unaware of the attractions, or the lack thereof, of other members of the fair sex. This particular female's only claim to beauty was her fine brown eyes. Her nose was snub and freckled, her chin round, her person not the least bit remarkable, being neither thin nor fat, short nor tall. She was, in all, an ordinary and very comfortable sort of female, which was a blessing, since none of the other members of the household were. "I also have brothers. Micah, the eldest, is the serious member of the family. Luke, my middle brother, is off somewhere fighting Frogs. I'm the youngest, and the most useless of the lot. For some reason, Aunt Syb is fond of me, and has made me her heir. Unless she's feeling cross, and then she bids me to Hades. Since I'm in her good graces at the moment, here we are, alone together in your bedchamber. You're safe with me, however. All those sisters, you see."

Oddly, Abby did feel safe. "You are not particularly frightening," she murmured sleepily.

Nigel wondered what it would be like to be frightening. He looked down at the hand he held in his. "You're not to worry about anything," he remarked, then paused reflectively. "Easy for me to say, I suppose. *My* memory is unfortunately intact. Do you remember anything, or is it all a blank?"

Unaware, Abby squeezed his hand. "I remember watching squirrels from a window. And I believe I feel strongly about sanitation, free trade, emigration and women's rights."

"Clearly you are a woman of dangerous principles," said Nigel. "When you are better, we will stand you in the pillory for an hour. Anything else?"

Abby tried hard to remember, but without success. " 'Faith is the assurance of things hoped for,' " she murmured, " 'and the conviction of things seen.' "

" 'A lively dog,' " Nigel responded, " 'is better than a dead lion.' Jael hammered Sisera's head to the ground with a tent peg and a hammer. Saul collected two hundred Philistine foreskins for David. Does any of this ring a bell?"

" 'God's will, inscrutable as it may sometimes be,' " Abby said faintly. "Forgive me, but you don't seem the sort of gentleman to quote Scripture, sir."

"That just goes to show you shouldn't judge by appearances," said Nigel, as he wondered why *she* could. "I may be a humbug, but I'm also a younger son, and was destined for the clergy until my grandfather took pity on my future congregations and settled a competence on me."

Abby pushed the dampened cloth off her forehead and peered up at him. "I can't imagine you reading a sermon." She paused. "Or perhaps I can."

Her eyes crinkled endearingly when she smiled. Nigel released her hand, and moved away from the bed. "Rest now. I'll be right here in the chair. There's nothing to worry about. Aunt Syb will see to everything. Whether you want her to, or not."

Abby didn't know what she wanted. How could she, when she didn't even know who she was? But her head did pound ferociously, and the conversation had exhausted her; Pontius was safe belowstairs, and the angelic gentleman had promised he would stand guard. She closed her eyes and slipped back into the dark.

FIVE

The Duchess of Charnwood peered over her teacup at her guests, one of whom had just inquired as to the color of her hair, and whether it was naturally streaked with different shades of yellow, or if she bleached it with beer, or alternately washed it with lemon juice and then sat in the sun; and the other of whom looked like she wished to sink through the floor. "You do *not* address Her Grace as 'Duchess,'" Lady Syb said sternly. "You are her social inferior, Annette."

Nit looked puzzled at the notion that anyone should be her superior. "Oh," she said.

"*And,*" added Lady Ysabella, "you do not ever ask a lady if she colors her hair."

Nit's lower lip quivered. "My mama colors hers," she protested. And she'd wager her favorite pair of garters that her aunt did also, but not even Nit was such a featherhead as to mention that. "I beg your pardon, Your Grace."

In truth, the duchess had not been Her Grace for long, and was not accustomed to the title yet. "It hardly matters here among ourselves," she soothed. "Did you know that Roman ladies used urine to bleach their hair, or that the Celts used lime?"

"Oh!" Nit looked fascinated. "I must tell Mama that. What is urine, please?"

"Never mind!" said Lady Syb, as their hostess looked amused. "I must point out that you are hardly an ordinary duchess, Elizabeth. In other instances, it might matter very much if my niece makes such a blunder. Pay attention, Annette! Only a social equal may address Elizabeth as 'Duchess.' To everyone else, she is 'Your Grace.'"

"Except for Nigel," murmured Her Grace, who was tall for a female and slender, with full lips and irregular features and brown eyes flecked with gold.

Lady Syb cast her a reproachful glance. "Pray do not confuse the issue! In speech, all ranks below duke are called 'lord' and 'lady' and never by their title. A duke is never called 'my lord,' but instead 'my lord duke.' Are you listening, Annette?"

"Yes, Aunt Syb," said Nit, somewhat untruthfully, for her attention had been on the large scarlet parrot sunning itself at the far end of the room. "Must I call him 'my lord duke' even after I have married him?" The duchess made a choking sound, and Nit looked back at her. "I mean to have a duke, or at the very least an earl, milady. Perhaps you will tell me how you got yours."

Lady Syb gritted her teeth. "*Not* milady: Your Grace, or ma'am. Do focus your attention, Nit!"

The duchess picked up the teapot. "Perhaps we should introduce her to Maman. It would serve them both right. I didn't get my duke, exactly, Annette; my mother got him for me."

"Oh!" Nit turned a hopeful visage toward her aunt. "*Dear* Aunt Syb, would you please get me a duke?"

Lady Syb shot a stern glance at their mirthful hostess. "I, on the other hand," she continued grimly, "am

Lady Ysabella, because I am the daughter of a duke. I am also the Right Honorable Countess of Witcham, because my last husband was an earl. Which makes me Lady Ysabella Witcham, because my rank by birth is higher than the rank I earned by marrying. Do you understand, Annette?"

Nit understood perfectly. "Poor Aunt Syb. You couldn't catch a duke, and so you settled for an earl. We must hope that I will have better luck."

The duchess's cheeks were pink with suppressed laughter. "We must, indeed. But there aren't a great number of dukes, my dear."

Nit frowned at this intelligence. "Are they all married, then?"

Elizabeth looked judicious. "I don't believe so."

"Then that's all right! And when I am a duchess, I hope my husband will buy me a gown just like yours, because it is very pretty. May I please feed Birdie, ma'am?" Annette was already acquainted with the parrot, which had for many years resided in Lady Syb's house.

Elizabeth nodded. "Mind your fingers." Nit picked up a biscuit and tripped to the far end of the room.

The duchess looked down at her simple white spotted India gown and murmured, "She admires my dress?"

"What she *meant,*" retorted Lady Syb, in equally low tones, "is that when *she* marries a duke, she will be considerably more grand. I've received vouchers for Almack's. It's my most fervent wish that you and Justin will also be there."

"Strength in numbers," said Elizabeth. "I perfectly understand. The child will create a sensation. Neither Justin nor I would miss it for the world."

"I wish *I* could miss it!" Lady Ysabella sighed as she rose from her chair. "I must go home and take some wine and water for my headache. Hopefully I may not turn into a sot before I get the chit married off. Come along, Annette! We have taken up enough of Her Grace's time."

Elizabeth also rose. "We have every faith in you, Lady Syb."

Nit made a pretty curtsy for the duchess. She was in an excellent mood as she and her aunt left the Charnwood's London house. London was such a very *stimulating* place. Already today she had taken tea with if not a duke, a duchess; had renewed her acquaintance with Birdie, and petted the family cat, which was soon to be a mama, though the duchess denied all knowledge as to how that had come about, which seemed odd to Nit, because the duchess was a married woman and therefore should know about such things. Although not all married people had offspring. Perhaps the baby getting business was like a lottery, or a roll of the dice. Although her own mama, who disapproved of gambling, had four daughters anyway. It was all very puzzling. And then Nit forgot all about her questions for the moment, because Lady Syb, in an attempt to elevate her own flagging spirits, decided that she wished to visit the Temple of the Muses, on the southwest corner of Finsbury Square.

In the middle of the shop was a huge circular counter around which a coach and six could have driven, so large were the premises. Nit stared in awe. A wide staircase led up to the lounging rooms and the first of a series of galleries with bookshelves. No great fan of the written word herself, Nit trailed after her aunt, who was apparently in a very Gothic frame of mind, for she purchased

Mrs. Radcliffe's *Mysteries of Udolpho* and Mr. Lewis's *The Monk.* Nit tugged on her sleeve. "Dearest Aunt Syb, do you think that we might have an ice?"

The child meant no harm, Lady Syb reminded herself as she looked into that exquisitely lovely face. 'Twas hardly Nit's fault if she hadn't the sense of a brick. Therefore the ladies went next to Gunther's Tea Shop, and enjoyed a sorbet as they watched the waiters dash across the road to take orders and deliver ices to customers waiting in their carriages. Refreshed by their treat, they then looked at patterns from Batavia, and inspected some imported French fashion dolls, for modishness remained of supreme importance, even if there was a war going on; and Lady Syb ordered up some buttons made to her specifications, and purchased lavender water and potpourri. Her spirits had improved considerably by the time Nit spied a false bosom made of wax. "But why may I not have one?" she persisted, when Lady Syb said a firm no. "It would look ever so nice."

Lady Syb eyed the appliance. "You have a perfectly nice bosom of your own."

"Yes," agreed Nit, "but I have always wished for *more*. If I had a larger bosom, perhaps I could look higher than a duke."

The only gentlemen higher than a duke were members of the royal family. Lady Syb shuddered at the thought. Nit poked the bosom with an inquiring finger. "It is very hard."

Lady Syb prayed for patience. "Of course it's hard. The thing is made of wax. Oh, do put it down!"

Nit frowned. "I don't think a gentleman would wish to cuddle a bosom that was hard."

Lady Syb dropped the pair of gloves she had been inspecting and frowned at her niece. "Annette, pray tell me you haven't allowed any gentlemen to, ah, cuddle you."

An agreeable creature, Nit wouldn't tell her aunt anything she didn't wish to hear. Besides, it had only been a small sort of cuddle, and probably didn't count. She giggled. "As if I would!"

Lady Syb suspected there was little her niece wouldn't do, if the notion came upon her. She took Nit's arm and escorted her firmly out of the shop. "To wear a such a device would be cheating. You wouldn't wish to cheat."

Would she not? Nit wasn't certain there was anything wrong with cheating, providing it netted her a duke. She tilted her head. "Maybe if Lady Augusta cheated a little bit, she might sometimes win at cards. Should I suggest that to her, do you think?"

Lady Syb thought that the sooner she got Nit settled, the better it would be for everyone concerned. "*Why* must you have a duke? Wouldn't an earl or a baronet do as well?"

Nit chewed her lip as she considered this suggestion. She didn't want to be unfair. "I wish to wear a tiara," she said obscurely. "But perhaps it wouldn't matter, providing he was very, very rich. He *must* be very rich, Aunt Syb."

Was Annette thinking of her younger sisters? Were she to marry well, they would be more easily disposed of in their turn. Lady Syb supposed she should applaud the girl's determination, but experienced a frisson of foreboding instead. She ordered her carriage turned toward home.

They found Augusta pacing the drawing room. Lady Syb raised her brows. "Conor is making further inquiries," Gus responded, with a slight shake of her head. "He thought I should wait here."

Nigel was sprawled on a sofa. "She means she quarreled with him again. By the bye, Aunt Syb, your houseguest woke up. Throckmorton is with her now. I've sent for the leech."

"Houseguest?" said Nit, with interest. "I didn't know you had a houseguest, Aunt Syb." She paused, then giggled. "Other than us, that is! Or maybe we don't count as houseguests, because we're family. Except Lady Augusta isn't family, or if she *is*, no one has told me about it. Were you talking about Lady Augusta, Nigel? Why does she need a leech?"

Lady Syb took a deep breath. "Her name is Abby," murmured Nigel, "and beyond that she don't know who she is. She seems to be a good sort of female, even if she does know her Bible and keeps a pig."

Lady Syb was briefly distracted from her niece, who in a spirit of good fellowship was acquainting Gus with every detail of a netted miser's purse she'd coveted today, made in silk with henna and yellow and green steel beads in a paisley and cone pattern, and a steel ring. "The Bible?" she echoed.

Nigel struck a pose. " 'There is not a just man upon earth, that doeth good, and sinneth not.' Damned if it ain't all coming back to me."

"Damned, indeed," said Lady Syb. She hoped Conor hadn't brought an evangelistic sort of female beneath her roof. Although if he had it would serve him right, since he was the one among them most in need of preaching at. "We will not subject her to your sister just yet. Keep Annette occupied while I check on our guest."

"After pausing to take some wine and water for your headache," Nigel said shrewdly. "I've found brandy to be the ticket, myself. Amazing, ain't it, how such a little bit of a chit can drive so many people to drink. And just think, the Season's only begun!" Lady Syb cast her nephew a glance of extreme displeasure and swept out of the room.

Unaware that she had been the topic of conversation, as she was unaware of so many other things, Nit was still attempting to discover why Lady Augusta required a leech. To that end, she was following Gus in her perambulations around the room, and chatting now about a pretty cap of embroidered mull trimmed with tucks and lace that would have been perfect for Lady Syb.

Gus hadn't the slightest interest in steel beads and embroidered mull. Still, the child didn't deserve to have her ears boxed for her attempt to be amiable. "It sounds like a very nice netted purse. Perhaps if you were to ask her, Lady Syb—Why are you staring at me like that?"

Nit gaped at the spiny bump in the crook of Lady Augusta's arm. An ugly spiny bump with whiskers and a black nose.

So *this* was why poor Gus required a leech. Nit reacted as would any young lady of exquisite sensibilities. She opened her pretty mouth as wide as it would go and let out a blood-curdling scream.

SIX

Conor Melchers' inquiries at Covent Garden market brought him little new information, though a middle-aged female portioning out some herbs remembered seeing his young woman, and a young boy struggling with a basket of apples recalled her pig. Neither had any notion, however, of who the young woman was, or where she had come from, or what had become of her valise. The thief, or thieves, were long gone into one of the many streets that opened off the piazza. Conor purchased four oranges for a penny from a little orange girl and made his thoughtful way back to Grosvenor Square.

An anxious-looking footman answered his knock on the door. "Conor Melchers to see Lady Ysabella," Conor said, and then, "What the devil is that racket? Don't bother to announce me, I know the way."

The footman, who was new to his post, found himself alone in the hallway, clutching the gentleman's topcoat and hat and oranges. Surely 'twasn't at all proper for the cove to go haring off like that without so much as a by-your-leave. Though it *was* common knowledge among the serving classes that there was no predicting the queer starts of the nobs.

Unaware that he had posed the footman a

dilemma—should he first inform the countess that a stranger had invaded the premises, or tend to the stranger's hat and coat and oranges instead?—Conor followed the shrill shrieks to the first-floor drawing room, where a startling scene greeted him. Miss Slyte was screeching louder than an Italian soprano, and jumping up and down. Lady Augusta was stretched out half beneath the settee, from beneath which issued additional high-pitched noises, her sweetly rounded gray-clad rump pointed up in the air, and her trim ankles twitching as if she'd like to give someone a good kick. Mr. Slyte lounged in an oval-backed chair, observing the scene with unholy glee.

He looked up as Conor stepped into the room. "Hallo, Melchers. In case you're wondering why Gus is on the floor, Nit thought your hedgehog was a rat."

Gus emerged from beneath the settee, in her hands the hedgehog, which was curled up in a defensive and very prickly ball. "It's not his hedgehog, it's mine. Do hush, you silly twit!"

Annette paused, midshriek, and stared at Lady Augusta in surprise. Though many people might wish to snap at Nit, few actually did so.

Of course Lady Augusta had not really meant it. Nit forgave her on the spot. She edged cautiously closer. "It looks very prickly. What is a hedgehog?"

"It *is* very prickly." The hedgehog's heart was beating so rapidly that Gus felt it in her hands. "Thanks to you."

Conor strolled across the drawing room to stand beside Gus. He touched a gentle finger to the little ball of spines. "*This* is a hedgehog, and a very splendid one, I'm told. Teeth good and strong for crunching beetles and earthworms and bananas. Ears nicely rounded.

Well shaped little tail. Notice the fine color of the quills. Bright clear eyes"—the hedgehog slowly un-curled itself under his touch—"proper number of toes." He tickled them, and the creature flattened its spines. Even a hedgehog found the damned man irresistible. Gus sniffed.

Nit extended a curious finger. The hedgehog growled and hissed. "No!" said Nigel, as Nit jumped and opened her mouth. "There is a gentleman present. Gentlemen do not like to hear ladies scream."

Nit looked puzzled. "But you have heard me scream before. Oh! You mean Mr. Melchers. I thought you said he was not a gentleman but a rakehell." Her beautiful blue eyes moved to Conor. "You're not really going to shoot Nigel, are you? I wish that you would not. Even if he isn't my favorite brother. Not that I wish you to shoot Luke either, but that isn't very likely, because he isn't here!" She paused, and when Conor said nothing, being involved in trying to sort out the intricacies of this speech, added, "Sir?"

Conor glanced at Nigel for enlightenment. That gen-tleman shrugged. "I told her that she wouldn't wish me to challenge you to a duel because you're the better shot."

"Why would you challenge me to a duel?" Conor in-quired blankly. Nigel raised his brows. "Ah, I see. I think I may safely assure you, Miss Annette, that your brother is safe. That is, unless he aggravates me beyond bearing, which is a distinct possibility." He glanced at Lady Augusta, who was cuddling her hedgehog against her bosom. "Although Gus may shoot him first. Have you named it yet?"

Gus wished Conor wouldn't smile at her. That lazy sinful smile was almost so irresistible as to cause her to forget that she was cross. And now he'd seen her on her hands and knees with her rump sticking up in the air.

Not that it would be the first time he'd seen a female in such a posture. He was a rakehell, after all. Probably the female had been naked. Probably *he* had been naked. Gus blushed.

"No!" she snapped. "How can I name the creature when I don't know if it's female or male?"

Conor picked up the hedgehog and flipped it gently over on its back. "Female," he said.

Gus regarded him with disfavor. "Of course you would know."

Conor was amused by her pink cheeks. "Of course I would. So would you, had you thought to look." Unfair of him to tease so easy a target. Gus's expression suggested that she wished he'd leave.

Oho! thought Nigel; sat the wind in that quarter? He opened his mouth to make a provocative remark. His sister, however, was unwittingly before him. "Prunes!" she said, and found Lady Augusta's scowl turned on her. "But that is what Aunt Syb says when you scrunch your face up like that!"

"You are not Aunt Syb!" Nigel said quickly, "and if you mention 'prunes' again to Gus she is likely to box your ears, and you wouldn't like that. Now apologize to her."

Nit wasn't certain why she was apologizing—Lady Augusta's face *was* scrunched up like a prune—but she did so, prettily. Then she beamed at Conor. "I am to go to Almack's, sir!"

Conor could think of nothing more insipid than an evening at Almack's. Still, the child's enthusiasm was endearing. It also made him feel as old as Methuselah. "How very nice for you," he said.

Gus snatched back her hedgehog. "Mr. Melchers isn't welcome at Almack's."

Conor turned his wicked gaze on her. "Will you miss me, sweeting?"

"Hardly." Gus sniffed. "Since I have no intention of setting foot there myself."

"The stakes at Almack's ain't high enough for Gus," remarked Nigel.

Not welcome at Almack's? Nit could imagine nothing more horrible than being denied entrance to that most exclusive of the temples of the *ton*. "Whyever are you not welcome at Almack's, sir?"

The child was all misguided sympathy. Gus almost smiled to think what havoc Conor might wreak among damsels newly introduced to the marriage mart. "Mr. Melchers may not go to Almack's because he is a—" She paused, remembering the last time she had tried to explain a rakehell. "Mr. Melchers is not the thing."

"Oh." Nit studied him. "Are you very wicked, sir?"

"I am, indeed," Conor said gravely. "Lady Augusta will tell you so."

Nit wasn't interested in asking Lady Augusta, who was scowling again. Nor was she, unlike her brother, sufficiently astute to muse upon why Lady Augusta was so certain that Mr. Melchers was steeped in sin. "Perhaps if you were to stop being so wicked you could go to Almack's. Have you thought that you might reform?"

Conor had an excellent understanding of the workings of the female mind. "You will not lack for dancing partners," he said. "And I don't wish to change my ways. I enjoy being wicked. As do the ladies that I'm wicked with."

Now Lady Augusta was frowning so hard her eyes

were almost crossed. "It all sounds very queer to me," Nit said doubtfully.

" 'Can the Ethopian change his skin, or the leopard his spots?' " murmured Nigel. The subject was best changed before Gus boxed Conor's ears and thereby gave Nit some unfortunate ideas. "I take it your inquiries were unfruitful, Melchers? Your damsel in distress is tucked away safely abovestairs. Her name is Abby, or at least part of it. She don't recall the rest. The leech says she'll do well enough, providing she don't start convulsing and foaming at the mouth. Which she may do anyway when she sees how much of her hair he has shaved off."

Gus turned her frown on Nigel. "Can you be serious about nothing?"

"I *can,* but I don't care to," retorted Nigel. "You're serious enough for all of us. I'll take you to see Abby, Melchers. We've all been parading through her bedchamber, so I don't see why you shouldn't do the same. Gus can stay here with Nit."

"No, Gus can't!" said that lady, as Nit stared at her reflection in the carved mirror over the fireplace and puzzled over the odd notion that someone she didn't know was sleeping in the house. "Why don't you go to your room, Annette, and look at all the nice new things Lady Syb has bought you since you came to London? Perhaps you might decide what you like best. No, I don't want to see them again. Remember, I was there when most of them were bought." Lady Syb had indeed been generous. Morning and afternoon and evening dresses, ribbon-and-feather-trimmed bonnets, gloves and shoes and a chemise trimmed with white on white eyelet embroidery that Gus coveted for herself.

The mirror's gilded frame had holders for a number

of candles. "I wonder," pondered Nit, "if a wax bosom would melt."

The other three occupants of the drawing room regarded her with fascination. "Surely Lady Syb didn't buy you a wax bosom!" said Gus.

"She said it would be cheating." Nit turned away from the mirror. "What do you think, Mr. Melchers? If you are so very wicked, you must surely know about bosoms, sir."

Mr. Melchers bit back any number of *risqué* rejoinders. Though it was as natural for him to flirt as it was to draw breath, Nigel's sister did not appeal to Conor in that way. Not that he had anything against virgins, and of course the little goose was a virgin; she would have never been able to keep it secret were she not. Although there was little more delightful than enlightening a lady about such matters, Conor preferred females he could at least discuss the weather with in between explorations of the amatory arts.

Nor did he care to be shot by either Nigel or Gus, both of whom were waiting with bated breath for his response. "I think," Conor said, "that you needn't concern yourself about such things, puss."

He had waited so long to reply that Nit had quite forgotten her question. What of all the things Aunt Syb had bought her *did* she like best? It was a perplexing choice. She would have to look at everything again. And practice with her pretty rosewood and ivory fan, because 'twould be a terrible thing if she let it rest against the wrong cheek, thereby saying no when she actually meant yes. Deep in her own thoughts, she curtsied and left the room.

Conor watched the door close behind Annette, then

glanced at Nigel. "You have my sympathy. Are there any more at home like that?"

"Three of them," Nigel said gloomily. "You see why I prefer to cast in my lot with Aunt Syb, who is bearing up remarkably well under the strain, even if she has shut herself in her room to drink herself into insensibility. I'll take you to visit the invalid. Abby, that is, not Aunt Syb."

"I'm going with you," Gus said, promptly. "You and Conor alone with a lady in her bedchamber—Unthinkable! She'll need a chaperone. Besides, I haven't properly met her yet."

With heroic effort, Nigel withheld comment. "Maybe seeing Melchers will jog her memory."

"Doubtful," said Conor. "Since it's unlikely she saw me before the accident. If it *was* an accident. I can't help but wonder what she had in that valise."

SEVEN

Abby wakened to once again find a gentleman by her bedside. This was becoming a pleasant habit, she thought. Not that anyone would mistake *this* stranger for an angel, for he was tall and broad and dark, with lines of dissipation around his handsome mouth and lazy eyes. Lucifer sprang to mind, along with Sodom and Gomorrah. Here was a gentleman who had eaten from the Tree of the Knowledge of Good and Evil, and relished every bite.

He was watching her. "Hello. You're looking better than the last time I saw you."

This man would be used to seeing females in—or out of—their nightgowns. Abby resisted the impulse to yank the bedclothes up to her chin. "Are you the gentleman who brought me here?"

"One might quibble with the use of the word 'gentleman.'" Nigel strolled forward. "This is Conor Melchers. He is indeed the valiant knight who rescued you when that wagonload of cauliflower fell on your head. And over there is Gus. She'd probably prefer to be called Lady Augusta, but we don't pay attention to that. We ain't named the hedgehog yet."

Abby turned her head to look at the woman, who stood on the other side of the bed. Lady Augusta might have been very attractive, were she not scowling so dreadfully. Abby remembered that Nigel had said this Gus was rather prickly. "You have a very nice hedgehog. What's her name?"

Lady Augusta looked surprised. "You knew she was female?"

It wasn't difficult to tell the difference, thought Abby, but didn't say so out loud. "I must thank you for taking me in. I am feeling much better now."

"It ain't Gus who took you in," interjected Nigel. "And you ain't going anywhere, because you still don't know who you are. Unless you've remembered?" He paused, and Abby shook her head. "Then Aunt Syb won't hear of it. You needn't mind being an object of charity. Gus is an object of Aunt Syb's charity, and so is my sister, and so for that matter am I. Melchers ain't, but not for lack of Aunt Syb's trying. She's always had a soft spot for a rakehell."

Abby could hardly blame her. Mr. Melchers' smile alone was enough to warm a woman to her toes. "I think you should name the hedgehog Helen," she said to Lady Augusta. "After Helen of Troy. She is a very fine hedgehog, after all."

Gus wasn't certain she wished people to be abducting her hedgehog, or waging war on her behalf. 'Twas as good a name as any other, however, and better than any she had come up with herself. "Helen it is," she said, as she moved closer to the bed, the better to observe Conor charming yet another female.

He *was* charming. Even she couldn't deny that. Gus wondered how many highflyers he had under his protection at this particular moment in time.

Abby wondered why Lady Augusta wore so very sour an expression. Perhaps the poor woman had heartburn. Angelica seeds crushed and added to cold water, then boiled and strained and drunk as tea, were an excellent remedy for heartburn. Then Abby frowned herself as she wondered how she knew such things.

The hedgehog liked Abby. Its little nose was pointed in her direction, its whiskers all a-twitch. Since Helen seemed so fascinated, Gus set her down on the bed. The hedgehog climbed up onto Abby, found a cozy spot, curled up, put a paw over its face, and went to sleep.

Conor glanced at Gus. "They think that if you can't see their faces, they're safe," he said.

Did he think she hid her face behind a frown? Gus opened her mouth to utter a scathing retort. "Children!" interjected Nigel, in excellent imitation of his aunt. "Must I remind you that we are in a sickroom? Don't listen to Melchers, Abbess. He'll lead you into bad habits, such as baiting Gus, which is a pastime I prefer to reserve for myself."

Abby blinked at him. "Abbess?" she said.

"Nigel nicknames everyone." Gus sat down gingerly on the edge of the bed. "Except Conor. I wonder why that is."

"Simple." Nigel draped himself against a bedpost. "I'm afraid of him."

Abby doubted Nigel was afraid of anyone. "Why Abbess?" she said.

"Because you can quote Scripture," retorted Nigel.

Abby considered him. " 'He that troubleth his own house shall inherit the wind.' "

Conor smiled his lazy smile. He liked the girl, Gus thought. And why should he not? Abby wasn't suspicious and cross-grained.

" 'Let he who is without sin pitch the first rock,' "

said Nigel. "Or something like that. King Solomon had seven hundred wives and three hundred concubines. I still remember my Oxford studies, or those studies I attended to when nothing more interesting presented itself. I don't suppose you know if you was ever at Oxford, Abbess?"

"'I have been a stranger in a strange land,'" murmured Abby, as she ran a gentle finger over the hedgehog's quills. "No, I don't know where I've been."

Gus supposed it was better to have memories one disliked than to have no memories at all. "What *do* you remember?" she asked.

Abby shook her head. "I remember Pontius. And then I woke up here. Everything else is disjointed, fragments of this and that."

Nigel settled himself more comfortably against the bedpost. "Tell us about it! Spare no detail, no matter how trivial."

"I'm afraid it's all trivial." Abby sighed.

Trivial Abby's recollections may or may not have been, but they were without doubt fragmented. Bell ringing and choir practice and boiling up bars of soap; the opinion that the government spent less time on educating the poor than was spent annually on horse-racing and keeping the opera house open; the fact that the singers were told not to sing the Response to the Communion Service, and did so anyway. Furthermore, she had strong opinions on sanitation, annual Parliaments, free trade, emigration, abolishment of slavery and prison reform, universal suffrage and women's rights.

"The pillory is too good for you," said Nigel. "Clearly it must be the Tower. No, no, *I* don't believe women are by nature inferior to men. I've lived with too many of them. I doubt Melchers thinks women are inferior either, considering how many of them he's had in his keeping, but you'd have to ask him that."

Abby had no intention of asking Mr. Melchers anything of the sort. All the same, she glanced at him.

His expression was sympathetic. "It must be very disconcerting, misplacing your last name. Never mind, we'll find it for you. You said you remembered your pig."

"I remember that I *have* a pig." Abby frowned at the snoozing hedgehog. "And that he is very large. And I also remember that he wasn't always so large, so I must have had him for some time. But I still have no idea why Pontius and I are in London. We don't live here, I think."

"You do now," Nigel said cheerfully. "Fortunately for us, because we were tottering on the verge of boredom when you came along. Tell you what, we'll smuggle your pig upstairs when Aunt Syb ain't looking. Maybe he'll jog your memory."

Conor interrupted. "Can you recall if you had anything of value in your valise?"

"I don't remember that I *had* a valise." Abby pounded her fist on the bedcovers. "Blast!"

The hedgehog huffed. Protectively, Gus scooped up her pet. "I'm sorry." Abby sighed. "I don't think it is in my nature to loll about in bed."

Conor looked wicked. Abby flushed. Gus scowled. "Lot's daughters took turns getting him drunk and sleeping with him," remarked Nigel. "'I am a brother to dragons, and a companion to owls.'"

"You are worse than a plague of locusts," said Lady Syb, as she swept into the bedchamber with Sir Edmond Jessop at her heels. "And as noisy. Stop stirring coals or I shall disinherit you again." She approached the bed. "I'm glad to see you are awake, my dear. I am Lady Ysabella Witcham. Nigel's Aunt Syb, for my sins."

Lady Ysabella bore a definite resemblance to her nephew. Golden curls and bright blue eyes and a hint of mischief in her expression—"What's *that*?" she asked, as her gaze fell upon the hedgehog.

"Teeth good and strong for crunching," offered Nigel. "Proper number of toes. Meet Helen the hedgehog, Aunt Syb. Melchers gave her to Gus."

How very queer of Conor. Lady Syb eyed him speculatively. Then she observed the hedgehog, which in return twitched its nose and huffed gently at the smell of her perfume. "Does it occur to anyone that there is a certain injustice in the circumstance that I rid myself of a parrot only to find myself providing shelter for a hedgehog and a pig?"

"Nit thought it was a rat," Gus offered.

"That explains the screams," said Lady Syb.

Lady Ysabella was also providing shelter for a stranger, who despite Nigel's earlier disclaimers was very uncomfortable at finding herself an object of charity. "I am so sorry to inconvenience you," said Abby, then flinched as the physician began to remove the dressing from her head.

"Our Abbess," offered Nigel, "don't like to presume on your good nature, Aunt Syb. I told her she shouldn't give it a second thought, since the rest of us do it all the time."

Lady Syb regarded her nephew with disfavor. "Sometimes I think that you are as great a rattlebrain as you pretend to be." She turned her shoulder on him and studied Abby. "You have been given a nickname, my dear, and are therefore already one of the family, which you will probably come to regret. As for inconvenience—piffle! We were in sore need of distraction, and you have provided it, as you will understand when you have met my niece."

"I told you you'd be sorry," murmured Nigel at her elbow. She frowned at him. "Well, I did!"

Sir Edmond cleared his throat, and suggested that he might better examine his patient in private. Lady Syb, who couldn't imagine that such a directive included her, banished the other visitors from the chamber and moved to the foot of the bed.

Abby winced as Sir Edmond examined his handiwork. "You're coming along nicely," he said. Then he asked a series of questions to which Abby answered yes and no. No, she had not vomited. Yes, she had drunk some barley water, and her head still hurt, but not so badly as before. No, her vision was not blurred. And other than that her name was Abby, and that she could quote from the Bible, and owned a pig named Pontius, she knew nothing about herself.

Sir Edmond looked grave. "Loss of memory is not unheard-of in cases such as this. We must hope that your awareness will gradually return. You must not try and force matters. Most of all you need to rest and regain your strength." He began to replace the dressing on her head.

"May I get up?" asked Abby.

"No," the doctor said, firmly. "However, I think we may arrange that you to have something nourishing to eat."

Lady Syb moved closer. She still had her own headache, but generous amounts of wine and water had rendered her considerably more philosophical. "We're happy to have you with us, my dear. I noticed when we were undressing you—Perhaps you may tell us what this is?" She touched the plain gold band that Abby wore on a chain around her neck.

EIGHT

Almack's! The word alone was enough to make Annette's heart skitter in her chest. And now she stood at the portal of that holiest of citadels of the *ton*, where tickets of admission were so jealously guarded that many hopeful young ladies denied entrance had thought their lives ended, and at least one had attempted (fortunately without success, for she had gone on to make an unexceptionable match) to end her life with an overdose of laudanum. Nigel had threatened something similar when informed he was to also be granted this treat, but brightened when he learned that the Duke and Duchess of Charnwood had promised to attend. On her brother's arm, Nit followed Lady Ysabella up the grand staircase that led to the ballroom.

Aunt Syb seemed to know everyone. Ladies and gentlemen alike bowed and paused to exchange a word or two and scrutinize her charge. Recipient of so many strictures on her conduct that she was terrified of making an error of precedence, Nit curtsied when it seemed appropriate, and otherwise remained mumchance. Aware of what had caused this phenomenon, Nigel wondered how long it would last. Nit would make a cake of herself. It was just a matter of waiting to see *how*. Nigel counted on his sister to enliven what was bound to otherwise be a curst flat affair.

Nit stared in awe at her surroundings. The ballroom stretched one hundred feet long, and was almost half as wide, decorated with gilt columns and pilasters, classic medallions, mirrors which reflected countless lighted wax candles with bedazzling effect. Lining the walls were sofas, one at the upper end of the room for the exclusive use of the patronesses.

Ropes marked off the space reserved for dancers. The orchestra was tastefully adorned with garlands of flowers. Already the ballroom was crowded with people, young ladies dressed in chaste white, accompanied by their more colorful mamas, gentlemen in knee breeches and black coats, military and naval uniforms. Nit clapped her hands together. "Jupiter!" she said.

Nigel smiled down at her. "Think you died and went to heaven, do you, puss?"

She cast him a puzzled glance. "Are you laughing at me again? I wish you would not. But oh, Nigel! It is so very grand."

He supposed it was, to her. For all his mischief, Nigel had no particular desire to spoil his sister's pleasure. Therefore, he did not point out that a great many of the misses and mamas present were as desirous of snagging an eligible bachelor as she was, and many had more to recommend them than a lovely face. "It is indeed grand," he said gravely. "And you will do very well so long as you remember what you've been told. Look, Aunt Syb has chosen a spot where you may be seen to advantage. And if I'm not mistaken, Lady Russell is bringing young Harcourt to you for the next dance."

Mr. Harcourt appeared to be in his midtwenties,

with artfully arranged brown curls, amazingly high shirt points, and a blush upon his cheeks. "*Mr.* Harcourt?" Nit echoed doubtfully.

"Good family, moderate expectations. He doesn't need to marry a fortune," said Lady Ysabella, who'd overheard this last remark. "You will be polite to him even if he doesn't have a title, Annette."

Of course she would be polite. Nit hoped she was not without a heart. Never had she been rude to any of her admirers—and Nit had had admirers from the day she first opened her eyes and smiled a dazzling albeit toothless smile at the little pageboy who'd just happened to be passing through the room—and turned on Mr. Harcourt a smile of such brilliance that the young man tumbled head over heels in love with her on the spot.

"A pretty-behaved gel," judged Lady Russell, with a grave smile and a nod. The patroness then went on her way to see what other matches she might make, leaving Nigel mute with merriment, and Lady Syb fluttering her fan. Lady Syb was dressed this evening in purple, as befit an older woman, but had hedged her bets by choosing a changeable silk that shifted from purple to blue, and had placed atop her golden curls a turban lush with ostrich plumes.

"I see you are doing your duty by your sister," came a voice from behind him, and Nigel turned toward the Duchess of Charnwood. Elizabeth looked very lovely in a short-sleeved high-waisted gown of white lace over green silk, deeply décolleté, her hair drawn back in a Grecian knot with a profusion of tiny ringlets escaping to cluster around her face. Completing the costume was a diadem, necklace, and earrings of emeralds set in diamonds and hung with immense pear pearls. Nigel blinked.

Elizabeth touched a massive pearl. "I am very duchesslike tonight. Maman would approve, don't you think? Don't look so horrified; she isn't here. Maman does not care for Almack's."

It was doubtful that Elizabeth's starched-up mama would approve of her daughter's neckline either. "It's a good thing Melchers ain't here to admire that dress, Duchess."

Elizabeth grinned. "That's the only reason Justin let me wear it. And you're not supposed to call me Duchess. Lady Syb has explained that you're my social inferior."

Nigel smiled back at her. "Met Nit, have you? Ah, there's Justin. Marriage seems to agree with the two of you. Good God, is that lemonade?"

The Duke of Charnwood was a tall man with short chestnut hair, cool gray eyes, stern aristocratic features, and an admirable physique. "Lemonade for Elizabeth," he said, as he handed her a glass. "And claret punch for Lady Syb."

Lady Ysabella took the glass and drank. "You are a most astute gentleman, Justin. I have always said so. Why aren't you dancing with your wife?"

The duke eyed the duchess's *décolletage*. "I dare not, ma'am, for fear her dress would fall off. I am self-ish, I admit it. The sight of Elizabeth without her dress is a pleasure I prefer to keep for myself."

Elizabeth laughed and took her husband's arm, snuggling closer than was perhaps appropriate in sur-roundings so august. The duke and his duchess did not often appear in public, being much more interested in pursuing those activities so enjoyed by newlyweds. "Gus isn't with you tonight?" she asked.

Nigel lowered his voice. "Gus has her own fish to

fry. Although she won't cook up as big a batch as she might like, if I know Aunt Syb. We have another house-guest. I call her the Abbess. Conor brought her home."

The duchess choked. The duke looked intrigued. "Not *that* sort of abbess!" said Nigel. "Shame on you for suggesting Aunt Syb might run a bawdy house. Although she'd do a good job of it if the notion struck her, so we must pray that it does not!" He proceeded to tell the fascinated Charnwoods the tale of Conor and Abby and the pig. Lady Syb meantime engaged in a good gossip of her own concerning the domestic battles of the Prince and Princess of Wales—*he* had proposed a reconciliation, which *she* had refused, and wisely, because at the same time he was breaking off with Lady Jersey and wooing Mrs. Fitzherbert once again; although how wise was her own flirtation with Junior Minister Mr. George Canning remained to be seen—while keeping a sharp eye on her charge.

Nit was trying very hard to follow the rules, display-ing pretty animation and graceful movements while conversing politely with her partner when they were brought together by the movements of the dance. Unfor-tunately, no one had thought to tell her that there were restrictions on the topics of a young woman's discourse. Therefore, Nit was enthusiastically discussing cow hocks and bowed tendons, cribbing and a twitch. Mr. Harcourt did his best to uphold his end of the conversation. He al-lowed that Miss Slyte knew her horseflesh.

Of course, Nit knew her horseflesh! Her papa said she was as bruising a rider as any of his sons. Why, if she wasn't a female, Nit would be a member of the Four-Handed Club. Nor was she one of those useless sorts of females who didn't know how to saddle her own mount. If Nit had never mucked out a stable, exactly, she'd certainly seen it done. And due to her tendency to hang around those stables, she'd also seen a stallion turned into a gelding, which was a terrible thing indeed, because it meant the poor thing could no longer sire little horses, and furthermore it had looked so very painful that she had felt squeamish for an entire week. (Although Nit might not have known how a man and woman made a baby, she knew what happened when a stallion mounted a mare. If most young ladies might see a certain similarity between the situations—well, this was Nit.) Why her confidences should have also made Mr. Harcourt look squeamish, Nit could not imagine, and decided he must be a very paltry sort of gentleman.

The dance ended. Mr. Harcourt returned Nit to her aunt. Such familiarity, and upon such a subject—Mr. Harcourt didn't know what to make of it. He murmured something unintelligible, and beat a hasty retreat. Nit immediately forgot him. Considerably more interesting than squeamish Mr. Harcourt was the tall gentleman standing beside the Duchess of Charnwood.

Elizabeth correctly interpreted Annette's admiring glance. "This is *my* duke. I don't wish to share him. You must find one of your own." Nit giggled and fluttered her lush eyelashes at Justin, all the same.

Nigel returned from the refreshment room, where a table had been set out with tepid lemonade and weak tea, tasteless orgeat, thin slices of bread and butter, and stale cake. He presented another glass of punch to Lady Syb. "How very ungenerous of you, Duchess! Yes, I know I am her inferior, Nit, because she has already told me so."

"Your brother has special dispensation," explained the duchess. "Because he is a humbug. You needn't defend him. He told me so himself."

Nigel made a moue. "Hoist with my own petard."

The duke looked unsympathetic. "'Tis no more than you deserved."

"What is 'dispensation,' please?" asked Nit. And then she wondered why her question made everybody laugh.

The duchess smiled at her bewilderment. "We're only funning, my dear. I hope I'm not the first to say that you're as fine as fivepence tonight."

Nit would be even finer than fivepence had she anything so magnificent to wear as the duchess's diamonds and emeralds and pearls. Not to mention that low-cut dress. Earlier, Nit had thought she looked quite splendid in her white gloves and satin shoes, gown of white gauze with silk appliqués, her mama's pearls clasped around her neck and wound in her hair. She hadn't even minded her brother's remark that she looked like a virgin sacrifice. Now, in light of all the other hopeful white-clad misses present in the crush of people, each and every one of them wishful of attracting the interest of an older son with a title and fat rent rolls, she wished she'd worn bright red. Not that Nit doubted she would be a success, despite all the competition, and despite Aunt Syb's warning that suitable husbands didn't grow on every bush.

Lady Syb had also warned her niece against ambitions set too high, but that particular piece of wisdom had passed in one of Nit's lovely shell-like ears and right out the other side. The family was depending on her not to make the same mistake as her older sisters, who had not married as well as they might have. Not that either of those elder sisters had been the beauty that Nit was, which stood to reason, because they had a different mama. Beatrice and Cynthia were not antidotes, far from it; all the Slyte siblings looked alike. Nit frowned as she wondered why that was. Perhaps because they all had the same papa.

"Stop air-dreaming!" hissed Lady Syb, and for good measure poked her niece with her fan. "Try to look as if you're enjoying yourself."

"I *am* enjoying myself!" protested Nit, bewildered as to why her aunt might think she wasn't. The crowd parted at that moment, and she caught a glimpse of a late arrival. Auburn hair, chiseled features, a very bored expression on his handsome face, eyes a glacial gray—"Jupiter!" she breathed.

"Now *that's* a puzzle!" said Nigel, as Lady Syb tutted at her niece. "Last time I saw Duke he swore he was going to ruin himself and thereby put off all the matchmaking mamas. Although how he was to ruin himself without either gaming away his fortune or compromising himself into marriage, he hadn't decided yet. There's no use looking at him like you'd like to gobble him up, Nit. Duke was married once, and his wife gave him a pair of sons before she died. He vows the twins are offspring enough for any man. Says he sees no other reason to marry. I doubt even you will change his mind."

So bewitched was Nit by the gentleman's person and demeanor—his features were those of an Adonis, and he was a very Apollo in form, or had she got it the wrong way around? Whichever, he was remarkably handsome and old enough to be interesting, unlike poor Mr. Harcourt, and furthermore looked quite bewitchingly bored—that only the teeniest fragment of her brother's speech penetrated her brain. "Duke?" she echoed.

Nigel saw disaster looming. "Short for Marmaduke. He's only a viscount. Bad-tempered sort. Ain't interested in young women like yourself." He caught his aunt's eye. "Why are you frowning at me, Aunt Syb?"

The Duke of Charnwood had himself once been relentlessly pursued for his title and fortune, and therefore might have been expected to feel some compassion for another gentleman in the same fix. "Viscount Daventry is rich as Croesus," he offered perversely. "His fortune is immense. The family lays claim to Plantagenet blood. Only Brummell counts for more in society."

Nit's eyes widened. What, she wondered, was a Plantagenet? A Brummell, a Croesus? It all sounded very intriguing. Before she could give voice to these questions, the duchess pinched her husband's arm; Lady Syb bade them go away and amuse themselves elsewhere; and Lady Russell reappeared, having selected another partner for Miss Slyte, one Sir Francis Braceborough, who Nit thought must be at least her own papa's age.

Obediently, she stepped out onto the dance floor. Sir Frances was very amiable, if a little creaky from the corset that he wore, and Nit returned his conversational gambits with polite absentmindedness, as she craned her neck to watch Viscount Daventry pause and speak with Nigel, and smile quite nicely at Aunt Syb.

A mere viscount, perhaps, but wealthy, and splendid as one or another of those ancient Greeks. Perhaps Nit would lower her expectations just a little bit. She didn't take seriously her brother's warning that the wealthy viscount didn't like young ladies. He just hadn't met the right young lady yet. That young lady being herself.

But how to bring herself to his attention without breaking one of Aunt Syb's countless rules? Once the viscount had vanished into the card room, or the refreshment room, she could hardly trail after him. Or she *could*, but Aunt Syb wouldn't like it one little bit. No, Nit must make her move now, before he moved on.

Oh! He had glanced at her! Perhaps Nigel or Aunt Syb had explained why they were present at Almack's tonight. Or perhaps he had noticed her simply because she was the most beautiful young woman in the room.

Whatever the reason, Nit must make use of this instant in which she had his attention. She cast about in her mind for an idea. Due to her abstraction, one foot slipped slightly on the highly polished floor. With just a little effort, the rest of her followed, gracefully.

'Twas a splendid accident. Those not privileged to be present heard all the particulars over their morning chocolate cups. One misstep by a provincial miss—a lovely creature she was, and not at all to be blamed if the French compound rubbed on the boards made them slippery as glass and most unsuited to the vigorous steps of a country dance—resulted in another, for the gentleman with whom she had been dancing had hold of her hand and also tripped. Two other dancers could not stop in time and joined them, and then yet another couple, until six highly mortified dancers ended up in a pile on the floor. It was noted by numerous observers that the damsel responsible for the contretemps comported herself the most admirably of the lot, for where the other young ladies shrieked, and the gentlemen sputtered, she merely sprawled where she had fallen, smack at Viscount Daventry's feet, her hands clasped to her bosom and her beautiful blue eyes raised soulfully to his face.

NINE

While Miss Slyte was draping herself at the feet of Viscount Daventry, and Lady Ysabella was wishing for her vinaigrette, and Mr. Slyte was biting his tongue lest he say, "I told you so," Conor Melchers was making his way through a series of gaming establishments. These were not the sort of establishments usually graced by Mr. Melchers; he was more often to be found at White's, or Brook's, or the Cocoa Tree. Not that Conor was a gamester. Though he was as beloved by Madame Fortune as by any other of his ladies, Mr. Melchers was not a devotee of games of chance. Any man who found pleasure in playing risked the chance of losing. Any man, or woman. Conor took his pleasure, frequently, elsewhere.

Gaslight flared above the portal of the fifth hell he'd visited that night. A wary eye inspected him through the grille. Conor waited while the eye squinted, apparently decided he was neither a representative of the law nor a spy, and swung open the door to allow him within.

Conor climbed the staircase to the first floor, where a series of rooms were crowded with men and women, some fashionable and some not, engaged in various games of chance. Gambling houses such as these were supported at considerable expense, for they were open all night and every night, providing supper and refreshment and a livelihood for not only the many employees required to run the place, but any number of sharks, sharpers, lack-legs, Greeks and rooks who stole from other nests to feather their own. Conor had no doubt the wink had been given when he first stepped into the room. Wink, shrug, nod, ahem; every motion of the hands and arms and feet; every word and gesture here was the covert language of fraud.

Conor was no lamb for the slaughter. Not only had he considerable skill at games of chance, he was a billiard player of the first class, no mean hand at skittles, and a pugilist of no small renown. He also enjoyed chess for the opportunity it afforded him to exercise his mind.

A waiter hovered at his elbow. Conor asked for a glass of claret, then paused to watch an E.O. table being set in motion by a young woman. Clever to have hired a female elbow-shaker, he thought. Conor put on the E, and it came up, then on the O, and he won again. The young woman smiled at him. Conor winked at her, but spent no more time watching the gyrations of the table. It was commonly the way of E.O. banks to win.

Faro, piquet, écarté—the players were intent on their games, countless playing cards scattered on the floor around them, for it was common practice to open a new deck at the beginning of each game. Not that the practice prevented cheating. *Chevaliers d'industrie* paid their expenses at the cost of dupes. Wondering if this visit would also prove fruitless, Conor entered yet another room and glimpsed his own errant lamb seated with several players around a large circular table, over which was suspended a lamp. There was good reason why the game they played was called hazard. It made a man or unmade him in the twinkling of an eye.

She picked up the dice box, lay a sum of money on the table, which had a deep beveled edge. The other players placed their own bets. "Seven," she said, and threw a five.

"Five to seven," called the groom-porter, who occupied a somewhat elevated position by the table, and whose duty it was to call the odds and see that the game was played properly.

Five had become the lady's 'chance.' If she could succeed in repeating it before she threw her 'main,' or seven, she would win. Otherwise, she would lose. Play would continue until she threw one or the other. Meanwhile the odds were calculated, and additional wagers laid.

The groom-porter declared odds of three to two: There were three ways of throwing seven, and two of throwing five. The lady increased her stake by ten pounds. The other players covered the bet by putting down two-thirds of the amount, and awaited the turning up of either chance or main.

So intent was the gambler on her game that she was unaware of Conor's interest. Others were not so blind. The nod of a head, the nudge of an elbow, and she dropped the dice. The player who had caused the mishap apologized profusely, and the groom-porter provided another pair of ivories. She took a deep breath, shook the box, cast the dice—and turned up a five.

Extraordinary runs of luck sometimes occurred at hazard. Conor had himself seen a player throw five, seven, and even eleven main in one hand. This player, however, was not known to be on intimate terms with Lady Luck.

Giddy with victory, she gathered up her winnings.

When she saw Conor, the smile faded from her face. "I suppose Lady Syb has sent you to bring me home," she snapped.

"To take you home was not my intention." Conor clasped her elbow. "My door is always open to you, however, if you've changed your mind."

Gus was surrounded by people who took pleasure in baiting her. And not unsuccessfully, because she couldn't help but wonder what would happen if she took Conor up on his invitation to visit his residence. Not that she would, of course.

If only he wouldn't look at her as if he knew just what she was thinking! "Are you trying to stare me out of countenance?"

"No," Conor said amiably. "I was thinking that you look exceptionally fine tonight." A pity that the flush on her cheek and sparkle in her eye had been inspired by the dice.

The flush currently on Gus's cheeks had nothing to do with gambling, and everything to do with the man standing beside her. "Are you saying that Lady Syb *didn't* send you?" she inquired.

Lady Syb was as determined to see Gus cured of her compulsion as to see her niece make a good match. Conor wondered if she would achieve either. "Not precisely. Perhaps we might speak more privately. My carriage is outside."

Gus waited silently while her cloak was fetched. Lady Syb would have her head for combing, and it wouldn't be the first time. Glad as she was that her cousin the duke had found himself a bride with whom he was besotted, Gus was consequently left without a home again, because kind as Lady Syb was being— although "kind" hardly seemed a fitting word for the

formidable Lady Ysabella—Gus could hardly stay
with her indefinitely. Perhaps she should save up her
allowance and track down her feckless brother and
strangle him.

As if she *could* save her allowance. Although no one
realized it, Gus had tried. But Gus had gambling fever,
and once she started to play she couldn't stop until she
had lost all her money, and sometimes not even then.
After which she wallowed in self-loathing until the
compulsion struck again. She glowered at Conor as
he placed her evening cloak around her shoulders. "I
might point out that I *did* win!"

"Only because the owners of the establishment were
afraid I might peach on them for running a crooked
game." He handed her up into his carriage. "Sweeting,
you are a flat."

What was wrong with her? Just the touch of Conor's
hand on Gus's arm made her entire body flush with
heat. Perhaps it was all the wine she'd drunk. Although
considering the effect Conor had on females of all ages
and persuasions, it might simply be the man himself,
so potently sensual that he beamed temptation out
about him like rays from a lighthouse.

Conor signaled to his driver, and settled on the opposite seat. "You can't stop me from playing," Gus
persisted. "I'm of an age to do as I please."

What she pleased to do, thought Conor, was to follow her brother's same pathway to perdition. He was
wiser than to mention this aloud. "You're of an age to
be turned over someone's knee. Try not to be so
prickly. I have a proposition for you."

"What sort of proposition?" Gus was grateful for the
shadows. Her cheeks burned hotter at the thought of
being turned over Conor's knee.

How suspicious she was of him. How appalled she would be if she knew how amused he was by her. "I have this evening visited a number of establishments that I did not particularly enjoy," Conor said. "Because Lady Syb knows that you have taken to stealing out of the house, and has determined that I am to keep you under my eye. Therefore, I thought I would escort you to some establishments that might be more to both our tastes." She hesitated. "If you are determined to journey through the fleshpots, there can be no better guide than myself. I know them so well, as you have any number of times pointed out."

Journeying through the fleshpots with Conor Melchers had an allure that he hopefully couldn't imagine. "Why would you do that?"

"The alternative is to have Lady Syb ring a peal over me. Which do you think I would prefer? Too, it would allow me the pleasure of your company." She snorted and he leaned closer. "I've realized why you're angry with me."

It was dark inside the carriage, and Gus was feeling the aftereffects of good wine and better play. Therefore, she spoke with more frankness than she might otherwise have shown. "You kissed me. And then, if you will recall, you ran off with my cousin's first wife."

Conor winced at this reminder. "That was a long time ago. Charnwood has forgiven me. I have even dined with him and Elizabeth. He has also forgiven Magda. Why should you—" He broke off. "Ah. I see."

Gus clenched her fists in her lap. "I am *not* angry because you didn't kiss me again."

"Of course you aren't," soothed Conor. "And I would be happy to see the matter rectified."

His voice was pure seduction. A lesser female would

have leapt across the carriage and straight into his lap. Gus dug her nails into her palms and stayed right where she was. "You have kissed too great a number of females between then and now."

'Twas the first time his experience in matters amatory had been held against him by a lady. Conor was bemused. "I'm sorry you feel that way. Perhaps you might be induced to change your mind."

Perhaps she might, and then she would have to strangle him. Gus didn't wish to strangle Conor, annoying as he was. Nor did she care to contemplate the cause of her reluctance. "And pigs might fly!" she snapped.

Conor was far too experienced with the ladies to think this lady's irritation meant that she disliked him. "Speaking of pigs," he said, "I haven't yet had the pleasure of meeting the fabled Pontius."

Gus *had* experienced that pleasure—and it says much for the eccentricity of Lady Syb's household that two of her intimates saw nothing untoward about the inclusion among their numbers of a swine. "Pontius is a very *large* pig, and growing more so daily, because he's become a great favorite with the kitchen staff. He had a lovely wallow in the mud today, after he was done rooting through Cook's vegetables. I heard her muttering to herself about a nice recipe for suckling pork. However, I believe she relented, because when I last saw the pair of them, she was roasting a blackcock, and he was enjoying a nice belly rub." She thought, shockingly, that she might fancy a nice belly rub herself.

Conor chuckled: a cozy, lazy chuckle that made her wish to make him laugh again. Lord, would the carriage ride never end? Gus sought to change the subject. "Helen is very clever. I think she might like to learn some tricks."

Helen? Tricks? The shadows hid Conor's startled expression. How did Gus know about his ladybirds? A moment's reflection caused him to realize that everyone knew about his ladybirds, and Gus was hardly a sheltered girl. Conor searched his brain, but could think of no way his companion might have learned about the little opera dancer who had so admired his toes, as well as the rest of him, not too long ago; who had already shown him a great number of tricks, the likes of which Gus definitely shouldn't know about, sheltered girl or no. "Helen?" he echoed.

"Abby named her that because she is so beautiful," said Gus. "After Helen of Troy. You sound very strange, Conor. Have you got something stuck in your throat?"

Very nearly his foot, thought Conor. "Ah. The hedgehog. They are nocturnal creatures, you know."

"I know it now. She spends a great deal of the night pushing a ball around the room." Gus pulled back the leather curtain and looked out the carriage window. "This isn't the way to Grosvenor Square."

"No. Since you are so determined to play, I am going to teach you to protect yourself." Conor paused just long enough for Gus to wonder what sort of things he meant to teach her, and if it involved turning her over his knee. "You are about to make the acquaintance of a colorful individual known as the Dimber Daddle, 'dimber' because he is a pretty fellow, and 'daddle' because he has a very nimble pair of hands."

TEN

"I'm not entirely certain," grunted Nigel, as he applied his shoulder and heaved, "that this is a good idea! Perhaps I have not yet recovered from last night. Was that a snicker I heard, Mortimer? Lady Syb would tell you that it is not good *ton* to snicker at your superiors."

Mortimer could not help but snicker, bad *ton* though it might be, at the sight of Mr. Slyte and Lady Augusta trying to persuade a pig to mount the stair. Indeed, he did worse than snicker, a shocking breach of etiquette that went unnoticed because the pig was shrieking loud enough to wake the dead. The butler disguised his chuckle with a cough, and ventured, "Perhaps Master Pontius might respond more readily to honey than to salt."

Gus, who was at the front end of the pig, paused her fruitless tugging. "Would you like some honey, you handsome brute?"

Pontius was panting almost as much as she from their mutual exertions. He whuffed at her. "Yes, I know this is all very trying, but you will be happy to see your mistress," said Gus, and scratched his head. Pontius appreciated this demonstration of affection so much that he decided to sit down and enjoy it, to the dismay of Nigel, who was propping up his other end.

Then came a knock at the front door. A goggle-eyed footman opened the portal. On the doorstep stood a handsome auburn-haired gentleman. "Good God," said Nigel. "Surely you ain't come to call on Nit!"

Viscount Daventry stepped into the hallway. So great was his self-possession that he didn't even blink an eye at the sight of Nigel sitting on the marble floor with a large pig in his lap. "I thought it only polite that I inquire as to your sister's health after all the effort she went to on my behalf. Hello, Gus. What are you doing with that pig? I heard him halfway down the street."

If Duke was not quite the paragon that Nit beheld him to be—his nose was slightly crooked, the result of a youthful misadventure; there was a curious scar above the corner of his left eyebrow; and his lips were thinner than found on the average Greek god—he was still a fine figure of a man, neither too tall nor too short, nicely put together, five-and-thirty years of age. He was also an acquaintance of long-standing. Gus sat down on the nearest step and took Pontius's head into her lap. "We are trying to get him upstairs before Lady Syb returns. Annette isn't here. She's been taken to visit Lady Ratchett as penance for her sins. Have you met Elizabeth? Justin's bride? Lady Ratchett is her mama, poor thing."

"Poor Lady Ratchett, she means," explained Nigel. "Our duchess has discovered a certain pleasure in doing what her mama thinks she should not."

Viscount Daventry eyed Lady Augusta, and Nigel, and the pig, and wondered why the devil they wanted a pig upstairs. "Have you tried tempting it with a turnip? I understand pigs like turnips beyond anything." The footman was dispatched to fetch a turnip and several of his fellow servants. Having made his small contribution to the venture, Duke took his leave.

Queer, mused Nigel. What was the most sought-after bachelor in London doing on their doorstep? Surely he wasn't so lacking for entertainment as to dangle after Nit. Nigel didn't think he wished his sister to be the source of anyone's entertainment. Save his own, of course.

The footman returned with the turnip. Pontius lumbered to his feet. Gus snatched the vegetable and backed up the stairs. Pontius followed, assisted by several brawny footmen. "That's a *good* pig!" said Gus, as she dangled the turnip in front of his damp and eager snout.

Damned if she didn't seem to be enjoying herself, which was most unlike Gus. Nigel wondered what she had been up to while he and his aunt endured Nit's misadventures at Almack's. He doubted she'd stayed home with a good book. No book that Nigel had ever encountered had left him with such an air of suppressed excitement, or sparkle in his eye, not even *The Lust of the Libertines*.

Gus continued backward up the stairs, keeping the turnip just out of the pig's reach. Pontius squealed and grunted, while the footmen pushed and shoved; Nigel offered words of encouragement from a safe distance behind. The rest of the household paused in their various tasks to titter and stare. Even Abby was drawn by the ruckus to climb out of her bed and venture into the upper hallway, where she became so dizzy that she plopped down on the rug.

Nigel climbed the stairway several steps at a time, and bent over her. "You ain't going to convulse, are you, Abbess? Or foam at the mouth?"

She ignored his nonsense. The procession reached the top of the stairs. Pontius spied his mistress. Turnip forgotten, he squealed and barreled toward her. Abby opened her arms. The pig ran into them. 'Twas the most touching of reunions. Even Gus was seen to smile.

Nigel waved away the fascinated footmen. Whatever Abby's history—and Nigel had many theories about that, each more outlandish than the one before, from her having been a female posing as a parson to the speculation that she might have escaped from a lunatic asylum, in which case she'd leapt from the frying pot smack into the fire—she showed no embarrassment at receiving visitors in her nightdress. Not that those visitors hadn't seen her in her nightdress before. However, now all of her was on view. And a nice all of her it was, Nigel noticed, though due to his many sisters he was of course immune to such things.

"As you see, he's fit as a fiddle. And a devilish ticklish task it was getting him up those stairs." He held out his hand to her. "This hallway is damned drafty. Not to mention public. Perhaps we might move this touching reunion into your room."

Abby looked up to see Lady Syb's usually discreet servants openly gawking at the sight of her and her pig. She grasped Nigel's hand and let him draw her to her feet. Pontius trotted beside her into the bedroom. Gus followed and firmly closed the door.

Abby was shockingly weak. Only Nigel's strong arm kept her upright. "Thank you. For everything," Abby murmured, as she sank into the chair.

"Don't thank me, Abbess!" Nigel brushed pig bristles from his jacket. "I do nothing that isn't in my own interests. In years to come, I shall receive great pleasure from telling the tale of our Abbess and her pig. There, now, don't fret! Your memory will come back."

Abby touched the gold band that hung from the chain around her neck. Whose ring had it been? Husband, lover, friend? "And if it doesn't?" she said quietly.

"Then you shall be Aunt Syb's salvation." Nigel stepped away as Gus slipped a pillow behind Abby's back. "Keep her from racketing herself to flinders, or alternately getting bored. Do a great service to us all."

Be an object of charity, thought Abby. She couldn't imagine anyone preventing Lady Ysabella from doing exactly as she wished. She looked at Pontius, his heart-shaped pink nose and curly tail and long droopy ears, round cheeks, and twinkling eyes. He was gazing at her with intense concentration. "My little piggershins," she murmured. Pontius sighed blissfully and lay down on his side. She rubbed his belly with her foot. Nigel had never realized that sight of bare toes tickling a pig's belly could be so erotic. Hastily, he looked away.

Gus wasn't similarly affected. "I didn't know that pigs could smile," she said.

Lady Augusta was also smiling. She was actually quite lovely, in an unconventional manner, with her hair coming unpinned and tumbling around her face, her patrician nose and high cheekbones. How Abby envied those cheekbones, having none to notice of her own. "Pigs can do many things. If you see Pontius running about with straw in his mouth, you may expect it to rain. I left Helen sleeping on my pillow. It was very generous of you to leave her to keep me company."

Gus turned to the bed, scooped up the hedgehog, and cuddled it against her cheek. "I've made her a play area in a hip bath, as you suggested. Empty, of course! And a cave from a flowerpot, with straw bedding and a piece of an old blanket. Helen is so very smart that she soils only one corner of her quarters, the clever girl."

Abby saw nothing untoward in doting on a hedgehog. She herself doted on a pig. "Helen will also like to play in shredded paper. Be alert, because hedgehogs can find entry to the strangest places, and like to explore."

Gus drew up a stool beside Abby's chair and perched upon it, thus bringing her hedgehog in close proximity to Abby's pig. Helen opened one eye and regarded Pontius. Pontius also regarded her. He grunted, she huffed; then Pontius returned to the pleasure of his belly rub, and Helen to her nap. "What a very good girl!" said Gus.

Women! He would never understand them. Since there was nowhere else in the room to sit, Nigel stretched out on the rumpled bed. "I don't mean to interrupt your reunion, Abbess, but Aunt Syb will return home before too long, and if she catches Pontius in your bedchamber we'll be in the suds along with Nit. Has sight of this fine fellow perhaps jogged your memory?"

Abby looked down at Pontius, the picture of porcine bliss. "A present of four hundred needles, four papers of pins, and two thimbles. A pond full of toads. Feeding sheep with cabbage. Planting peas and beans and radishes and Spanish onions in my garden. But I don't know where the garden is. 'The male is by nature superior, and the female inferior; and the one rules, and the other is ruled; the principle, of necessity, extends to all Mankind.' I can quote Mary Wollstonecraft as well as Aristotle. 'It is a farce to call any being virtuous whose virtues do not result from the exercise of their own reason.'"

" 'All wickedness is but little to the wickedness of a woman,'" responded Nigel. "Equality of the sexes, female sexuality and awareness, vigorous exertion of the feminine intellect—definitely you are a radical."

Abby regarded him. "Even more curious than my knowing such things is that *you* do. Priding yourself on your uselessness as you do."

"Ah, but I *am* useless." Nigel positioned himself more comfortably upon the pillows.

"'A merry heart doeth good as medicine,'" murmured Abby, and was fascinated to see him flush.

So might Gus have been, and even more so, had she been paying attention to the conversation. Instead she was scratching Pontius's back and thinking about her adventure of the previous night, which had taken place in the back room of a tavern, or as Conor called it, a flash house. Conor knew all manner of strange individuals, which was on reflection not surprising, because he was a rakehell as well as a gentleman, and therefore could do anything he pleased. The Dimber Daddle had turned out to be a slender man with delicate features whose real name was Jeremy. Conor explained that Jeremy was a bully-trap, a sharper or a cheat, whose effeminate appearance made him appear an easy mark.

How Conor came to know the man had not been explained. Jeremy had shown her many things, while Conor sat by silently and enjoyed what appeared to be a mug of ale: a preparation of the playing cards called *biseautage,* where one end was made narrower than the other, enabling the shark to remove various cards from the pack and clasp them in the necessary order so that they might be slipped into the hand of an operator; cards briefed, slipped, or covered, packed or cut or even swallowed for purposes of concealment, in one instance between two slices of butter and bread. He introduced her to the ways of throwing used by doctors of the dice, such as the stamp, the dribble, and the long gallery; demonstrated the use of "cramped" boxes, by way of which the sharper "cogged" or fastened dice in the box as he dropped them in, so that he could drop them out with the required face upward. Then there was the "eclipse," the fraudulent manipulation of a die, done by the little finger, which led to the eclipse of the victim by the sharp. "A gentleman might be damnably bubbled, if he ain't being sharp," Jeremy said, at the end of the lesson. "Or a lady likewise."

It had all been most fascinating, and when she had thanked Conor—and very prettily, moreover—he had merely made her a mocking bow. Gus wondered why he was being so obliging. Impossible, despite his claims, to believe he feared displeasing Lady Syb. Conor being Conor, it was perhaps best not to know.

Abby and Nigel were trading Bible quotations. "'Like a gold ring in a pig's snout is a beautiful woman who shows no discretion,'" said Nigel. "I refer, of course, to Nit. Aunt Syb is both beautiful and discreet. Gus is sometimes neither, and sometimes both. Whereas you, Abbess, are an unknown quantity."

Whatever Abby might be, she wasn't beautiful, as she knew very well, having looked into a mirror. "Abraham tried to pass off his wife as his sister, so if men lusted after her he could give her away instead of having his property stolen. And no, I don't know how I know that, but the fact that I *do* know it might explain why I also know the works of Mary Wollstonecraft."

Nigel propped himself up on one elbow to regard her with interest. Abby was unlike any female he'd ever known, which was not surprising, since few females combined a knowledge of Bible study and the ravings of Mary Wollstonecraft with a face that looked like it belonged to a wholesome country miss. "Whatever else you may be, Abbess, you're game as a fighting cock."

Before Abby could respond to this provocation— "They shall be a thorn in your side" and "Miserable comforters are ye all" came to mind, along with the realization that she knew a great deal about fighting cocks, such as that they were paired by weight, and trained for their task, and often had inch-long metal spikes strapped over their own spurs to insure a fight to the death—a footman scratched on the door. "A message for Lady Augusta," he announced, and presented a silver tray.

Gus opened the note and scanned it. Conor suggested a tryst. His carriage would be waiting that evening at the end of the street.

How clandestine. And how intriguing. Gus tucked the note away. Then she scowled at the two people regarding her with curiosity, one from the bed, and the other from the chair. Three people, if Pontius was included, because the pig had raised his head to see why his back was no longer being scratched. "Is there perhaps a Biblical quotation about minding one's own business?" she snapped.

ELEVEN

"I didn't do it on purpose!" protested Nit. "Truly! My foot slipped!"

"Now you're telling clankers," retorted her brother. "You should be ashamed. And it didn't do you any good at any rate, because Duke paid you no more attention than a flea that had bit him. I already told you he ain't on the dangle for a wife, being as he already has his heirs. And you *don't* want to meet them, because they're not cute little fellows you wish to chuck beneath the chin, but hell-born brats who go through nursemaids like mice through cheese. No, there ain't any mice here, or if there are you ain't like to see them, so don't screech! And don't try and change the subject, either. I told you how it would be."

Everyone was very busy telling Nit how things would be. Lady Ratchett had certainly had a great deal to say on the subject—"No demeanor, whether in a princess or a country girl, can be comely that is not grounded in female delicacy," for example, whatever that meant.

Lady Ratchett had also said she didn't know why anyone should have chosen Aunt Syb for a chaperone, considering—Aunt Syb had shushed her at that point, with a reference to little pitchers and big ears, which

Nit thought very unfair, because her ears were as nicely formed as the rest of her. Had not a number of young gentlemen told her so? "I don't think it's very nice of you to compare me to a bug." She sulked.

Nigel wasn't to be distracted. "Besides, I thought you said you wanted a duke or at least an earl."

"I did say that. I remember it," Nit replied, with dignity. "But I am a female, and it is my prerogative to change my mind."

Lady Syb, who sat forward in the box, turned and frowned at them. "Shush!" she said.

Nit didn't know why she should shush when in all the surrounding boxes people were paying more attention to each other than to the action on the stage. Aunt Syb had explained that *Pizarro* was an antiimperialist melodrama written by Mr. Sheridan, owner of the theater, who had strong feelings about Britain's reassertion of control over Ireland's government. Nit didn't understand what Ireland had to do with Peru, where the play was set, but her understanding of geography was not great. Obediently, she gazed at the stage, where a Peruvian landscape was being excellently portrayed, and the hero, Rolla, was crossing the trunk of a tree thrown over a ravine.

Her attention did not stay long with the action. If Viscount Daventry hadn't been impressed with her—and Nit was not at all convinced of that—other gentlemen had been, judging from the posies and invitations arriving at Aunt Syb's house. Nit started as Rolla threw the tree bridge down into the stream. Poor Gus, missing the excitement. Nit nudged her brother. "Is Lady Augusta ill?"

Nigel gave up all hope of watching the play, not that he was especially enamored of Peruvians, although he was a friend to Sheridan, whose outstanding oratorical

skills were unfortunately not matched by his abilities
at theater management. "If Gus is ill, it's not of some-
thing a leech can cure," he said. "Don't go tearing up!
She ain't at her last prayers yet. Did you know that
Drury Lane was where King Charles II first set eyes on
Nell Gwynne?"

Nit did not. She didn't know who Nell Gwynne was,
and was uncertain of King Charles. Nigel delivered up
a history lesson about Charles I and Oliver Cromwell
and the abolishment of the theater, which was seen as
ungodly and licentious entertainment, only to return to
favor when Charles II restored the monarchy, fatefully
as it turned out, because the King became enamored
with an orange girl with a talent as a light comedienne.
Since Nit appeared mildly interested, Nigel also explained how the careful use of light and shadow set off
the caves and recesses and gloomy woods of the stage
background; that the waves of the sea were made by
dozens of extras on their hands and knees heaving
about beneath a blue cloth; and that a prompter stood
behind the proscenium to the actor's left, alert lest
someone forget his lines.

Forget his lines? What a shocking thing. Why would
anyone who was forgetful go upon the stage, although
the theater was very exciting, with all the splendidly
dressed people, and the buzz of conversation, and the
smell of the candles and lamps. Nit was splendidly
dressed herself, in a gown of white gossamer satin,
sleeves and hem decorated with rosebuds, as was the
cap she wore. Lady Syb was even more magnificent in
a dramatic dress of black slashed to reveal the white
satin worn beneath, and a magnificent turban fes-
tooned with flowers, tassels, and a rope of pearls. For
his part, Nigel had chosen an evening coat of dark

green, breeches of drab kerseymore, a white waistcoat embroidered with gold thread, natural-colored
stockings, buckled shoes, and an intricately tied cravat.

Mrs. Jordan, herself considerably less exquisite as
the beleaguered Cora, raised her voice in song:

> "'yes, yes, be merciless, thou tempest dire;
> Unaw'd, unshelter'd, I thy fury brave:
> I'll bare my bosom to thy forked fire,
> Let it but guide me to Alonzo's grave!'"

Bare her bosom? Surely not! And if Mrs. Jordan *did*
bare her bosom, Nit didn't care to see. Her attention
was caught by a figure in an opposite box. Was it Viscount Daventry? Could it be?

It was, and he had seen her, judging from the re-
signed expression on his handsome face. Nit raised one
hand and wiggled her fingers at him.

"Silly chit!" said Nigel, witness to this byplay. "Ain't
you heard a word I said? Duke ain't going to be a pre-
tender to your hand, so don't go and make a cake of
yourself again."

"I didn't!" wailed Nit. "I wasn't! And no one ever
told me I shouldn't wiggle my fingers at someone."

Lady Syb was considerably more interested in the
play than either of her companions. She turned to
frown at them. "You are not to wiggle anything!" she
said sternly. "Just sit there quietly and think of all the
things Lady Ratchett said to you."

Nit didn't want to think of Lady Ratchett, who
hadn't seemed to like her one little bit. "The timid, the
retreating step, the cast-down eye, the blush—" Well!
Nit couldn't imagine why a gentleman would like a
lady who couldn't say boo to a ghost.

Lady Ratchett had also made a great many comments about deportment and delicacy and demeanor. Even Aunt Syb's eyes had glazed over. "A pretty face may be seen every day, but grace and elegance, being generally the offspring of a polished mind, are more rare." Nit didn't think her mind was polished, nor would she care for it to be, because Lady Augusta's mind probably *was* polished, and look how miserable she was. Although Gus had seemed to be in high spirits today. Nit wondered why that was. She realized that Viscount Daventry was no longer in the opposite box, and felt fairly miserable herself.

Intermission came. Visitors flocked into the box, for Lady Syb was popular, and Nit had drawn no little attention to herself with her mishap at Almack's. Nigel abandoned the ladies in favor of the Green Room backstage, joining the gentlemen chatting with the cast in the general dressing room amidst makeup tables and wig stands, where he put forth a grave opinion that the drama might have benefited from the inclusion of a chorus of fifty singing witches, like Kemble used in *Macbeth,* and flirted with both Mrs. Siddons and Mrs. Jordan before settling into a semiserious conversation with Mr. Sheridan, who hoped to persuade Mr. Kemble to resume management of the theater, even though that gentleman was not likely to soon forget he had once been arrested for one of Sheridan's own debts.

Visitors crowded Lady Syb's box, including young Mr. Harcourt, who had overcome his shock at hearing Miss Slyte speak so casually of castration, and was eager to pay his respects; and Sir Frances Braceborough, who hadn't minded falling on her one little bit. Nit was entertaining her admirers with tales of her horse Fancy, a palomino with a white stripe down her face, who had an excellent conformation and a sweet disposition, now that she had been cured of baulking and bolting, although she still had the habit of cribbing when bored. She was lamenting the impropriety of females riding astride when Viscount Daventry stepped into the box.

Fortunately, Lady Syb was not listening to her niece, else she might have had no other recourse than to resort to her vinaigrette. She broke off her own conversation and looked quizzically at Duke. He bowed and introduced his companion, Bartholomew Heath, the Right Honorable Earl of Ormesby, Tolly to his friends. Lady Syb raised her brows. "He is a marital prize of the first order," Duke murmured into her ear.

Lady Syb eyed the earl, who had wrestled himself a seat beside Nit, and was hanging on her every word. "Ormesby is a mooncalf," she murmured. "If you mean to distract my niece, you will have to do better than that."

"I would prefer to distract *you*," Duke murmured, with a pointed glance that caused Lady Syb's other companions to move a discreet distance away.

"Tiresome creature!" Lady Syb regarded her professed admirer with amused exasperation. "You wish to flirt with me because you know I have no desire to marry you or anyone else. You must be desperate indeed if you attempt to empty the butter dish over a lady old enough to be your mama."

"Not at all," retorted the viscount, and pressed a kiss into her palm. "Granted, I *am* desperate, but you surely aren't old enough to be my mama."

Lady Syb glanced at her niece, who was looking sulky, and rapped him with her fan. "Gentlemen do not comment on a lady's age. Even when the lady brings up the matter first."

Duke pointedly refrained from looking at Nit. "Age is irrelevant," he said.

Age was irrelevant only to those who weren't familiar with its progress in the mirror. Gently, Lady Syb wafted her fan.

Viscount Daventry was an enigma: a very eligible, very elusive, very handsome gentleman who showed great adroitness in sidestepping the hopeful young women paraded endlessly before him. Had he loved his wife? Syb could hardly remember the girl. For whatever reason, Duke had never shown the slightest interest, despite all the lures cast in his direction, of taking another bride.

Lady Syb was far too wise in the ways of the world to attach any significance to his flattery. However, if he sought a brief respite from matrimonial machinations, she could provide it easily. She patted his hand and set out to amuse them both with a fine wicked gossip about Mrs. Jordan, currently playing the part of Cora—it would be said of her, alas, that she was very bad in a wholly unsuitable role—who while touring the provinces frequently sent a portion of her earnings through the post to the Duke of Clarence, with whom she lived as man and wife in all but name.

Nit didn't understand. Why was Viscount Daventry talking to Aunt Syb instead of her? Not that he *could* talk to her, really, with so many gentlemen flocked about. Mr. Harcourt and Sir Francis were tussling over her as if they were two dogs and she a bone, while Lord Ormesby seemed content just to sit and look at her. Nit supposed she should be gratified by the gentlemen's attention, but each was so eager to impress her that she was unable to overhear a word of what Viscount Daventry was saying to her aunt, whom she was rapidly coming to consider as a snake clutched to her breast.

She must marry a title, Nit reminded herself. A title, accompanied by wealth. Viscount Daventry was not the only gentleman to possess both. Lord Ormesby certainly had little enough to say for himself. She fluttered her lashes at him.

Miss Slyte seemed to Tolly a goddess, so golden was she, so fair. Her hair was yellow as straw, her eyes like blue marbles, her mouth—Imagery failed him, but her teeth were as shiny as any teeth he'd ever seen. As for her person, it made a fellow think he'd never really looked at a female before. And if she wished to ride astride, why shouldn't she? Were there no horses handy, he would be pleased to offer her himself. Shocked at his own wickedness, Tolly blushed bright red.

Nit watched in fascination as color flooded Lord Ormesby's cheeks. He did not look to her like she thought an earl should look, for he was only of medium stature, the buttons on his waistcoat strained by a tendency toward girth; his hair a nondescript brown, his features unremarkable.

But his expression was genial, and he was clearly full of admiration for her. Nit smiled, thereby causing Tolly to blush all the harder, and asked his opinion about what was best done in the case of a capped hock. If Tolly had no opinion on the matter, generally leaving such business in the capable hands of his groom, Mr. Harcourt saw an opportunity to draw Miss Slyte's attention back to himself, and leapt in with an astute remark regarding the use of ice to limit inflammation, followed by the application of a soothing poultice. Not to be outdone, Sir Francis shook his head, and said that the bursa must be tapped, and the fluid withdrawn, and a medicinal salve applied. The longer a capped hock went untreated, the greater chance that the inflamed tissue might become permanently thickened, resulting in a lifelong blemish, which would be a sad thing.

Viscount Daventry was fascinated by this conversation. "Capped hocks?" he murmured to Lady Syb.

She glanced over her shoulder. "You can't think Ormesby will do for her," she murmured. "He has yet to say a word."

"He's moonstruck," Duke said gravely. "As he is a slowtop, and she is a pretty widgeon, they might do very well. In truth, I only meant Tolly as diversion. I wished to speak with you without having her fall again at my feet." He winced. "I sound like a coxcomb."

"Yes," said Lady Syb. "But I know you aren't one, so never mind. Unfortunately, I doubt your scheme served its purpose. Annette may be speaking to Ormesby, but she keeps throwing impassioned glances in your direction. You only whet her interest by ignoring her, for young women are prone to want what they're told they may not have. Don't ask me about older women, or I shall have to scold."

"You have piqued my curiosity." The viscount rose from his chair. "However, since intermission is ending, I must collect Tolly and take my leave. 'Twas a pleasure being rescued by you, Lady Ysabella. I am in your debt."

Lady Syb regarded him over the top of her fan. "Twaddle!" she said.

Nigel returned to the box, having had his fill of Sheridan's laments about players so ungrateful as to ask for their salaries, and tradesmen indignant about unpaid bills, to find his aunt fluttering her eyelashes at Viscount Daventry while his sister ignored her own admirers to stare. Those admirers scattered on the reappearance of her brother. Nigel wondered if he was expected to defend her honor by demanding pistols at dawn, and devoutly hoped not.

"So you've met Tolly," he said, as he reclaimed his seat. "He's a good sort. Not only an earl, but rich as well. He seemed taken with you. What did you think of him, puss?"

Nit looked at the stage, where the afterpiece—*Hannah Hewitt, or The Female Crusoe*—was under way. "His understanding is not powerful, is it?" she said, thereby providing her brother with an excellent instance of the pot calling the kettle names.

TWELVE

Nit need not have pitied Lady Augusta for missing the excitement of seeing the intrepid Rolla hurl his tree bridge into a stream. Gus was enjoying some excitement of her own, in a gaming hell, where Jeremy explained that the trick to winning at play was to avoid games that were purely chance, that most gamesters had neither the ability nor desire to calculate the odds, and therefore her chances of winning would be greatly improved by remembering what cards had already been played. He showed her how the deck could be fuzzed by continuously stripping off the top and bottom cards, added several new words to her vocabulary—the swag; Sir Hugh's bones; down-hills (false dice which ran low); bulking (a cogger's term for cheating by confederacy and obstruction)—and bade her practice until she could made a shuffle behave properly. He then taught her how to slip a card, an "old gentleman" being a card somewhat larger and thicker than the remainder of the pack, and an "old lady" a card broader than the rest; and related the tale of a foreign sharper of distinction, a foreigner, whose hand was thrust through with a fork by his adversary, with the cool remark, "I ask your pardon, sir, if you have not the knave of clubs under there." "Nine-tenths of the people who play live by it," Jeremy warned her, then related several chilling tales of gentlemen who had been roused from gambling fever to find themselves over head-and-heels in debt. One blew out his brains with a pistol; another suffocated himself with charcoal fumes; yet another quitted this world by stabbing himself in the neck. One gentleman was so thorough a gamester that he left instructions in his will that his bones should be made into devil's teeth, and his skin prepared as a covering for dice-boxes.

Gus raised her hands. "Enough!"

'Twas no concern of Jeremy's if the lady remembered his warning no longer than the next time the fever struck. He had done as he had been asked, and shown her how to bite the biter, cheat the cheater, rob the rogue. Because he liked her, he additionally warned her of the danger of going double or quits with a gambler who could afford to keep losing until he won; and told the story of a clerk who, having nothing left to play with but his ears, cut off the fleshy part of one and flung it on the table, to the consternation of his fellow gamblers.

Lady Augusta winced and touched one of her own earlobes. "Never let me stir again if I lie to you!" said Jeremy, and sat down to a game with her, which he let her win, as an example of how luck was dependent on the behavior of the cards, for he could have as easily turned up a winning hand for himself.

Gus's eyes were sparkling as she and Conor left the hell, her cheeks flushed, her lips curved in a smile. Unkind to take her home now, when her blood was thrumming with excitement, and sleep was the last thing on her mind. Since it was not in his nature to leave a lady wanting more, Conor took her instead to Vauxhall.

The pleasure gardens were situated a mile and a half from London, on the south side of Lambeth, and con-

sisted of several acres of tree-lined avenues and grav-
eled walks, wooded valleys, exotic Turkish minarets
and Arabian columned ways. Thousands of lamps
twinkled in the trees, their flames tinged with reds and
blues and greens. A double row of globes were
arranged in perpendicular lines on the pillars of the entrance, and met with other rows along the arched roof
of the passageway.

Ahead of them lay the Rotunda, a large building of an
orbicular figure, with a row of windows around the attic
story. Inside, the vast amphitheater was decorated with
gay paintings and gildings, four grand portals in the
manner of ancient triumphal arches, and four times
twelve boxes in a double row with pilasters between.
Conor procured a supper box decorated with statues and
arches and a cascade, a romantic view painted on the
wall. To the sweet strains of an orchestra, he and Gus
dined on two tiny chickens, slices of ham as fine as
muslin, assorted biscuits and cheese cakes, and a fair
amount of arrack punch, a particularly potent beverage
formed by mixing flowers of Benjamin with rum.

Gus drained her glass and set it down, licked the last
drop of liquid from her lips. She had never sampled arrack punch before, and found it very fine. As, indeed,
was her companion. Conor, with his amused dark eyes,
his lazy tempting smile; his sensual mouth, the dark
hair tumbled on his forehead that a person itched to
brush back into place—

No wonder the man had had a thousand mistresses.
He was as potent as the arrack punch.

Gus looked different tonight, thought Conor, as he
watched her tap one silk-shod foot in time with the
music. Her chestnut hair was arranged not in its customary ringlets but pulled up into an elegant chignon

that complimented her slender, graceful neck; her lips quirked in pleasure instead of being drawn in their usual stern line. The silver-shot gray silk gown she wore brought out the color of her eyes. "What are you thinking, Gus?"

Wicked, irresistible Conor, whom she had once known so well, and who was now as far above her as the stars in the night sky. Faithless, mocking Conor, whose warm caressing gaze melted the most determined lady's defenses and left her mizzy-mazed.

Mizzy-mazed or no, Gus would stick a fork in her own hand before she told him what was on her mind. "I was thinking it a pity Tony never had the advantage of acquaintance with someone like Jeremy."

Gus seldom spoke of her brother. Conor suspected this moment's candor was due to the arrack punch. "Doubtless Tony encountered someone like Jeremy, but not in a student-teacher role. Has he contacted you?"

She pulled her shawl closer round her shoulders. "If *you* were my brother, would you dare show me your face? I would rather he does not. Still, I wonder where he is, and if he is well. Or if he's managed to fall into another scrape. Don't let's talk of Tony, or I shall become cross again! Walk with me, Conor. I wish to see the temple of Pythia, and have my fortune read."

Conor loved the ladies, and the ladies loved him back, and since none of Conor's ladies expected him to love her exclusively, or forever, they all rubbed along together very well. And then there was Gus, who wished him to escort her along Vauxhall's dark walks, not for purposes of dalliance, but to have her fortune told. Conor rose from his chair and offered her his arm.

Somehow she had amused him, and Gus didn't care. Tonight she wasn't angry, embittered Lady Augusta, but someone gayer and more adventurous. Someone who was enjoying herself more than she had in years. If ever. Probably ever. "We took Abby's pig upstairs today," she said, as Conor assisted her from the supper box. "I wonder if she could be shamming her illness? Yes, I know I have a suspicious nature. Still, even I can't imagine Abby will murder us all in our beds."

"I doubt housebreakers are generally accompanied by pigs." Conor guided his companion through the promenading crowd into a gravel-strewn avenue lined with arched elm trees. "However, I do have doubts as to whether her mishap was an accident at all. I keep thinking of that missing valise."

Gus looked up at him. "You think it may have contained something valuable?"

"I don't know what to think," replied Conor. "Except that your eyes are silver in this light."

Gus blinked, then turned away, possessed of a sudden absurd wish to cry. In the distance, a fountain bubbled. Nearby, music played. "I think Nigel is quite taken with our Abbess," she remarked, for want of anything else to say.

Conor touched a curl that had escaped its moorings to lie upon her nape. "Do you mind?"

Gus glanced back, as startled by his question as by the touch of his hand. "Why should I mind?"

He slid his hand down her arm and took her fingers in his. "As I recall, Nigel was once quite taken with you."

His hand was strong and muscular. And warm, even through her gloves. Gus forced herself to concentrate. "I think we may safely say that Nigel has changed his mind. And it was I who didn't wish to marry him, if you will recall."

Did Gus regret that long-ago decision? Had old feelings resurfaced now that both she and Nigel dwelt beneath Lady Ysabella's roof? Along with a hedgehog, a pig, and a mysterious young woman. Conor was half tempted to move in with Lady Syb himself.

They were too late to view the fireworks—the dazzling display had culminated in a grand Buffette of three Mutations, consisting of illuminated Wheels, Palm, Branches, Fire-Trees, and six Pot d'Agrettes—and there was no circus exhibition tonight, so Conor and Lady Augusta were denied the spectacle of men and women performing acrobatic feats on unsaddled horses, playing with balls and knives, jumping through paper and over boards. Still, crowds thronged the avenue, gathered around the band playing merrily from an elevated platform covered with a splendid canopy. Some people stopped to watch; others joined in the dance.

One of the revelers broke away and danced up to Conor. She was painted, masked, and very buxom, her gown cut so low that the tops of her rouged nipples showed. Conor smiled, and shook his head. With a disappointed glance, the girl turned away.

Gus scowled. Conor was here with her tonight not of his own volition, but because Lady Syb had asked it of him. If Gus *weren't* here with him, he would probably be dancing with that bit o' muslin now. Dancing, if not more. Lady Syb seemed to be overlooking the fact that it was hardly proper for Gus to be going about chaperoned by a rakehell. Not that it hardly mattered if her reputation was sullied, since she was not likely now to wed. Nor were the doors of the *ton,* save those of the highest sticklers, likely to be closed to the cousin of the Duke of Charnwood.

"What?" said Conor, because Gus was frowning at him, and he didn't know why she should, unless the encounter with a lightskirt had set up her back, and a lady who cheerfully visited a gambling hell was unlikely to be such a prude. "Would you care to join the dancing? Even respectable ladies sometimes mix in."

Gus thought of all the things she could never be, or have, simply because of who and what she was. Respectable. Past her youth. Stuck away on the shelf to wither and gather dust.

If all that, however, she was also a gamester, and this was a lucky evening, which soon enough would end. "Conor," she said abruptly, "I have decided I would like you to kiss me again."

She looked stubborn, and determined, and perhaps a little shy. Her dark lashes feathered her cheek as she refused to meet his gaze. Conor took her hand and drew her into a secluded grove. "Does this mean you have finally forgiven me for the first time?"

As if she could ever forgive him for giving her a glimpse of something she would never have. Gus succumbed to temptation, and brushed his thick dark hair back from his forehead. It was silky soft beneath her hand. "I'm considering it," she said.

There was an odd note in her voice. Conor wondered if it was truly he she wished to kiss. Conor was not unaccustomed to standing in as proxy when a more proper gentleman would not oblige.

A different thing, however, when the lady involved was Gus. Not that he would forbear kissing her. Conor was a rakehell, after all. He drew a lazy finger along the line of her jaw, then caught her chin in his hand and brushed his lips across hers.

Gus had closed her eyes in anticipation. Now she opened them to scowl. "Not that sort of kiss. I want you to kiss me like you once did. Even better, kiss me as if I were that dollymop who wished to dance with you. And I doubt very much that was all she wished to do!"

Gus was jealous. Why, Conor couldn't imagine, since he had his own suspicions about her reasons for wishing to be kissed. However, it was not his habit to argue with ladies who wanted kissing, especially since he felt very much like properly kissing Gus. He laid his hand against her cheek. She turned her face into it. The gesture moved him strangely. "Are you certain, Gus?"

Gus had never been more certain of anything. Conor was a lighthouse, and she was a ship about to smash herself on the rocks trying to get close to his bright blaze, which now that she considered it was a metaphor worthy of Nit. Appalling, the effect this man had on her. "If you refuse to kiss me properly, then who will? I don't wish to die without ever having had a proper kiss."

Had she muttered something about a lighthouse? Surely he hadn't heard her right. Or perhaps he had. Although it might be unfair to say Gus was a trifle bosky, she was definitely under the influence of the grape. He himself was not unaffected. Conor slid his hand from her smooth cheek, along her graceful neck, and rested it on her nape. Her skin was the softest he had ever touched.

With his other hand, Conor clasped her slender waist and drew her closer to him. "Are you planning to die soon?" he murmured, as he rained lazy kisses from her temple to the fine line of her jaw.

Faithless, wicked, irresistible as sin . . . His thumb traced lazy circles on her skin as his lips moved closer to hers. So seductive was his touch that Gus thought she might melt into a puddle at his feet. Mizzy-mazed, she reminded herself, and said faintly, "One never knows about that sort of thing."

Her voice was unsteady, as was the pulse that beat beneath his hand. Conor was experiencing no small degree of anticipation himself. If Gus wished to have a proper kiss, then she would have the best of him. He lowered his lips to hers.

As kisses went—not that Gus had much experience in that area—this one was memorable. Heat shot through her, starting at the crown of her head and sizzling its way down to the soles of her feet. That long-ago kiss had been nothing like this. Gus slid her hands to Conor's shoulders and pressed herself against him, wanting more.

His tongue traced her lips, and they parted for him. She tasted intoxicatingly of passion and arrack punch. Her body was soft and yielding and feminine, and fit perfectly into his arms. When he started to draw back, she wound her hands through his thick hair and kissed his face, his chin, his jaw. He took a harsh, quick breath. "What's wrong?" Gus whispered.

"Nothing," he said, as he moved his lips along the smooth line of her neck. She clutched his arms and let her head fall back. His questing mouth moved down her throat to the cleft between her breasts. She caught her breath. Conor slid his hand down her slender back to clasp her hips.

Gus sighed, and moved against him. The sensation was delightful. Without conscious thought, she molded her body to his.

Heat? A conflagration. Pyrotechnics far surpassing any seen ever at Vauxhall. Gus's senses were sent spinning like a Catherine wheel. She gasped, and broke the spell.

What the devil was he doing? Conor caught himself. Of course he knew what he was doing, but what the devil did he mean by doing it with Gus? Gus, whose mouth he'd just plundered as if she were an opera dancer. And if she hadn't made a noise, he would have plundered even more of her.

Not Gus, he told himself. Surely even he was not that depraved. Perhaps he might blame his aberrant behavior on the arrack punch. He had suffered an attack of the passions brought on by his surroundings, and the arrack punch; had consequently become so caught up in the moment that he forgot whom he was kissing, and had gone considerably further than he might have had he been in his right mind.

No excuse was sufficient for his behavior. Conor was a scoundrel, through and through. He was supposed to be Gus's mentor, not her downfall. Lady Syb certainly had not intended him to escort Gus to the pleasure gardens, nor to kiss her as he had just done. Hopefully, Gus would never know how close she'd come to being ravished in one of Vauxhall's dark walks. He could not deny himself the painful pleasure of holding her a moment longer against his body. Then he set her away from him, and waited to be slapped, which was no more than he deserved.

Her knees were shaking. Her heart was pounding fair to pop right out of her chest. Gus fought to regain her balance as Conor released her. She struggled even harder not to hurl herself back into his arms.

She disapproved of Conor, Gus reminded herself. He was a rascal and a rogue. And there he stood, in the moonlight, looking as tempting as Eve's apple and watching her quizzically.

She licked her swollen lips. "You have definitely been practicing," she said.

Gus sounded as bemused as he felt. Conor rewarded

her with a ravishing smile. "Consider me at your disposal, sweeting. Should you feel the need to be kissed again."

Gus felt the need in that very moment, damn the man. "I trust you will not hold your breath for that event," she snapped. And then she remembered that she had quite forgot to breathe when Conor was kissing her, and no wonder, considering *how* he had kissed her, and blushed a charming shade of rose.

THIRTEEN

Outside the blue-hung windows, the day was gray and gloomy. Inside the bedroom, a cheerful fire burned in the hearth. Abby sat propped up against her pillows. Nigel sprawled in the bedside chair. Pontius snoozed on the rug, occasionally grunting as he dreamed of turnips and cauliflower.

"'Whatsoever thy hand findeth to do, do it with thy might,'" quoth Nigel, "'for there is no word, nor device, nor knowledge, nor wisdom, in the grave, whither thou goest.'"

His irreverence made Abby laugh. "Very nice, but what earthly good *are* you?" she said.

"Life on earth is unimportant," Nigel replied cheerfully, and stretched out one booted foot to give Pontius's back a scratch. "One should contemplate the hereafter instead of taxing one's brain with pernicious doctrines such as you espouse."

"Humbug!" retorted Abby.

Nigel paused in his pig-scratching. "If you wish to insult me, Abbess, you will have to do a great deal better than that. Might I suggest lollpoop, or nigmenog?" Their conversation today had thus far ranged from prison reform—Abby believed that the punishment should fit the crime; Nigel conceded that he had little faith in the existing penal system as a means of re-forming criminals—to the inequity of the current system of parliamentary representation and the need for social reform. Nigel confessed to being a member of the House of Commons. Abby must not hold it against him. Even in the harvest field, there would be found weeds.

Weeds! Abby smiled. Nigel was as easy to talk with as he was to look at, and she suspected there was con-siderably more to the man than he cared to admit. "I cannot imagine you as a member of the clergy." She touched the ring that hung from the chain around her neck.

Nor could he imagine her as a member of the clergy, or posing as one rather, so Nigel had abandoned that idea. Currently he was toying with the theory that she had some nefarious reason for hiding from the law. "Lack of religious conviction need in no way interfere with the supervision of parish activities," he said solemnly. "Hasn't anyone ever told you that women should confine their interest to the domestic sphere?"

" 'A fool uttereth all his mind,' " said Abby, and threw a pillow at him, just as a knock sounded on the door. The maidservant displayed no reaction to the sight of Nigel clutching a pillow: she had been among the audience previously privileged to see him sat upon by a pig.

"Sir Edmund Jessop is wishful to see you, ma'am."

Nigel settled the pillow comfortably behind his back. "Enter the leech!"

Sir Edmond entered, but not alone. Trailing after him was Nit, who gazed upon Abby and said, "Ha! I knew there was a stranger in the house, even though everyone said there wasn't, and why they should tell me whoppers, I don't know, because when *I* try and tell a whopper, everybody scolds. I am Miss Annette Slyte, Nigel's sister, ma'am. Aunt Syb is cross with me because I wiggled my fingers at Viscount Daventry, but I did not know that was something I should not do, and I wished to draw his attention to myself. Viscount Daventry is as handsome as Croesus, you see!"

Among the odd things Abby knew was that Croesus was legendary for being not handsome, but rich. No question but that before her stood the legendary Nit, dressed in a long-sleeved cherry-striped chintz gown trimmed with matching ribbons and a flounce. "Did it work?" she asked.

Nit blinked her beautiful blue eyes. "The tumble," Abby explained gently. "Did you gain the attention of your viscount?"

"He's not my viscount," Nit said gloomily. "Aunt Syb has stole a march on me, I think, which will sound very queer, because she is quite *old*. It is also very selfish, because she has had oh so many husbands, and I want only one!"

"Aunt Syb ain't that old," countered Nigel, to Sir Edmond's gratification, because the physician disliked to hear Lady Ysabella so maligned. "And there ain't no use in sulking because Duke chose to gossip with Aunt Syb instead of making sheep's eyes at you. I told you he ain't wishful of stepping into a parson's mousetrap."

A mousetrap? Nit looked cautiously around her. Seeing no rodents in attendance, she sat down on the bed with a little bounce, causing Abby to wince, and Sir Edmond to frown. "You make marrying me sound a horrid fate!"

"I'm sure he didn't mean it that way," Abby said quickly, before Nigel could compound his mischief with another provocative remark.

Nit looked more closely at the young woman on whose bed she sat. Rather it was Lady Syb's bed, but Nit knew what she meant. If not tallow-faced, exactly, the stranger was not at all out of the common way, with all those freckles, and that unmanageable curly hair, which was a very ordinary shade. She also had something wrong with her head, poor thing, because why else would Sir Edmond be poking at her like he was?

"Who are you?" Nit asked. "And why has Aunt Syb hidden you away like this? Are you hiding from someone?" Her eyes widened. "Oh! Are you a *criminal*?"

Nigel disliked to hear his current theory voiced aloud, not that he believed a word of it himself. "Her name is Abby, and she has been injured, as you could see if you ever looked anywhere but in a reflecting glass!"

As he had intended, this slur distracted Nit from her speculations. "Beast!" she wailed, and reached over to swat at him. "Gracious! Is that a *pig?* Whatever is a pig doing in the bedroom?"

Sir Edmond had wondered the same thing, but hesitated to inquire. "It is my pig. His name is Pontius," said Abby, as if that explained everything, which of course it did not. "Is my head healing properly, Sir Edmond? Pray tell me I may get out of bed."

"Perhaps tomorrow," said the doctor, and snatched his medical bag away from Pontius's quivering nose, for now that Nit had awakened him, the pig was curious about this new article, and wished to smell and push at it, and see what its purpose was. "Your injury is mending very well. As to the other"—he glanced warily at the fascinated Nit—"has there been any, ah, change yet?"

"No." Recollection of serpents eating dust and the magical powers of mandrake hardly gave Abby any better notion who she was.

"Don't fret yourself about it." Sir Edmond said briskly, and prepared to leave. "In time, all will be made clear."

The strange young woman looked unhappy. Nit would cheer her up. "I am to go riding in Hyde Park with Aunt Syb. Lady Augusta is to accompany us. Perhaps you might wish to come along."

Did she ride? Abby didn't know. At any rate, she certainly didn't wish to ride today. "Out of the question!" said Sir Edmond, and regarded his patient sternly. "Gentle exercise only, my dear, and that does *not* include climbing onto a horse. Head injuries are not to be taken lightly. Things might go badly for you were you to take another fall." He took himself off to deal with more conventional patients who suffered merely from gout and the French pox.

Nit chuckled at the notion that anyone should fall off a horse while traveling at a sedate speed through Hyde Park. Then she stopped abruptly because a newcomer entered the room. The lady wore a traveling dress of periwinkle blue, a matching bonnet trimmed with pink roses and white lace, and a weary expression upon her pale face. Even Nigel abandoned his usual nonchalance to sit up and stare. "Cyn! What the devil are you doing *here?*"

The lady ignored him as she pulled off her bonnet and walked closer to the bed. "Mortimer told me all about Aunt Syb's latest project." She looked Abby up and down.

Golden hair mussed from her travels, blue eyes made no less fine by shadows beneath them, a lovely face marked with lines of strain—"You must be another of Nigel's sisters," Abby guessed.

Cynthia smiled, revealing a trace of Nigel's mischief. "I'm the homely one. My nose is too long, my mouth too wide, I have no bosom to speak of; I can't sing, or play a musical instrument, or paint a pretty picture, or even speak intelligible French. Even worse, I have an excellent head for business. My stepmama quite despaired of me. That's why I ran off with Duncan, damn his eyes." Her gaze fell upon Pontius. "What a handsome pig."

Abby watched with fascination as the elegant newcomer—who was as far from homely as chalk was from cheese—knelt down on the rug beside Pontius and proceeded to administer a good scratch. "Duncan is your husband? Is he with you?" Abby had grown accustomed to Nigel seeing her in a condition of undress, and even Mr. Melchers, who had probably seen more ladies undressed than not, but she was not prepared to entertain yet another strange gentleman in her boudoir.

"Not yet," said Cynthia, the blissful pig's head in her lap. "But he will be soon enough, because he'll wish to wring my neck once he realizes that I've left."

"Jupiter!" gasped Nit. "Cyn, you haven't run off *again*?"

Even Nigel looked startled. Quickly, he recovered his aplomb. "'As a day returns to its vomit, so a fool repeats his folly.' Proverbs 26:11. I perceive a certain irony. Cyn ran off to marry Duncan, and now she's run off and left him behind. You must know your own business best, Cyn, but as your favorite brother I feel obliged to point out that Duncan is going to be mad as fire."

"You're not my favorite brother!" retorted Cynthia. "That would be Luke. You *were* my favorite brother until the episode with Duncan's sporran. I haven't forgiven you for that yet."

"Unfair!" Nigel protested. "*I'm* the brother who helped you marry your Scots outlaw, not Luke."

"I'm not sure I've forgiven you for that either." Cynthia tossed her bonnet onto a table a safe distance from Pontius's quivering snout.

Nit gaped. Here she was, come to London in search of a husband, a more daunting prospect than she had anticipated, for thus far no one had sung under her window, nor had she received a single billet-doux; while ungrateful Cynthia left a perfectly good husband languishing at home. "But Duncan is very handsome!" she said.

"Duncan is a pigheaded Scotsman," retorted Cynthia, then gave Pontius a quick kiss on the nose. "No offense!"

Cyn would rather kiss a pig than her husband? How very sad. "But you live in a castle!" Nit reminded her.

"I do, indeed," Cynthia conceded. "A great drafty moldering pile."

Cyn was beyond ungrateful. Were *her* castle drafty, Nit would simply wrap herself in a heavy shawl. "You are a ladyship!"

"I am a ladyship who socializes with sheep and chickens and has more than a passing acquaintance with pigs." Wearily, Cynthia grasped the arm of Nigel's chair, and pulled herself to her feet. "I am older than you are, brother. Act the gentlemen that you aren't and let me sit down."

Nigel conceded her the chair, not because he was a gentleman, but because Cynthia *was* his favorite sister, and he disliked to see her looking like death's head on a mop stick. He wondered what the black-hearted MacDougall of Dunally had been doing to her. "Tell me you didn't travel all this way alone."

"I brought my maid with me." Cyn leaned her head back against the chair and closed her eyes.

Nit understood none of this. "Why did you come to

Aunt Syb instead of going home? Duncan will expect to find you there."

"Precisely." Cyn opened one eye to look not at Nit, but at her brother. "I'm thinkin' it'll be a temper that himself will be in after stravaigin' about the country in search of an errant wife. Which will serve the brute excellently well for saying he won't live under the cat's paw. Where *is* Aunt Syb?"

"Here, there, and everywhere. You know how she is." Nigel had taken up a position by the bedpost nearest Cynthia. He glanced at Abby, who looked concerned. "Ain't you glad you got knocked on the head, Abbess? Otherwise, you would have missed all this. And no she ain't really an abbess, Cyn. I just call her that."

"I didn't think she was." Cynthia smiled. "She appears to have great good sense. Not that I suppose the other sort of abbess wouldn't. But just look what excellent care she's taken of this pig."

"Better credit Cook for that," said Nigel. "She fed him the truffles we was supposed to have for luncheon. Says he is a great deal more appreciative of her talents than we are."

Nit was less interested in truffles than in husbands. "Why didn't you tell Duncan you were going away?"

Cynthia pulled off her gloves. "I had meant to tell him something else altogether, but he was much too busy to listen to me, as usual, so I decided that it was time to take matters into my own hands. Take my advice, and never let yourself be taken for granted, Annette. Every man, even the best of them, which I usually think Duncan is, needs occasionally to be reminded that a woman is not so predictable as a blackfaced ewe! Pray ask me no more questions, because the journey was long, and I am very tired."

Immediately, Nit was contrite. She hopped off the bed and hovered over her sister, offering to fetch lavender water for her head, or a nice basin of flower water in which to soak her feet, or barring all else, a nice cup of tea. Nigel leaned against the bedpost, and wondered how his aunt would respond to this latest development. Abby rested against her pillows and mused upon Jacobites and rack rents and Scottish blackface Highland sheep, which could thrive under the most adverse circumstances, producing wool that was coarse and heavy, and horn sheaths prized for the crafting of shepherd crooks and walking sticks.

FOURTEEN

Lady Ysabella had a headache. It was riding along-side her on a sorrel mare, and chattering excitedly about all the friendly gentlemen who had paused to speak with them, surely some of whom must be titled and wealthy and on the lookout for a bride. "You might do well to remember that you will be spending the rest of your life with the gentleman you marry," said Gus, who rode on Annette's other side. "A title does not necessarily make a comfortable bedfellow."

Nit's beautiful blue eyes widened. "Oh! Am I expected to *sleep* with him? What a shocking thing!"

Lady Syb and Gus exchanged glances. Neither felt up to explanations. "Not necessarily," said Ysabella. You will probably have your own bedchamber."

Nit looked bewildered. "Then why did Lady Augusta say what she did? Unless she meant to wind me up, which would not be very kind, but I suppose I should not be surprised, because Nigel does it all the time!"

Annette was a pretty horsewoman, which was why Syb had agreed to take her out today. Since Nit didn't know enough to get out of the rain, alas, Gus had been persuaded to come along. Not that it was raining, though the day was overcast. Too, Syb was curious as to Augusta's progress through London's gaming hells,

though the unobliging creature was stubbornly un-
forthcoming on that point.

She returned her attention to her niece. Although Nit
had promised to observe all the proprieties, Nit's
promises were only as good as her memory, which had
already proven as trustworthy as water in a sieve. She *did*
make a pretty picture, however, in her green riding costume, the jacket with a black velvet collar, and double
rows of buttons, on her curls a black beaver hat, with a
gold chain band around the crown, and a feather in the
front. For the occasion, Lady Syb had donned a riding
dress of blue cloth with a double plaiting of Valenciennes
lace around the neck, a black beaver hat embellished
with a gold band and tassel and an ostrich feather of
blue. Gus wore a habit of gray cloth with a waistcoat of
yellow silk, and since her white silk hat boasted two yellow feathers, she outshone them both. Nigel had seen the
ladies off with several remarks about birds of a feather
flocking, and fine feathers making fine birds. He had not
accompanied them, claiming their splendid plumage
would cast him into the shade.

Hyde Park was the rendezvous of high society at this
fashionable hour. Ladies drove out in superbly ap-
pointed carriages, attended by liveried footmen and
coachmen in wigs and three-cornered hats. Gentlemen
drove, or rode, or in case of dire necessity hired a good
horse from Mr. Tilbury in Mount Street.

The park's history was colorful. Henry VIII had ap-
propriated the property from the manor of Hyde,
which belonged to the Abbot of Westminster, and
turned it into a private deer park. Oliver Cromwell's
corpse had once dangled in a cage at Tyburn gallows,
at the treeless northeast corner of the park. During the
Great Plague of 1665, many of London's citizens fled

the city and Westminster to camp on the park's great open spaces. William III caused three hundred oil lamps to be erected along the Route de Roi to light his way from Kensington Palace to St. James's.

It was along Rotten Row that the ladies now rode. Here the ranks of society who preferred horse exercise displayed themselves on ground carefully laid down in tan and gravel for their use. "Oh!" cried Nit. "There is the Duke of Charnwood. If only you had snapped him up before Lady Ratchett did, Aunt Syb!" She twinkled at Gus. "You will not mind if I speak so, because you know how very handsome your cousin is."

Her cousin handsome? Gus supposed he was. She also supposed she should be grateful to him for restoring her dowry after her brother had gambled it away, but it was difficult for Gus to be grateful to anyone, even Lady Syb, who had made it possible for her to wander through the fleshpots with Conor, and be soundly kissed, with the result that now she could think of precious little other than when she might be kissed again. "Justin married an heiress," she said, dampeningly. "It was only later that they discovered they had made a love match."

"Don't pucker up!" Lady Syb added hastily, with a stern glance at Gus. "You will give yourself lines." Immediately, Nit smiled, and noticed that the Duchess of Charnwood, who wore an enviably form-fitting costume of amber color that matched her eyes, was *not* wearing the obligatory ostrich plume. "Hello, Gus," said the duchess. "You've been playing least-in-sight."

Elizabeth was not a friend, not really. When Gus thought about it, she had no real friends, save Helen, and it was not entirely satisfying pouring out one's heart to a hedgehog. Not that she would pour out her heart to Elizabeth, but Gus felt the need to confide in someone, a clear indication of the sorry state she was in, which was all Conor's fault, because she couldn't help but remember how she had felt when Conor kissed her, and held her against him, and how she hadn't wished him to let her go.

Indeed, she had thought about it all night. She was thinking about it now, while Elizabeth regarded her curiously. Gus scolded herself. Conor Melchers hadn't earned his shocking reputation by saying no to curious females.

The ladies had dropped back behind the other riders. The duke rode ahead with Lady Syb. Elizabeth watched Nit coquette with one admirer, then another; the gentlemen swarmed around her as if she were a honey pot. "You were not at Almack's to see Annette throw herself at Viscount Daventry's feet."

Gus wouldn't have cared just then if Nit threw herself into the nearby Serpentine, a small narrow lake that curved diagonally through the park, which was used for swimming and boating and fishing, as well as mock sea battles, to the dismay of the resident ducks. "Lady Syb took her to visit your mama as a penance," she remarked.

"I know. Maman does not approve of her. Or of Lady Syb." Elizabeth grinned. "Nor does she approve of me! Ladies apparently are not to wear their hearts on their sleeves. Doting on one's husband, especially in public, is considered gauche."

Gus looked steadily before her, afraid of what Elizabeth might read in her face. "At the time of Nit's *débâcle* I was at a gaming hell, being instructed on the proper way to play. Did you know that within two short years after attaining his majority, Prinny had lost eight hundred thousand pounds?"

The Duchess of Charnwood knew full well that Lady Augusta was addicted to play. She had herself once accompanied Gus to a gaming hell, which had mightily displeased her husband, not only because he disliked his cousin's gambling, but also because he had been present with a lady other than his bride. "Forgive me for saying so, but I thought Lady Syb was supposed to prevent you from visiting gaming hells."

Gus glanced at Elizabeth. "I believe the expedition was Lady Syb's idea. She hasn't time to deal with me herself, being busy trying to prevent Nit from landing in the suds. Don't look so astonished. You know Lady Syb must have a finger in every pie."

Elizabeth could not help her fascination. "Lady Syb sent you to a gaming hell."

Gus contemplated her horse's ears. "Lady Syb sent me to a gaming hell with Conor. It's not the same thing."

The duchess's amber eyes opened even wider as she assimilated this information, and observed the telltale color that stained her companion's cheeks. "I thought you didn't like Conor," she said, cautiously.

Gus's color deepened. "I don't *approve* of Conor. That's quite a different thing. Although when you come right down to it, I don't know who I am to approve or disapprove of anyone."

Here was a strange mood in which to find Augusta. "Fiddlestick!" Elizabeth said, bracingly. "Tell me all about it, pray!"

Gus would not tell Elizabeth about the kiss, of course, much as she might long to. Instead, she entertained the fascinated duchess with instructions on how to fuzz the deck, and how to slip a card, the description of a perfect shuffle, the information that it took five to seven shuffles to totally randomize the deck, and the tale of the sharper who had his hand thrust through with a fork; the upshot of all this being that she would not have to eat playing cards with butter and bread, she hoped.

Elizabeth marveled. "*Conor* showed you all this?"

"Jeremy showed me all this, at Conor's request." Gus paused. Perhaps she was feeling the aftereffects of overindulgence in arrack punch. Perhaps that was why she didn't wish to strangle Conor, but rather to kiss him again. Again and again. Until he was as mizzy-mazed as he had left her.

To the devil with discretion. "He kissed me," she said.

The duchess's curiosity overcame her. "Which one?"

At the thought of Jeremy kissing her, or any other lady, Gus had to smile. "Conor, of course. I asked him to. It was very nice."

Elizabeth suspected, from Gus's expression, that "very nice" was an understatement of considerable degree. Some comment seemed called for. "Oh, my!" she said.

"He gave me a hedgehog." Gus looked almost shy. "Conor, not Jeremy! I have named her Helen. Or rather, Abby has."

Though it was not for her to question Lady Syb's wisdom, or Conor's intentions, Elizabeth hoped that Gus was not in the process of exchanging one addiction for another, with stakes even more ruinous. But Gus was looking as if she already regretted her confidences. "How glad I am that you have brought up the subject," the duchess said cheerfully. "I am most curious about Nigel's Abby and her pig!"

* * *

Lady Syb was questioning her own wisdom in escorting Nit to Hyde Park. She had hoped to gain the girl additional admirers, since none of the crop currently flocked around her would suit. However, though other gentlemen aplenty stopped to speak with Annette, her trio of beaux guarded their privileged places jealously.

Mr. Harcourt was amiable enough, and wouldn't lead the girl into bad habits, but he had neither a title nor sufficient wealth for Nit. And how on earth did he manage to turn his head with shirt points so high? Sir Frances Braceborough was amiable, sometimes boring, upright and honorable and entirely too old for the chit, who would doubtless lead him into an early grave. Since Nit had only to favor Lord Ormesby with a smile to render him tongue-tied, it was unlikely he would be able to check her starts. Annette needed a strong hand on the reins, due to no innate ill temper, but to youthful high spirits and a total want of common sense. Hands such as Viscount Daventry might possess. Lady Syb asked Lord Charnwood his opinion of Duke being brought up to scratch. Unlikely, thought Justin, but one could never tell when Master Cupid would choose to let loose a fatal dart, as he could attest to himself.

Nit's hands on the reins were light, her posture graceful and relaxed. Due to the many hours she'd spent on horseback, Nit was more comfortable in the saddle than anywhere else, and could manage her horse and carry on a conversation simultaneously with perfect ease. That conversation at the moment concerned fistulous withers and poll evil and parrot mouth. Mr. Harcourt put forth his opinion about stringhalt and overreaching. Sir Frances spoke solemnly of various equine vices he had known, not only kicking and weaving and biting, but also wind-sucking, blanket-tearing, and halter-pulling. Lord Ormesby merely stared soulfully at Annette.

Graitfying as it was to be admired, Nit was growing a trifle unnerved by Lord Ormesby's unrelenting gaze. Perhaps if she tried very hard, she might persuade him to speak to her. "I understand the Four-Handed Club meets in the Ladies Mile."

Four-Handed Club? Tolly frowned in an intense effort to understand what his goddess was talking about. "You mean the Four-in-Hand Club," Sir Frances said indulgently. "I'm a member myself."

"*Are* you?" Nit abandoned her effort to set Lord Ormesby at ease—the poor thing really was a knock-in-the-cradle—and beamed at the older man. "Tell me all about it! I have always wished that I might join."

Sir Frances, who was very jealous of his own right to wear the ankle-length drab coat and yellow-striped blue waistcoat of the club, tut-tutted at the notion that a female might drive a carriage pulled by four horses, an exercise requiring considerable strength and skill. "A pretty little thing like yourself—Why, 'twould be unthinkable! Better you allow the gentlemen to drive you about."

It took a great deal to rouse Nit's temper, but this dismissal of her abilities made her mad as fire. "What an unjust thing to say!"

Mr. Harcourt saw his opportunity. He offered Miss Slyte his own team to drive. "Yes, but are there *four* of them?" she demanded. Lord Ormesby roused from adoration announced that he would be happy to lay his own matched four at his goddess's feet. Annoyed by these efforts to upstage him, Sir Frances bade Lord Ormesby not to talk like a nodcock, and told Mr. Harcourt that only a saphead would allow his ribbons to be tooled by a female. Mr. Harcourt retorted that Miss Slyte might do anything with his ribbons that she wished, and furthermore he would go with her to watch a horse being gelded if that was her wish. Sir Frances doubted the fidelity of his own ears. "Being *what?*" he gasped.

The road was wide enough to easily drive three carriages abreast, and crowded with fashionable ladies and gentlemen, roans and bays and blacks and grays, carriages the splendor of which Nit had never before seen. Ladies and gentlemen young and old greeted one another, or snubbed one another, made assignations and broke them, exchanged the latest *on-dits* and made up new ones on the spot. The milling throng did not overwhelm her, for Nit had been taught from her girlhood to mount and dismount expertly, ride gracefully, shake hands with friends from the saddle, and control her horse so as to avoid accidents in a crowd. As her admirers quarreled among themselves, Nit stared at a passing gentleman who had a poodle perched beside him on the carriage street, and another dressed all in a bright green that matched his curricle. And then Nit glimpsed an auburn-haired gentleman mounted on a fine black steed. Viscount Daventry saw her also, and nodded politely, but gave no indication that he meant to stop.

Well! He meant to pass her by? Nit thought otherwise. A slight flick of the rein, a nudge of the knee . . .

The sorrel mare was gratifyingly responsive. Eagerly, she broke into a trot. Nit dropped the reins, and shrieked.

FIFTEEN

Conor Melchers was having a stern talk with himself. What the devil had he been thinking to kiss Gus? She wasn't in his usual way—she wasn't in anyone's usual way—and kissing her now had been considerably, startlingly different from kissing her when they were both young.

Conor had definitely taken too much of the arrack punch. Why else would he have kissed Gus in the manner that he had? Not to mention the other things he'd done to her, all of which had felt damned fine. And not that he regretted an instant of that embrace, even while admitting he should not have done it, but he didn't doubt Gus would be cursing him today, not only for the kiss, but for her overindulgence in the grape. Therefore, he was presenting himself at Lady Syb's residence in Grosvenor Square, so that he might apologize, and Gus might box his ears, since he could not do it for himself.

She was in the drawing room, which on first glance appeared filled with flowers, the sweet scent of the blossoms heavy in the air. "Hello, Melchers," said Nigel, who lounged in one of the oval-backed chairs. "You will think someone has died. Unfortunately, she ain't." He regarded his younger sister unappreciatively.

Nit's lower lip quivered. Teardrops trembled in her eyes. "I am in disgrace, Mr. Melchers, which isn't fair, because I didn't mean to take a tumble, or if I *did*—and I don't say that I did, mind you!—it was only because I wished Viscount Daventry to *look* at me."

Gus was standing by the fireplace. She caught Conor's glance, and her cheeks turned as pink as the pretty gown she wore. She *did* regret the kiss, he thought, then was surprised to realize he had hoped she would not.

Nit was looking at him expectantly. Ah, the viscount. "And *did* Duke look at you?" Conor asked.

"I suppose so." Nit made a *moue*. "Certainly everyone else stared! I don't know if you can imagine how it feels, sir, to know that you are an excellent horsewoman, and still fall off your mount."

Not for the first time, Conor was grateful for his wicked reputation, which kept young ladies, for the most part, from making cakes of themselves on his behalf. "When did this, ah, mishap occur?"

"Today," said Nigel. "In Hyde Park. As result of which, none of us will attend Lady Brock's assembly, which for my part I consider a blessing, but Nit is inclined to sulk."

"I am perfectly well enough to dance!" Nit squirmed. "Although I do have a dreadful bruise, but I mustn't say where!"

Conor glanced at Gus, who refused to meet his eye. Whether Conor would go about his usual activities this evening remained unclear. He was uncertain how he felt about that circumstance.

Conor was uncertain about Gus altogether. Memory of their embrace haunted him, which was a most unusual thing. Possessed as he had been of a myriad of ladyloves, Conor could not recall that one had ever before invaded his dreams. Not that Gus was his ladylove. Maybe that was what made the difference. Conor didn't think he had ever felt about a female the way he felt about her.

It would pass, of course. Passion always did. Even passion as profound as any he'd experienced before. Although, considering Conor's legions of ex-lovers, it wasn't impossible that he should have forgotten how he felt about one of them. Which made him feel obscurely ashamed of himself. Dammit, he wished to speak with Gus, and without all these other people in the room.

"I have not fallen off a horse since I was five years old!" Nit continued, with a pretty pout. "And then it was because Nigel let go of the leading rein."

"'*Mea culpa, mea culpa, mea maxima culpa!*'" muttered that gentleman. "You can't blame me for today's contretemps, because I wasn't there!"

Nit didn't see that her brother's absence absolved him of responsibility. "Why is everyone pinching at me? You'd think I'd tied my garter in public." She peeked through her lashes at Conor. "I suppose I should not have said that to you, since you are so wicked, sir."

"No, you should not!" said Cynthia, entering the room to hear that last remark, with a pale Abby on her arm. Pontius was not with them, nor Helen, because Lady Syb had banned both creatures from her drawing room. "You have already sent Aunt Syb to bed with the headache, you ungrateful child. And you might have a thought for those three gentlemen with all their posies, each one of them feeling as guilty as if it was his fault you tumbled off your horse! Hello, Conor. You won't mind if I speak freely in front of you. I assume that you've met Nit."

Conor knew the older Slyte siblings, for they had, along with the Duke of Charnwood and his cousins, grown up on neighboring estates. "I have had the privilege," he said politely.

Nit *did* feel a tiny bit remorseful that Mr. Harcourt and Sir Frances Braceborough and Lord Ormesby had reacted with such horror to her fall. If only Viscount Daventry had been equally concerned! Instead he had appeared to consider her horse worthy of more concern than herself. "I don't know why everyone must make such a great to-do over a simple mishap," she muttered.

"Mishap, my eye!" retorted Cynthia. "What do you think Papa would say to all this, pray?"

'Twas very *unfeeling* of her siblings to be so cruel when Nit was sore and bruised, which was a testament to what a very good rider she was, 'else she might have broken her neck in such a fall, and surely Nigel hadn't meant it when he'd expressed a wish that she had. "The same thing he'll say when he finds out you ran away from your husband!" she retorted. "That he doesn't know why the Lord blessed him with so many daughters, and we shall between us send him to an early grave. And I should think running away from a husband is surely a great deal worse than falling off a horse!"

"It is in some ways quite similar." Cynthia sat down beside Abby on the settee. "You are looking well, Conor. It was very thoughtful of you to rescue Abby and bring her to Aunt Syb."

"It isn't fair!" protested Nit. "Abby takes a tumble, and Mr. Melchers rescues her. *I* take a tumble, and not only does Viscount Daventry rescue my horse instead, Aunt Syb calls me a cabbage head!"

"That's because—" Nigel broke off under the combined stern glances of his sister and Gus.

"Just think of all the gentlemen who *were* concerned for your welfare," soothed Abby. "I have never seen so many visiting cards." In point of fact, she didn't remember seeing any visiting cards before, but saw no need to point that out. Distracted from her grievances, Nit surveyed the cards, and tried to recall what it meant when the upper right-hand corner was turned down.

Conor studied Abby. She wore a pretty round gown of figured dimity with a narrow flounce, and a ribbon in her curls, which had been artfully arranged to cover the area where her hair had been cut away. "You look very well today, Abby. I'm glad to see you out of bed."

Nigel was not long silenced, no matter how many censorious glances were cast in his direction. "That's a compliment indeed, Abbess, because with Melchers it's generally the other way around."

Gus moved from the fireplace to stand by a damask-draped window. "Annette, perhaps you might like to show Abby the painted velvet reticule that Lady Syb bought you the other day. Would anyone care for tea?"

Nit wrinkled her brow in concentration. "The reticule?"

"The reticule," Gus said firmly, as she rang for a servant. "Abby will like it above anything."

If Lady Augusta said there was a painted velvet reticule, then there must be one, whether Nit remembered it or not. And if Abby liked the reticule, then perhaps her sister would also, and Nit would give it to her, and Cyn would stop cutting up so stiff. Somewhat cheered by this prospect, Nit set out for her bedchamber.

The room was briefly quiet. *"Is* there a painted velvet reticule?" Cynthia inquired.

Gus smoothed her skirts. "No. But it will keep her occupied for a time."

She was very cool, composed, and distant. Conor remembered the warmth of her beneath his hands. He must be even more depraved than he was generally considered to be, thinking of seducing Gus. However, he *was* thinking about it at that moment, which shocked even him. In search of distraction, he glanced at Cynthia. "You look tired, Cyn."

"I look like the devil, and I know it. Don't fuss, Conor, I'll be fine." Her eyes twinkled. "That's a very nice hedgehog you gave Gus."

Conor wondered what else Gus might have confided in Cynthia, and found he didn't wish to know. He turned to Abby, who was fingering the soft material of her gown. "I feel like a fraud," she murmured. "Lady Ysabella said my own clothes had been damaged beyond repair, and that furthermore she disliked to see anyone but herself in black. But this is much nicer than I am accustomed to, I think."

The tea tray arrived. Cynthia prepared the beverage. Nigel refused to curdle his insides with such stuff, but prepared Abby a selection of tea cakes, one of which he popped into his own mouth. "She ain't to exert herself," he said, in response to Conor's quizzical glance. "Lest she rupture the substance of her brain, in which case we may see an apoplectic seizure, and stupor, or paralysis, or all of them at once. Tell you what, Abbess, maybe you shouldn't be hefting that teacup!"

"Twaddle!" retorted Abby, as she lifted the cup with

ease. "I shall have to exert myself a great deal more than this, I think, if I am to discover who I am."

"Fascinating!" remarked Cynthia. "Perhaps we may all help you. Like a treasure hunt. Leaving no stone unturned."

Abby doubted there was treasure to be found. "You are very kind."

"Now, that we ain't!" Nigel said bracingly. "What we are is a family of meddlers. Well, look at Aunt Syb! Furthermore, we will do anything to escape ennui. Cyn has run all the way from Scotland because she was bored with sheep and drafts. I periodically present myself in the House of Commons, and put forth shockingly radical ideas. It is very well for *me* to have radical ideas, you see, Abbess, because I am a man. While Gus—not that Gus is a member of the family, but she might as well be—well, Gus will have to tell you herself what means she takes to keep boredom at bay." Despite her every intention not to do so, Gus glanced at Conor. There was a question in his dark eyes. She looked quickly away.

If neither Cyn nor Nigel had noticed this byplay, being intent on Abby, Abby wondered what lay between Mr. Melchers and Gus. "I know how to change surgical dressings," she said slowly, "and I believe I must have been exposed to smallpox. There is something lurking in the corner of my mind, but I cannot bring it out into the light." A fisherman who built his own rod and made his own flies. And wore a blue dressing gown.

She touched the ring that hung around her neck. "Perhaps I am a widow. But I don't feel the least bit sorrowful, which seems a shocking thing in me. If I had a husband, I must have cared for him. Surely, if I knew who I was, I would be missing him more than a little bit."

"Not necessarily," remarked Cynthia, who had barely sipped her tea. "I don't miss mine at all."

"Liar!" said Nigel. "Perhaps you had him beheaded, Abbess. Like John the Baptist and Salome. Which is surely preferable to a bloody death involving dogs."

Abby smiled to think of the irreverent Nigel speechifying in the House of Commons, or even more absurdly, conducting the daily services of morning and evening prayer. "I've made some inquiries," he added. "And there's no word of a parson recently popping off."

"But it wouldn't necessarily be recently, would it?" said Cynthia. "Which might explain why you aren't overwhelmed with grief, my dear. Now we have made you sad, which is very bad of us. Shall I tell you about Scotland? I have learned a great deal about the wretched place since I married the bloody MacDougall of Dunally."

"Married him over the anvil," Nigel reminded her. "Our father had forbidden the match. Not that anyone could blame him for it. Nit has the right of it, you know. All *she* did was fall off a horse."

"Shut up, Nigel," said his elder sister. "The Mac-Dougalls are descended from the eldest son of Somerled, one of the most celebrated of Celtic heroes." She went on to talk of how the Highlanders had made a living from stealing their neighbors' cattle for over a thousand years.

Conor had particular interest in neither Scotland nor the lairds of Dunally, though he was concerned to see Cynthia's fine features so drawn. He moved casually to the window where Gus stood. "I owe you an apology," he said quietly.

She looked not at him, but out the window. "No, you don't. And if you tell me you're sorry, I really *won't* ever forgive you."

Conor glanced over his shoulder, but the others were entranced by Cynthia's tales of a MacDougall ancestor fighting naked and painted blue, screaming like a banshee as he chopped off the heads of his enemies, which he later used to decorate his home. "I'm not the least bit sorry," he murmured. "Are you?"

So far was Gus from sorry that she longed to know when she might be kissed again. Right now might be nice, if there weren't so many other people in the room.

She dared not look at Conor. "How can I be angry when I asked you to—" Prudence reared its head. "You know."

If she stared at the window with any more intensity, the force of her gaze might break the glass. Conor touched her shoulder, and she turned toward him. He smoothed one of her raised eyebrows with a gentle fingertip. "I would have done it anyway, sweeting. Whether you asked me to or not."

He had *wanted* to kiss her? Gus stared at him. Conor was smiling at her disbelieving expression when Nit tripped back into the room. Her earlier sulks forgotten, she was holding a flower-bordered Norwich shawl.

"Are you *quite* sure Aunt Syb gave me a painted velvet reticule? Because I cannot remember it, and could not find it anywhere, and when I asked her about it, she told me I was a nuisance, and that I should go away. I do not think that she is ill, whatever you may say, because surely no one who is ill can be so very cross! I'm sorry I could not find the reticule, Cyn, but perhaps you might like this instead." She draped the shawl around her sister's shoulders, then glanced at Conor.

"Why do you have Lady Augusta stuck over there by the window, sir? You look like you are going to push her out!"

Gus stepped quickly away from him, and Conor dropped his hand. "He's trying to prevent her *jumping* out," said Nigel. "Which she has threatened to do if you don't stop throwing yourself at Duke."

Nit blinked. "Does *she* want him, too? Well, that is very bad! It is also very unfair, because no one is scolding *her,* even though jumping out a window is surely more shocking than falling off a horse!"

Nigel laughed. Gus rolled her eyes. Conor flicked her cheek with a lazy finger and murmured, "Tonight."

SIXTEEN

If Lady Augusta thought Mr. Melchers had arranged for an assignation with intentions of a dishonorable nature, she was to be disappointed, for the result of their clandestine meeting—clandestine because he knew she would prefer it; Lady Syb would hardly have minded if he'd called at the front door—was that he escorted her to a gaming hell. This was not one of the places where she had learned about bully-sharps and *biseautage,* but the Maison de Bonheur, an exclusive establishment in Pall Mall.

The façade was elegantly Palladian, the servant who granted them entrance liveried and bewigged, the stout front door promptly bolted and barred behind their backs. "Should officials of Bow Street manage to enter armed with warrants, players may still escape by way of a subterranean passage, through a long range of cellars, terminating at a house in Shug Lane," explained Conor, with that odd ability he had of sensing a lady's thoughts.

The footman led them up a grand staircase to the first floor, where the rooms were beautifully paneled, and the furnishings of the finest quality. Dazzling chandeliers hung from intricate plaster ceilings that were as superbly fashioned as the rugs on the gleaming floors. Mirrors and silk and gilt gleamed everywhere.

"There is a billiard room on the upper floor," Conor added. "And smaller rooms that are put to use for more private games." Gus thought of what manner of private games she might play with Conor, and fixed her attention on the glittering throng of bejeweled women and handsomely dressed men, some of them of the gentry and others not, for all that was required to gain entry here were lips not prone to preach or babble, and pockets deep enough to stand the heated pace.

Gus was not here to play tonight, but merely to observe. She glanced at her escort, who looked like a fallen angel in his dark evening coat, and perfectly at home in the raffish crowd. A fallen angel? Lord! Abby and Nigel were rubbing off on her. She smiled.

Perhaps because it was so rarely seen, Gus's smile was particularly sweet. She was enjoying herself in this place, as Conor had expected she would. If only he could stop himself from thinking of the various ways in which he might enjoy her, a feat that might have been more easily accomplished if she weren't wearing a gown of gray-green silk that complimented her coloring and clung to her slender curves. He was a rascal and a rogue, Conor reminded himself. Gus deserved far better than a jaded libertine. He fetched her a glass of iced champagne from a passing waiter, and they strolled through the rooms.

Whist, deep basset, faro—The owner of the establishment had taken his nightly stand at the hazard bank. Tables were placed about the rooms, and stands for the punters' glasses and their rouleaux. Where once she would have wished immediately to play, now Gus shrewdly watched the players. Many were the tricks employed by professional gamblers to communicate among themselves: the use of a handkerchief during a game was evidence of a good hand, and a snuffbox the opposite; affected coughing the assurance of so many honors; rubbing the left eye an invitation to lead trumps, and the right eye the reverse.

They paused by a table where a game of piquet was under way. Piquet was played with thirty-two cards, two to six of each suit being omitted from the deck. The game consisted of six deals called a *partie*, with the deal alternating between the two players. Each hand was played in five parts: blanks and discards, ruffs, sequences, set and tricks. The game continued until one of the players scored one hundred points. There were ways to cheat at piquet: Short cards used for cutting; the aces, kings, queens, and knaves being marked with dots at the corners of the cards. Gus watched intently for signs of cardsharping, then turned as she felt someone's gaze on her.

Conor glanced around also. He had been enjoying the intensity with which Gus observed the players, and studied the cards. "Stafford," he said coolly to the tall and stern-featured man whose attention was fixed on Gus. There was nothing for it but to make introductions, and he did so. "You were acquainted with Lady Augusta's brother, I believe."

Jack Stafford was a man of no more than average height, but still he managed to seem sinister. His hooded eyes were as dark as the coat he wore; his hair as black as Conor's, but unrelieved by white. If Conor was a fallen angel, this man was the devil incarnate. There was an unnatural stillness about him, an innate coldness that Gus fancied she could feel even through her gloves.

He held her hand longer than was strictly proper. His thin lips twisted in what might have been intended as a smile. "My sympathies, Lady Augusta. I was indeed acquainted with your unfortunate brother. A pity Tony wouldn't let Charnwood bail him out of the River Tick."

Tony would have shot himself before he appealed to Justin for rescue, not because the duke would have refused to pay his vowels, but because by so doing Tony would have lost his cousin's respect. Not that Tony had retained anyone's respect by acting as he had, but at least he had spared himself seeing the look on Justin's face. Gus, who had not been so fortunate, could not blame her brother for that. And Stafford was as easily blamed for ruining him as a reptile for its fangs.

Gus greatly disliked reptiles. As soon as she could politely do so, she slid her hand from Stafford's grasp. "I believe," she murmured to Conor, "that I would like to leave now."

Conor was more than willing. He collected his coat and hat from the servant at the front door, and draped Gus's wrap around her shoulders. "I would never have brought you to this place if I'd thought I would find Stafford here," he said, as he helped her into the waiting carriage. "The man is notorious for the unerring certainty with which he wins from all who venture to play with him."

Gus settled back on the carriage seat. "Like Tony," she said. Odd to find herself suddenly pitying her reckless brother for falling into a cardsharper's hands.

She did not want to think of Tony. Instead she looked at the man seated opposite her, his long legs stretched out before him. If she shifted positions only slightly, her leg would brush against his. It was a heady thought. Even though she had already brushed against a great deal more than Conor's leg. The way he had kissed her—

She should have been shocked. She *was* shocked. She was also avidly curious. Gus screwed up her courage. "Conor. I wish—"

"I know, sweeting," he interrupted. "I wish it, too. I can only apologize to you."

Apologize? Gus stared at him. "I believe I told you *not* to apologize to me!" she said.

His lips curved. "I regret taking you somewhere that you encountered someone who reminded you of your brother. Surely you will allow me to apologize for that."

Gus would allow Conor to do about anything, a circumstance that she was trying to convey to the wretched man. She tried again. "Conor. You will recall that I, ah, asked you to kiss me at Vauxhall?"

Of course he remembered it. Frequently. Vividly. In point of fact, Conor was hard-pressed to think about anything else. His fingers itched to reach over and stroke her smooth, soft flesh. "I remember." He slouched back in his seat.

Why did he sound angry? Gus moistened her dry lips. "I realize that I told you not to hold your breath. However, I have changed my mind. I *would* like you to kiss me again, if you please."

She wanted to be kissed again. So did he. Conor reminded himself that it wasn't really he she wished to kiss. And if she did, she shouldn't, which amounted to the same thing, for she of all people knew his far-from-blameless reputation—God knew she reminded him of it often enough! Although he could hardly be held at fault if the ladies had been running mad for him since he turned fifteen. Nor had they paused noticeably in the years between then and now. Odd that a natural inconstancy should be irresistible to most women, but there it was. Each seemed to think that she would be the one to reform him, and though Conor was horrified at the notion someone *should* reform him, he was incorrigibly fond of the ladies, and willing to let them try.

Except for Gus. Even he was not guilty of that much wrongheadedness. And if he was, he would not act on it, even though every nerve in his body screamed at him to reach over and pull her onto his lap and kiss every other thought out of both their heads.

Gus didn't really want to kiss him, he told himself; she only thought she did because he had kissed her in a way no gentleman ever would have, and the fact that he didn't regret it for one instant just showed how lost to shame he was. Better she should have Duke, or even Nigel. Duke would probably never kiss her in the way that Conor had. Nigel certainly would not. Thought of either Duke or Nigel kissing Gus caused Conor to grind his teeth.

Conor had been too long silent. Gus stared at his profile. Now that she had compared him to Lucifer, she could not cast the image from her mind. Beautiful, fallen Conor, whose lips were so intoxicating, and whose hands she wanted to feel on her again. "What's wrong?" she asked.

What was wrong was that Conor found himself in the unusual position of refusing further advances to a lady who wanted them, and to whom, furthermore, he wished to make advances. He shook his head to clear it of that muddled thought. Conor knew that he was selfish, and hedonistic, and extremely unfaithful; and, fortunately, wealthy enough to indulge his baser self.

Denying Gus might be his first—and probably only, considering how much he disliked it—unselfish act. "I'm not worthy of you, my darling," he said.

Gus turned to stare out the carriage window. She was to have nothing that she wanted, it seemed. Not that she had ever thought she might have Conor for any prolonged period of time, but still—

A kiss. She had only wanted a kiss. Well, to be truthful, she had wanted considerably more than a kiss, but a kiss would have made a good start. "Take me home," she snapped.

Conor had hurt her, and he regretted it, and he could think of no words that would make things right. He could pull Gus onto his lap, perhaps, and soothe and caress her; could say that it wasn't that he didn't want to kiss her, but that he wanted to kiss her too much—but in that event, he *would* kiss her, because he was an unprincipled rogue, and then they would be back where they had started, and this entire exercise have gone for naught.

The devil! Conor wasn't enjoying his newfound nobility of character one little bit. He said nothing, and neither did Gus, until the carriage drew up in front of Lady Syb's house.

Conor stepped down from the carriage, and helped her to alight. When Gus refused to meet his eyes, he touched a knuckle to her chin. She did look up at him then, and drew back her hand, and slapped him hard across the face. Then she turned on her heel and strode with immense dignity into the house.

Past the startled footman at the door she stalked, then picked up her skirts and ran up the stairs. In the safety of her room, Gus flung herself on the bed. She had slapped Conor because he didn't want her, but hadn't slapped him when he did. He would think her as paper-skulled as Nit. She *was* as paper-skulled as Nit. Conor would know exactly why she had hit him. Gus didn't know whether she wished to break something, or burst into tears.

Tears were foreign to her nature. She had nothing of her own worth breaking, and hesitated to damage anything of Lady Syb's. Gus contented herself with pummeling a pillow until her fury passed.

She sat up and looked about for Helen. The hedgehog was nowhere in sight, which was hardly surprising in view of Gus's display of temper. The poor creature had probably hidden beneath the bed.

Then came a scratching at the door. Gus opened it to find Throckmorton standing there. Not by a twitch did the abigail betray that she'd been roused by an excited footman with the intelligence that Lady Augusta was acting as loony as Miss Nit. "Do you require assistance, Lady Augusta?" Throckmorton said politely. "The family has retired, save for Miss Abby. I believe you will find Miss Helen keeping her company in her room."

"No, thank you, Throckmorton. I will see to myself tonight." What a picture Gus must make, with her tousled hair and rumpled gown. Still, she would not be the queerest sight Throckmorton had seen during her years of employment with Lady Syb. Gus stepped out into the hall. A light shone from beneath Abby's door. She raised her hand and knocked.

"Enter!" called Abby. Gus stepped into the room. Abby sat propped up among her pillows, amusing the hedgehog with a ball of wadded paper. Pontius snoozed on the rug beside the bed.

"You're still awake." Gus already regretted the impulse that had brought her here.

Lady Augusta looked rumpled and tousled and altogether cross. Abby wondered why. "I've been lying here trying to remember who I am. With a remarkable lack of success, I might add."

Gus sat down on the bed and rolled the paper ball toward Helen, who chased it with great enthusiasm and then pounced. "I have been at a gaming hell. With Mr. Melchers. Don't look so appalled. I didn't play."

Abby had nothing against gaming, which now that she thought of it, seemed a trifle odd in her. "I don't seem to be appalled by much of anything," she said, as Gus got up off the bed and began to pace the floor. "I wish you would tell me what has upset you."

Gus could hardly explain that she was upset because Conor hadn't wished to kiss her. Still, she could not seem to prevent herself from saying the man's name. "I know he has been kind to you, Abby, but Conor Melchers is a rakehell. A roué, a libertine, a seducer of females. It is folly to become too friendly with such a man, who has only one thing on his mind, except when he doesn't. Oh, I am making no sense whatsoever!" She sank down on the chair.

That she was herself no maiden, Abby was certain. No maiden would be as aware of the nature of Conor's charm as Abby was. "I see."

Gus was annoyed by the violence of her feelings. And glum to think that she was fool enough to desire so faithless a man. For of course she wanted Conor, had wanted him for as long as she could remember, and had always been at great pains to keep him from suspecting her weakness for him. Well, he knew it now, and she could only blame herself.

Still, despite the disappointments of the evening, she could not regret that not-to-be-repeated kiss. Unless she had mistaken the matter, Conor had wanted her in return. A great deal, from all indications. And wasn't it just like a man to change directions as easily as a weather vane.

The image amused her, in spite of her ill temper. Gus slipped off her shoes and rested her feet on Pontius's belly, plumper surely now than when he had arrived in Grosvenor Square. The pig snuffled in his sleep. Abby scooped up the hedgehog from her coverlet and held it out.

Difficult to be wholly in the dumps with a hedgehog climbing up one's arm and a snoring pig warm beneath one's feet. And then there was her memory of the satisfaction she'd received from slapping Conor's face. Were Nigel with them—and Gus was glad he wasn't—he would surely be prepared with an appropriate Biblical quote. *Abstain from fleshly lust, which wars against the soul.*

Abby was gazing at her with concern. Gus sighed. "Never again," she said, "shall I drink iced champagne."

SEVENTEEN

Lady Ysabella glanced up and down busy Oxford Street, once the route taken by convicted criminals on their last journey from Newgate Prison to Tyburn Gallows, now the venue of elegant shops displaying muslins and chintzes and a dazzling array of other commodities dear to a lady's heart. Accompanying her were her nieces and nephew, as well as her reluctant houseguest, who was just now staring with appalled fascination at two headless gentlemen posed in the window of a tailor shop, one wearing a hunting coat, and the other a dressing gown. "Nothing strikes you as familiar, my dear?" asked Lady Syb.

Abby shook her head. She wasn't familiar with London, or unfamiliar with it either, for she was aware of Monmouth Street and Holywell, where secondhand garments were sold; and of a small area in the vicinity of Drury Lane where piece-brokers purchased old clothes and cut from them such scraps as might be sound enough to patch up other garments to wear; she knew also of Temple Bar, and the Inns of Court. Doubtful that the elegant Lady Syb, in her gown of blue embroidered muslin, and her interesting bonnet formed like an ancient helmet ornamented with zebra trimming and rose knots in the front, had ever explored

such areas. "I don't think I'm accustomed to so many
people in one place," she said.

More the wonder if she had been, thought Nigel, as
he put forth an opinion that the legendary Tower of
Babel had nothing on the confusion of Oxford Street,
which took at least a half hour to cover from end to
end. Providing, that was, that one didn't tarry in the
shops, and try on gloves and sniff perfumes, and
hunger for a white gown spangled with scarlet, as Nit
had done until informed by her sister that the red
speckles were probably intended to represent blood
spattered from the severed heads of guillotined aristo-
crats, which quite put her off her desire to visit Mrs.
Salmon's Waxworks and view the exhibition of his-
torical tableaux and horrific scenes in wax.

Nit also wore a pretty hat, with a blue rosette in front
and blue ribbon round the crown, tied down with the
same colored ribbon in a bow beneath her chin, which
she was holding high, determined that she wouldn't let
it quiver, no matter how much anyone might scold.
Abby and Aunt Syb were deep in a conversation about
Mary Wollstonecraft's belief that the rights of men and
women should be one and the same thing, which to Nit
sounded very queer, because she for one didn't want an
education, and she'd be very surprised if any gentleman of her acquaintance wished to learn needlework.
Although now that she thought about it, she wasn't a
dab hand at needlework herself. She wasn't a dab hand
at much of anything, except looking lovely, and apparently she wasn't good at even that, because Viscount
Daventry didn't seem to like her one little bit. Perhaps
Nigel was correct in predicting that she had given him
a disgust. Perhaps she had also given Lady Augusta a
disgust and that was why Gus had refused to come

with them today, saying that she'd rather stay home and brood.

Nit didn't see why Gus should be in the dismals. *She* was the one who had been pinched at and scolded and told she was a grievous disappointment until a lesser damsel would surely have sunk into a fatal melancholy. "I don't understand," she muttered, "what Lady Augusta has to brood about."

Both Lady Syb and Abby had their own notions on that score, which neither volunteered. "Gus was ever prone to the megrims," said Cynthia, who was a little prone to the megrims herself, due to the failure in appearance of a certain irate spouse. Perhaps Duncan had encountered a water kelpie and gotten tangled in her hair and been dragged to a watery death, which was a kinder fate than his wife would grant him, had he been dallying in her absence with females other than herself.

A long array of carriages was drawn up in the street near a Ladies' Bazaar for the Sale of Miscellaneous Articles, which also boasted galleries for the display of works of art. Lady Syb ushered her companions into a vestibule containing a few mediocre sculptures, then up a flight of stairs to a range of rooms occupied by a picture gallery, and from there to the upper floor. On one side was spread out a toy bazaar; on the other an aviary, and an adjacent conservatory where plants were displayed in neat array. Nit was immediately enchanted with a toy dog that squeaked, and an elephant that wagged its tail. Lady Syb inspected a set of nestling boxes. Cyn touched a finger to a large wooden horse, and smiled to see it rock.

Abby looked about with an expression of wide-eyed wonder. 'Twas certain she'd never before found herself in such a place. Nigel escorted her into the conservatory, in the center of which played a fountain, its basin filled with gold and silver fish. Among the plants and evergreen shrubs and flowers hung caged creatures for sale: parrots, love birds, singing birds, as well as lories, squirrels, and white mice. Perched in the branch of one tree was a tame macaw.

Abby sank down on a bench. Nigel raised his arm and the macaw stepped onto it. As he gave the bird a scratch, he studied Abby, who looked quite the lady in a calico dress forced on her by Lady Syb. A ribbon-and-feather-trimmed bonnet perched on her unruly curls.

She also looked pale. "Are you growing weary, Abbess? Do you wish to go home?"

"Probably I would, if I knew where home was." Still, it was very pleasant to sit here in this oriental setting, with birds and plants and flowers all about, watching Nigel scratch the blissful parrot, while sunlight coming through the window cast a halo around his undeserving head. "I'm not the least bit tired. It's nice to be out of the house. Not that I'm not grateful to your aunt, because I am, but I don't think I'm accustomed to spending so much time indoors."

Nigel contemplated the golden freckles on Abby's pert little nose, which would have caused any young lady of fashion to run shrieking for A Wash of the Ladies of Denmark. Then he wondered if anyone had ever tried to count those freckles, and wished that he might.

Abby tilted her head. "You have the strangest expression on your face."

This was what came of spending too much time in the company of his sisters. Freckle-counting, indeed. "Perhaps you would care to inspect the rest of the premises," Nigel said, as he returned the parrot to its perch.

What *had* he been thinking? His handsome face was pale. How dispiriting to be around so many lovely people when she was herself so plain. *All is vanity,* Abby thought, as she placed her hand on Nigel's arm.

They descended another stairway to the lower floor, where counters attended by young females were laden with uncountable trinkets. On one was displayed articles of millinery, on another lace, on yet another gloves and hosiery. Cutlery, jewelry, sheets of music, artificial feathers and flowers, packets of soap and combs—It was a shopper's paradise. Nigel didn't appear the least bit discomfited by being one of the few gentlemen present, although he did glance askance at a piece of false hair plaited and wired to stand upright. "It seems odd that Lady Augusta never married," Abby said.

"It wasn't for want of being asked." Nigel abandoned the Apollo knot. "Why are you looking at me like that?"

Abby realized that she was staring. "So Lady Augusta and Mr. Melchers do have a romantic history?"

"Whatever gave you that notion? I doubt Melchers has ever wished to marry anyone. Stands to reason! Why should he? No, I was the one who wished to marry Gus. Thank God she refused me. I would probably have had to do away with myself long before now. Or fight a duel with Tony, and neither of us would have liked that."

Nigel and Gus? It was a startling thought. And one that explained any number of things, as well as raised more questions, such as whether Lady Ysabella was playing matchmaker by having them both beneath her roof, which now that Abby thought of it, made perfect

158   *Maggie MacKeever*

sense, although she had doubts about the eventual success of such a plan, unless bickering was a form of
lovemaking that she didn't know. Which led her to
muse upon what form of lovemaking she *did* know,
and how she might have learned.

His Abbess was distracted. She had an almost wist-
ful expression on her face. "Melchers ain't tried to get
up a flirtation with you, has he?" Nigel asked.

"Me?" Abby laughed. "Not particularly, although I
suspect that flirting, for Mr. Melchers, is as natural as
drawing breath. If he is getting up a flirtation with anyone, it is Lady Augusta, I think."

Nigel had far too many sisters to take a lady's comments at face value. Abby's offhand manner must
surely mean that she wished Conor would get up a flirtation with *her*. "Gus don't even like the man."

Interesting, thought Abby, how people developed a
selective blindness about certain things. Such as
Nigel's refusal to see what perched right beneath his
nose. "Lady Augusta likes Mr. Melchers well enough
to accompany him to gaming hells."

Nigel didn't care if Conor took Gus to gaming hells.
In his opinion, she couldn't be in better hands. However, he *did* care that Abby cared. Perhaps she wished
to go with Conor to gaming hells herself. "Melchers
ain't known as a seducer of respectable young females.
Not that Gus is young. For that matter, I ain't sure she's
entirely respectable, because Tony made a greater
scandal than Conor has ever done. Not that Melchers
ain't made his share of scandals! But he won't lead Gus
into habits worse than she already has. And if this ain't
all Aunt Syb's doing, I'll eat the feather off your hat."

He sounded cross, thought Abby. And who could
blame him, when the woman he fancied in her turn

fancied a rakehell? Abby wished she might console him. Since she could not, perhaps she might direct his attention elsewhere. "Tony is Lady Augusta's brother? Did you know him well?"

Nigel hadn't thought of Tony in some years, and didn't particularly wish to do so now. "Well enough, I suppose. Tony had a devil in him, and would dare anything."

Rather like his sister, mused Abby. "There's your aunt." Lady Ysabella was debating the relative merits of calamanco and dimity with a young saleswoman as they approached, while Cynthia contemplated a piece of patent lace, and Nit stood on her tiptoes to survey the crowd.

Abby paused by a display of hosiery. Nigel watched her touch a silk stocking as if she'd never worn such a thing. Perhaps she hadn't. Were she to make that omission known to Conor, he would probably purchase dozens of silk stockings, and put them on her himself.

Conor Melchers. Damn the man. Nigel hadn't thought of sensible, freckled Abby as being prone to romantical high flights. Still, she was a female, when all was said and done, and every female that he knew sooner or later fell victim to Conor's charm. If Nigel had thought Abby would prove the exception, then he was clearly mistaken, and as a result he didn't know with whom he was the most cross. At least Nit had the good sense not to be struck all aheap by a philanderer.

Not that Nit and good sense belonged in the same sentence together. She looked like a goose, craning her neck to peer into the crowd. She *was* a goose, albeit a lovely one. "You ain't going to find Duke in here," said Nigel. "And if you'll take my advice, which you ain't done yet, you'll stop throwing your handkerchief in that direction, because he ain't going to stoop to pick it up."

Nit quivered. Her brother was being unusually harsh with her today. "Oh! You are very cruel."

Lady Syb gave her nephew a reproving look. Cynthia withdrew her covetous gaze from a silk hair net. "What Nigel *means,*" she said, "is that you should not make Viscount Daventry the object of so persistent a campaign. Just think how cross *you* feel when your admirers are forever underfoot."

Nit looked about at the crowd of shoppers. Her lower lip trembled. "But they aren't! Not a single one!"

"Never mind," soothed Lady Syb. "They would be, if they knew you were here. When it comes to the gentlemen, my dear, sometimes it's best to be a little bit aloof, to pretend that you aren't interested, even though you really are."

Nit looked at her older sister. "Like you and Douglas?"

"Not a good comparison, perhaps," murmured Nigel. "But Aunt Syb has the right of it. Gentlemen like to think that the pursuit of a lady is their idea. And they don't care to be pursued themselves as a general rule."

Nit turned her curious gaze on her brother. "Has anyone ever pursued *you*?"

Lady Syb raised her brows. Cynthia coughed. "Oh, look," said Abby. "A painted velvet reticule."

Nit was immediately distracted. It was indeed a painted velvet reticule, like Lady Augusta had said she had already bought, but clearly she hadn't, because she couldn't find it anywhere in the house, and now here it was in the bazaar, which made her think that Lady Augusta must have the second sight, and so she said.

Before embarking upon this excursion, Lady Syb had fortified herself with calomel pills and Velno's Vegetable Syrup. Upon hearing her niece's garbled tale of the painted velvet reticule, she promptly made her a present of the thing.

Cynthia shook her head. Gloves at a shilling a pair, silk handkerchiefs at four—She didn't even wish to know what the painted velvet reticule had cost. Not that she begrudged it to her sister. Or if she did, it was only a little bit. What Cynthia really wished for was her laird. She pressed her handkerchief to her mouth, and inhaled the soothing scent of lavender. Lady Ysabella shot a sharp glance at the elder of her nieces, and purchased her a pretty gold comb.

Cynthia contemplated her present. Nigel engaged Abby in a conversation regarding the difference between Tories and Whigs. Nit chewed on her lower lip, trying very hard not to say or do or even think anything she shouldn't, lest her aunt punish her again. Nit could hardly find herself a wealthy and titled husband while shut up in Grosvenor Square. If she wasn't very careful, she would be forced to retire after several unsuccessful Seasons and become a sharp-tempered spinster like Gus.

Lady Syb regarded her small flock. They were all behaving exactly as they ought, including Abby, who was clearly a young woman of decent birth. Or as close to behaving as they ought as was possible for members of her family, amended Lady Syb, as Nigel snatched a glass ornament from a display counter and presented it to Abby. "Next you will say that to achieve true equality society must rid itself of the monarchy as well as religious and military hierarchies," he remarked.

Abby looked at the glass ornament, then set it back

down on the counter. "I don't know that true equality is achievable," she said. "Perhaps the best we can do is live our lives with all the fairness that we can, in our dealings with one another, and our view of the world."

Nigel picked up the glass ornament again, and paid for it this time. Then he presented it to Abby with a flourish. "Well said, Abbess. I stand rebuffed."

Abby looked appalled. "Lord! I didn't mean—"

"Of course you didn't!" Lady Syb took Abby's hand and drew it through her arm. "And if you *had,* it would be quite understandable, for Nigel would try the patience of a saint. Am I correct in assuming that none of this is familiar to you?"

Abby felt absurdly as if she were disappointing her hostess, who had been so very gracious. "I'm sorry," she said.

"Piffle!" Lady Syb patted her hand. "It doesn't signify. We shall merely proceed to the next step of my plan."

Her companions regarded her with varying degrees of trepidation. "And that might be?" Nigel inquired warily.

Lady Ysabella smiled. "Why, we shall take her with us to Carlton House," she said.

EIGHTEEN

Do something, Gus told herself, *even if it's wrong.* Kissing Conor had been wrong, and she had enjoyed it very well. Not that Gus expected to enjoy this adventure. Indeed, she could not help but wonder if she was making a terrible mistake. However, Dame Fortune had presented her with an opportunity, and she would regret it forevermore if she ran home now and buried her head beneath her pillows and bewailed her wretched lot in life.

Not that her lot was all *that* wretched. She had good food to eat, and a comfortable place to sleep. And a wardrobe that many would envy, including this muslin walking dress, made high in the front, with long sleeves, and the deep-brimmed bonnet that partially obscured her face. Though she was uncertain why, Gus even had friends of a sort. Abby seemed to like her, and Cyn, Lady Syb, and Elizabeth. Which said a great deal for their forbearance, for Gus knew herself to be prickly and cross-grained. Not to mention long past her first youth, as Nigel was prone to point out. She had no future, no fortune, no good name. Even rakehells didn't wish to kiss her. At least the particular rakehell by whom she wished to be kissed.

A far cry, this, from her adventures with Conor. If

only he were with her now. Not that Gus truly wanted
Conor with her, because she was cross with him, and
he was certain to disapprove of her intentions; but it
was one of the man's many contradictions of character that in his presence a lady felt safe. Or if not safe,
precisely, that no harm would come to her except
through him. Not that Conor had ever harmed anyone
that she knew of. Unless it was harmful to be introduced to the pleasures of the flesh.

Some would think so, surely. Gus stepped out into
the street. Not surprising that she was attracted to
Conor. Every female between the cradle and the grave
was attracted to Conor, whether he had gotten around
to kissing them or not. Gus wondered how many females Conor had kissed. She suspected she would
carry the memory of his kiss with her to her own grave.

That event hopefully lay far in the future. For the
moment, she must push Conor from her mind and concentrate on what lay immediately ahead. Perhaps her
plan wasn't wise—indeed, she knew it wasn't—but she
couldn't bring herself to care. Gus had been angry for
a very long time, and she was sufficiently weary of her
own ill-temper that she wished to see it end. 'Twas one
of the many reasons that she'd invited Conor's kiss.

But even Conor's kiss had not had the hoped-for effect. Although it certainly had others. Gus had not
hitherto known a person could tingle all the way down
to her toes. She almost wished she didn't know it now.
Conor had made it very clear there would be no more
kisses, and therefore Gus was even angrier. She could
not throttle Conor, who had introduced her to bone-
melting kisses and then done an abrupt *volte-face,* or
her brother, who had gambled away all their money
and then taken French leave; or her cousin, who had

bought himself a wife and left her without a home; but there was one member of the species upon whom she might still wreak a justly merited revenge.

Gus gazed at the Palladian façade of the Maison de Bonheur. The place looked disheveled in the bright daylight, a little tawdry and yet faintly menacing, like an old street whore after a long night's work. Before her courage could desert her, Gus marched up to the front door and raised her hand to knock.

The door of the Maison swung open long enough to grant her admission, then closed smartly behind her back. Gus glanced cautiously around the hallway. Entering a gaming hell alone was far different from visiting one with Conor by her side.

Conor would perhaps throttle *her* if he learned what she meant to do. Certainly Lady Syb would have an apoplexy on the spot. Abby would quote the Bible, and even Cyn would be shocked. Nigel alone might encourage her, from sheer perversity.

Even worse were her own demons, who were delighted to find her in such a place. Plato claimed that dice and gaming had originated with the devil Theuth. The Greeks and Romans gamed with the knuckle bones of goats and sheep. Gus wished she knew the location of the entry to the subterranean escape route.

The place was empty, save for the servants preparing for the evening ahead. The air stank of stale perfume, spilled liquor, perspiration and cigar smoke. Many gamesters, among them Gus's brother, seldom saw any luminary above the horizon other than the moon: During the day Tony had longed for night, while during the night he dreaded the return of day. A manservant led her up the grand staircase, past the first-floor gaming rooms, to one of the smaller chambers on an upper floor, where he left her alone.

Anxiety and apprehension and excitement mixed together until she thought she might be sick with them. Gus took firmer grasp of her reticule and looked cautiously around. The servants' efforts had not yet extended to this room, where candles had guttered in their crystal holders, and the ashes of a fire were scattered on the hearth. Comfortable chairs, a gaming table, a plush sofa—it didn't take much imagination to envision such scenes as might have taken place here the previous night. Or the many nights before that. Gus had entirely too much imagination. She perched stiffly on the edge of an upholstered chair.

She had not long to wait before the door swung open, and Jack Stafford walked into the room. Again he was dressed in black. The man looked as cruel and stern and sinister as some medieval representation of death.

He closed the door and leaned against it. Too late, now, to flee. Gus was very much aware that she was alone with a man in a potentially compromising situation, and while she had certainly been alone with Conor in such situations, this was a very different thing. Conor refused to take advantage of her, even when she had wished him to. Jack Stafford lived to take advantage of the gullible and naive. Jeremy's cautionary tales echoed in her ears, stories of gamblers acting like dogs biting a stone flung at them, eating up cards, crushing dice, breaking tables, damaging furniture and each other, one enraged player going so far as putting a burning candle in his mouth and chewing it up.

She wondered how many such excesses Jack Stafford had witnessed, and caused, how many young

men about town he'd led to their ruin. Not to mention
females, which she didn't care to think about just then.
"Thank you for seeing me, Mr. Stafford." Gus rose
from her chair.

His dispassionate gaze moved over her slowly, in-
sultingly. "Lady Augusta, surely you realize that it is
dangerous for you to come here."

Of course she knew the danger, which was not only
to her reputation. Jack Stafford was capable of unimaginable villainies. Gus was gambling that the prospect
of gaining further inroads into her cousin's fortune
would prevent him from dishonoring her on the spot.

If she was wrong, she'd have to kill him. However, it
was her intention to first try and persuade the man to
take her for a flat. "I am perfectly capable of taking
care of myself," she announced sulkily, and trusted he
would think she was not.

Appearing to accept her words at their face value, he
moved away from the door in a leisurely manner that
made Gus wonder if she had underestimated him. Or
overestimated her own ability to play a peahen. As he
moved closer to her, she forced herself not to back away.

He raised one hand to touch a chestnut curl. "My curiosity was piqued when I received your note. I had the
impression that you didn't much like me, Lady Augusta."

How astute of him. She detested the man. Due to
Jack Stafford, Tony was languishing God knew where,
and she was reduced to gaming with Lady Syb for buttons of silver, brass and bone.

Prunes! Gus told herself, and tried very hard to look
hen-witted. "That was for Melchers' benefit. I wished
to throw him off the scent."

The merest flicker of interest showed in those emotionless dark eyes. "You intrigue me, Lady Augusta. What might that scent be?"

Gus intended to more than intrigue Jack Stafford; and due to her knowledge of cramped boxes and old gentlemen and Sir Hugh's Bones, she thought she might succeed. The man was exceedingly dangerous, however, as well as clever, or he would not have prospered in his infamous profession so long as he had. Gus raised limpid eyes to his. "If I may be frank?"

She must have convinced him, at least partially, of her simplemindedness, because he stepped away from her to pick up a crystal decanter and pour liquid into a glass. "Please do."

Arrack punch, iced champagne, and now brandy before luncheon. Gus accepted the snifter, but did not drink. "I have a fondness for play, Mr. Stafford. My family does not care for me to indulge. Because of Tony."

Jack Stafford cradled his own snifter casually in his hand. "Your family may have a point."

Definitely her family had a point. Gus pouted, *à la* Nit. "It is unfair! Tony was a fearless plunger, willing to gamble on anything from the turn of a card to a race between flies crawling up a wall. I am not so green."

Nor was Jack Stafford. He insisted on looking the plumpest of pigeons in the mouth, even when she was positively panting to be plucked of her feathers and plopped into the cooking pot. "And Melchers?" he inquired.

"Doing Lady Ysabella's bidding by squiring me about and keeping me out of trouble," Gus said, with a nice petulance. "We have quarreled, however, and he will be expected to do so no more."

The deep dark eyes still rested on her. Gus would have given a great deal to know what was passing through the man's mind. "I am a gambler, Mr. Stafford. My cousin makes me an allowance. It is not enough."

"His caution is understandable, considering your brother's ill fortune." His expression was unreadable. "You will forgive my plain-speaking, Lady Augusta. What have you to offer me?"

What she *wanted* to offer him was a good clout on the side of the head. His gaze made her skin crawl. "A woman in my position could be a considerable asset . At a concert, an elegant dinner, a *soirée*. If you will forgive *my* plain-speaking, Mr. Stafford, to be seen with me would lend you a degree of greater respectability."

Stafford's eyes narrowed. "Your family would hardly approve of your association with me."

Gus lowered her gaze. Thought of how Justin or Lady Syb would react to her reckless behavior inspired her to sample her brandy, despite the early hour. "I hardly meant that we should put in an appearance at Almack's."

He didn't even smile at the absurdity of the notion. "Why should you take up someone who is shunned by the highest sticklers in society?"

It was a fair-enough question. Gus tried hard to summon forth a blush. "I thought that perhaps an association with you might allow me certain, ah, pecuniary advantages," she murmured, and recalled Jeremy's tale of a young gentleman of means who within fifteen months of the moment his hand first grasped a dice box was lying dead in jail, which considerably stiffened her resolve.

Jack Stafford set down his glass on the table, and walked across the room toward her. "You want me to stake you. Since Charnwood keeps so tight a hold on the purse strings."

This was the telling moment, when Stafford took or refused the bait: Gus was inviting him to encourage her to gamble for stakes, the ultimate prize her wealthy cousin, the Duke of Charnwood.

His silence was unnerving. Gus chewed her lower lip so hard that she brought tears into her eyes, which she then quickly raised to his face. "Oh! It is very bad of me!" she wailed, in tones that would have done Nit proud. "But I cannot stay away from the tables, and Justin will not stake me, and I cannot think what else I am to *do!*"

NINETEEN

It said a great deal for Lady Ysabella's standing among the beau monde that the Prince of Wales was delighted by her arrival at Carlton House, no matter how many uninvited guests she had in tow. Then, too, Prinny was known to have a weakness for ladies older than himself, and the countess was ravishing in richly embroidered lilac, black, and silver, atop her golden curls a headdress of Brussels lace embellished with a small plume fastened at the bottom with a diamond pin. Whatever his reasons, he saluted Lady Ysabella's hand and pronounced himself delighted to see her, greeted her "houseguest" with all the considerable charm of which he was capable, pinched her niece's cheek and pronounced Miss Slyte a comely miss who would have the young bucks falling all over themselves in an effort to see her smile. Nit curtsied prettily, and hoped he might be right. Lady Syb had threatened to send her home if she didn't behave unexceptionably tonight.

Carlton House was *en fête*, as was the Prince, in a scarlet coat richly and elegantly ornamented with gold lace in a very novel style. Abby looked about with wonder at walls covered with painted mandarins and fluted yellow draperies; peach-blossom ceilings and canopies of tassels and bells; carpeting with gold fleurs-de-lis on a blue background; imperial dragons darting from every chandelier. "Heavens!" she breathed.

"Tell me you don't find it familiar!" begged Nigel, by her side. "Because if you do, I shall be sadly disappointed in your taste. Prinny was given Carlton House when he attained his majority. The place takes its name from a certain Baron Carleton who died holding a fair duchess by the hand, and being fed with a fat chicken at the same time. Prinny began extensive renovations the moment he moved in. 'Tis said that Carlton House has cost, to date, over a million pounds."

Abby gazed upon a luster, fashioned of glass and ormolu, which looked like a shower of diamonds. She felt as if she'd stepped into fairyland, a place not entirely comfortable perhaps, but bewitching all the same. Even she was enchanted for the evening, bullied by her fairy godmother into a yellow silk ball dress trimmed with satin bows, the hem embellished with satin rouleau. "I'm certain I've never seen anything like this before," she said. "I probably disapprove of such excess, but Lord! It is all so very grand."

Nigel eyed a pair of candelabra with pedestals veneered in amboyna and mahogany, adorned with ormolu mounts, and reflected that Prinny's indulgences must seem grand indeed to a young woman who knew how to boil up bars of soap. He glimpsed the Duke and Duchess of Charnwood making their way through the glittering throng of men in court dress and elegant women enhanced by jewels and ostrich plumes. The duchess outshone them all in a low-cut lace gown, her train trimmed with two rows of fabric roses, her headdress of braided satin trimmed with feathers and pearls. The duke wore a besotted expression on his handsome face. "How fine we all are!" Elizabeth smiled at Abby. "Justin didn't wish to come, but I insisted, because I wish to see what Nit will do next." She winced. "That is—"

"You needn't explain." Abby glanced at Annette, who stood beside her aunt, trying very hard for a casual air of indifference. "I know exactly what you mean."

As did Nigel, and with dismay he glimpsed a familiar auburn head. Fortunately, Nit was staring in the opposite direction. In an attempt to delay the inevitable, Nigel excused himself and slipped away into the crowd. It had been too much to hope that Duke might absent himself from this affair, for Prinny liked Viscount Daventry, and would demand his presence at Carlton House.

He was surrounded by ladies. Duke was always surrounded by ladies, whether he wished it or not, and generally he did not. Upon glimpsing Nigel, he deftly extricated himself. "I suppose it is too much to hope that you are here alone."

Nigel observed the disappointed glances cast in their direction. "Damned if they ain't like a pack of hounds in full cry. Next thing we know we'll find you torn to bits." Having earned a scowl from his companion, he continued. "Of course I ain't alone. Come to think of it, I seldom *am* alone. I wonder if I'd enjoy it. Anyway, I thought you liked Aunt Syb."

Duke adroitly evaded a dowager who was headed in their direction, a marital gleam in her eye. "You know perfectly well that I'm not talking about your aunt."

Nigel would have much rather talked about his aunt. However, duty called. "Sisters are the very devil!" he said gloomily. "Damned if I don't sometimes think they set out purposely to cut up a man's peace."

Duke couldn't remember the last time he'd been at peace. Doubtless it had been before the birth of his sons. "I don't want your sister. *Any* of your sisters. In case you have any doubt."

"I know that!" retorted Nigel. "Everyone knows but Nit, and she'd know it too if she wasn't so stubborn, because even Nit ain't that much of a shatterbrain. Thing is, she's set her cap at you, and now she can't back down without losing face. And as long as she's got her cap set at you she won't look at anybody else. We need to get her settled before she drives all of us lunatic."

In Duke's opinion, certain members of the family hadn't far to go to achieve that state. He eyed his companion warily. "I suspect you're going to tell me that you have a scheme."

Nigel linked arms with the viscount, and beamed. "How clever you are! I've always said so. The thing is, Nit's accustomed to being doted on. That's your attraction for her, you see, because you don't. If you *was* to dote on her, she'd lose interest. Sounds queer, I know, but I've seen it happen before."

Duke blinked at this queer notion. The viscount was accustomed to being admired for his fortune, or his title, or even his looks; although he was no coxcomb, his mirror, and any number of ladies, had assured him that he was not hideous. But to be admired because he didn't dangle after a damsel? "I don't think I *can* dote," he said.

"Clearly you won't do for Nit!" retorted Nigel, as the gentlemen were caught up in a throng of guests admiring an assortment of Dutch and Flemish paintings hung on red satin damask walls. "Not only can't you dote, you ain't got sufficient humor to survive her for a week! It's a matter of pride with Aunt Syb to get Nit married off. Not that she'll give her over to someone who will mistreat her, or fail to appreciate her good qualities. You look doubtful. I understand it. I'd be doubtful too if I was in your place. But you may take my word for it that Nit has a good heart."

"That may be." Duke gazed without admiration upon a collection of Oriental porcelain. "I don't want her, all the same."

"So you say." Nigel tilted his golden head. "However, you don't wish her harm, I hope, because as her brother I'd be expected to defend her honor, since I'm the only one around." He shuddered. "I abhor bloodshed. Particularly when it's mine."

Viscount Daventry regarded his friend with exasperation. "Doing it rather too brown, Nigel. You know very well that I don't wish your sister—any of your sisters!—harm."

Nigel brightened. "You relieve me. Indeed, you've taken a prodigious load off my mind. However, you must see that due to her infatuation with you, Nit's unlikely to bring a single gentleman up to scratch. Except perhaps Ormesby, and Aunt Syb won't let Ormesby have her, because she says the world ain't ready for such offspring as they might produce. Nit may be a beauty, but she ain't got a great portion, and left to her own devices she'll manage one way or another to drive off every gentleman who might offer for her. She's already talked to young Harcourt about castration. Braceborough had the gall to tell me it wasn't the thing for my sister to know about such stuff, as if the whole thing was my fault."

Despite himself, Duke was fascinated. "Why should your sister wish to castrate Harcourt?"

"Not Harcourt," sighed Nigel. "I think. This is fair and far off! If you can't bring yourself to dote on her, I'll just have to tell her that you've lost all your blunt. A pity to have that rumor get about, but I fear it will. Even if I tell Nit to keep the business a secret, she'll forget."

Duke frowned at his companion. "You wouldn't," he said.

Nigel looked apologetic. "Ah, but I would. Nit thinks she must marry money. No help for it, alas."

The viscount contemplated the repercussions were the *on-dit* that he had lost his fortune to circulate around the town. "I'll dote," he said grimly. "But if this doesn't cure the little ninny of thinking she may bring me up to scratch, I vow I'll have your head!"

Unaware of her brother's efforts on her behalf, Nit stayed close to her aunt's side as they moved through the splendid public rooms. She tried very hard not to gape at her surroundings like the rustic that she was, and stored away descriptions of Chinese designs and Gothic furniture for the next letter she sent home. The two eagles and Prince of Wales feathers that formed part of the plaster decorations, she surely would remember; but she doubted her powers of description would do justice to the chinoiserie drawing room. Lady Syb was largely ignoring her, chatting instead with Abby and the Duke and Duchess of Charnwood, and exchanging pleasantries with such members of the Prince's set as Brummell and Alvanley, Lord and Lady Sefton, the Duke and Duchess of Devonshire. Even in her pretty dress, trimmed with clusters of yellow posies and bands of white lace, Annette felt out of place. She brightened when she saw Lord Ormesby. At least one of her admirers was present to keep her company. If only he would say something, instead of staring mutely at the wreath of flowers in her hair. And then she saw her brother making her way toward them, Viscount Daventry by his side.

Goodness, but the viscount was handsome. Heavens, but he looked bored. Indifference was tantalizing, claimed Lady Syb. Nit supposed her aunt must know whereof she spoke, for she knew a great deal about the ways of the world. Unless Syb knew so much more of the world that she meant to cut out her own niece and fix the viscount's attention on herself.

Very well, she would be indifferent. As Viscount Daventry approached, his cool gaze fixed on her, Annette turned her back on him and remarked to Lord Ormesby that above anything else in all the world she wished for an ice.

Tolly was delighted. Indeed, had she required it, he would have fetched Miss Slyte the stars and moon, although how he might have accomplished that, he had no idea. An ice, however, was definitely within his power. He offered his arm, and escorted her to the supper room.

"Astonishing!" said Justin, as he looked after them. "Never did I think to see Duke given the cut direct."

Neither had the viscount. Torn between amazement and annoyance, he regarded Nigel. "*Dote*?" he inquired.

Lady Syb had hoped to get through the evening without further embarrassing incidents: Nit had already become so excited talking to the Duke of Bedford about his racing stud that she'd stepped on Lady Hertford's hem. "This is my fault. I told Annette that nonchalance is appealing." She sighed.

Duke frowned at her. "Perhaps you might next explain the difference between nonchalance and rudeness to your niece. And pray coordinate your efforts with your nephew, because I'm damned if I'll be made a laughingstock."

The viscount was in a temper. He could hardly be blamed, for Annette's snub had been witnessed by any number of people, and quickly would be noised all about the town. Abby discovered herself to be most uncomfortable in the presence of a gentleman in a temper, which was something she must ponder. "There is Mr. Melchers," she said, with relief, as she glimpsed Conor in the crowd.

He made his way toward them. "Hello, Lady Syb. Abby. Nice dress, Duchess." Elizabeth turned to display the back of her gown, which dipped into a low V.

Justin placed a possessive hand on his wife's bare shoulder. Conor smiled, and said, "Where's Gus? And why is Nigel glaring at me like that?"

Nigel was glaring because Abby was clearly glad to see Melchers, and he would be damned if he let that notorious libertine treat her to silk stockings, and escort her to gaming hells. "I ain't glaring at you," he retorted, untruthfully. "Gus begged off with a headache."

Poor Nigel, thought Abby, to want a lady who wanted someone else. And now Mr. Melchers, who had belatedly noticed Viscount Daventry, was glaring at him in turn. Since it was clearly in her nature to play peacekeeper, Abby cleared her throat. "Lady Augusta received a note. I saw it." Conor turned his frown on her, and she faltered. "I thought it was from you."

TWENTY

Jack Stafford's carriage stopped discreetly around the corner from Grosvenor Square. Gus gathered her evening cloak more tightly around her as she stepped down into the street. She had survived her first evening unchaperoned in the Maison de Bonheur without having undone herself, hadn't been tempted to go double or quits, or been reduced to wagering an earlobe.

Gus didn't delude herself that this circumstance was due to any change of luck. She had been a pigeon among hawks. It was the practice of ivory tuners and Greek bandits to let a flat win the first time he visited a hell; and if this had not been Gus's first visit, it was the first time she had played. If perhaps she wondered that her secret purpose might make a difference in the thrill she experienced at the fall of a card, the roll of the dice, it had not. Fortunate perhaps that she possessed so slim a pocketbook, or she would still be plunging recklessly, deliciously, in company with an amiable young gentleman named Willy, who had been tempted first to gamble in the funds, and when that had not proved to his advantage, next became involved in difficulties during an unfortunate transaction at cards during the Lincoln races, and now sought to recoup his losses at the gambling house in Pall Mall. Jack Stafford

promised an infallible means of replenishing his funds.
Gus suspected that the young man would soon find
himself staking watches, rings, clothing, everything he
owned.

Fools, the lot of them, including Gus herself, who
had as good a chance of exposing Jack Stafford as of
breaking the Maison's faro bank. Closely as she had
watched, she'd never seen him reverse the cut or slip a
card. Gus couldn't help but wonder if perhaps her
scheme had been nothing more than an elaborate excuse to enable her to play. Now, even if she wished to
cut her losses, it was unlikely that Stafford would allow
her a graceful retreat. Gus reluctantly admitted that, as
regarded cardsharpers, she might have bit off rather
more than she could chew.

Nothing was accomplished standing here in the
darkness, gnawing on her lower lip and damning herself for a fool. What could Stafford do if she failed to
answer his next summons? Invade Lady Syb's house
and drag her, cowering, out from beneath her bed?

It was not beyond the man. To pretend to be his special friend had been difficult indeed, for he had taken
advantage of every opportunity to touch her hand, her
shoulder, her neck. Only with considerable ingenuity
had she avoided sharing a private dinner. Gus couldn't
help but think Stafford was playing a deep game, with
herself the stakes.

Stakes? Gus snorted. She was hardly anyone's prize.
Nor did she usually stand on dark street corners mut-
tering to herself. She started around the corner into
Grosvenor Square. It would have been nice to blame
Lady Syb for this muddle she had gotten into. Or
Conor. Unfortunately, Gus could not fairly blame any-
one but herself. In earlier days, unwanted female

relatives had been shut up in convents. Gus wondered how she might like convent life. And then she yelped, because a strong arm clasped her around the middle, and a hand pressed itself against her mouth, and she was swept up off her feet.

She kicked and flailed and struggled, bit the hand that remained clamped on her mouth. "Damnation, Gus!" said her captor, as he tossed her into a waiting carriage, and followed her inside. He closed the door firmly behind him and knocked on the roof to signal his driver to proceed.

Gus regarded her abductor with disfavor. "I don't suppose it would occur to you to simply ask me to get into your coach."

Conor inspected the teeth marks on his hand. "The last time we spoke, you slapped me. I decided on a more direct approach. Where the devil have you been?"

Gus wasn't about to explain where she'd been, or why. Especially not to Conor, who had gone to such efforts to save her from herself. What a cod's head he would think her. Gus didn't want Conor to think her a cod's head, even if she was. "In a game of chance," she remarked, "the oftener the same combination has occurred in succession, the nearer we are to the certainty that it will not recur at the next cast or turn up. This does not account for 'doctors' or false dice, high and low and clogged, or the cramped box; the different ways of throwing, like the stamp, the dribble, and the long gallery; or the experienced nurse of the dice who knows how to nick the main, or throw crabs. In case you might think I didn't pay sufficient attention to Jeremy."

Conor thought she meant to keep her secrets, and she would only grow cross if he demanded to know what she had been doing, and who she had been doing it with. He didn't know if he minded more that she might have been gambling, or that she might have gone out to meet a man other than himself. Who might have kissed her. If not worse.

Conor studied her indignant features. It hadn't been his intention to lead Gus into bad habits. He doubted it had been Lady Syb's intention, either, but one never knew with Lady Syb.

When he said nothing, Gus thrust out her chin. "Where are you taking me?"

"Nowhere in particular." Conor moved to sit beside her. "I merely wished to talk to you. Preferably in private, in case you decided to box my ears."

So much for her brief fantasy that he might take her home with him, there to turn her over his knee. Still, he was warm and solid and curiously comforting, and she didn't wish him to move away. "You might have *asked* me to favor you with my company, instead of willy-nilly snatching me. Talk to me about what?"

Conor picked up her hand, pulled off her glove, and wrapped her fingers in his. "What mischief are you up to, Gus?"

The gesture was curiously tender. Gus wasn't used to being touched. Or hugged, or kissed. Generally, she disliked such gestures. Conor, however, might with her blessing touch her anywhere he wished. "I don't think I'm a mischief sort of person," she muttered. "You must have me confused with someone else."

Unlikely that Conor would do that. He hadn't spared a thought for any of his ladybirds since he started going about with Gus, and almost groaned to think of the sort of mischief he might make with her. It would never occur to Gus to try and make him jealous, or even that she could.

Conor didn't recall ever feeling jealous before. He disliked the sensation a great deal. The feel of her hand in his was quite a different matter. That, he liked very much. Gus sat stiff as a fence post on the seat beside him. A lovely fence post dressed in an evening cloak of emerald velvet, and a yellow gown of antique quality with a closely fitted bodice and deep square neckline, gathered beneath the breast with a gold cord. Her hair was gathered up in curls high on the back of her head.

He wanted to plunge his hand into those curls and scatter hairpins everywhere, yank that bodice lower still, and press his mouth against her breasts. Conscience dictated that he refrain. In an attempt at distraction, he spoke easily about the years Gus and her brother had spent in the same country neighborhood as the Slyte family, Lord Charnwood, and himself. Conor had been the eldest, though not by many years. Gus smiled to recall amateur theatricals performed in the billiard room of Charnwood Hall, most especially the occasion on which Nigel had become so immersed in the role of Ophelia that he had almost drowned himself; and chuckled at the memory of Nigel's papa's unfortunate experiment with a machine-before-horse type of reaping machine that rotated a cheese-shaped cutter with a knife on its lower edge; and laughed aloud at Conor's account of the oxen-versus-horse controversy that resulted, when the gentlemen were a little overpowered by wine, with one assaulting another with the *pot-de-chambre* which traditionally resided in the sideboard. In addition there had been many shared hunting seasons, grand fancy dress balls, Christmas mummers in painted paper and floral headgear reciting traditional words while banging one another with

wooden swords; New Year's Eve wassailers and the traditional Yule log and kissing beneath the mistletoe.

Conor had never kissed Gus beneath the mistletoe.
Now he wondered why. He stroked his thumb along the
pulse beating in her wrist. "My mother shared your
fondness for play."

Gus had been lulled into a near stupor by the near-
ness of his warm, strong body, the music of his husky
voice. Not to mention the fascinating sensation of his
thigh pressed against her own. "I didn't know you had
a mother," she said, glancing up at him. "I mean, of
course you had a mother, but no one ever spoke of her.
I supposed she had died."

Conor appeared fascinated with the beating of her
pulse. "I vaguely remember her—she was gentle, and
smelled of vanilla, and liked to make me laugh. Then
one day, she simply wasn't there. When I asked about
her, I was told not to mention her name. I discovered
years later that my father had forbidden her to play and
she disobeyed."

"That's why you don't care to gamble." Gus turned
sideways on the seat to stare at him. "And why Lady
Syb—"

Conor squeezed her hand and went on as if she
hadn't interrupted. "He publicly announced he
wouldn't pay any more of her debts."

Gus recalled Conor's father, a scholarly, austere, serious sort of man who seldom had an approving word
for anyone other than his son, on whom he saw the sun
set and rise. "He cast her off?"

Conor turned her hand over and studied the palm. "I
didn't learn the truth until after his death. His solicitor
had instructions to keep track of her, make sure she had
a roof over her head, and enough to eat, but no more."

Gus suspected few others knew this story. Certainly Nigel didn't; he could never have kept it to himself. "Did you visit her?" she asked quietly.

He shook his head and looked at their clasped hands. "She was gone by then. I have, however, visited her grave, in Somerton. She was known there as Mrs. Milby, a widow with a small competence who did extraordinarily fine needlework."

Of course his mama had done fine needlework. It was one of the graces expected of a lady. Gus sewed a nice seam herself. If Jack Stafford ruined her, perhaps she could make a living by it. "She never remarried?"

Conor shrugged. "How could she? They never divorced. Perhaps she hoped that in time my father would relent."

But he had not, and since Conor had learned firsthand how much a man could damage a woman, he had determined to be an instrument of pleasure rather than pain. "It's a pity your mama could not have known Jeremy," Gus said lightly. "He could have taught her about probabilities. For example, one has an even chance of throwing eight. Odds are thirty-five to one, however, against throwing any particular doublet, and six to one against throwing any doublets at all. As well as seventeen to one against throwing any two desired numbers, and four to nine against throwing a single number with either of the dice, and—Oof!"

Conor had pulled her onto his lap. His hands rested on her shoulders. "Haven't you heard a word I've said to you?"

He looked as if he wished to shake her. "Yes," retorted Gus, with remarkable self-possession, considering his proximity. "And I have listened to every one. You might try and have a little faith in me. I'm not going to come to grief."

He feared she was going to find herself in the devil of a fix, unless she could be brought to confide in him. But Conor's efforts to gain her trust had only made her angrier. If only Conor might take all that passion and put it to a better use.

He definitely was wrongheaded. Depraved. And since he was demonstrably a roué as well as a rake, a philanderer without the least pretense to nobility of character, he might as well act the part. He plunged one hand into her hair and with the other pulled off her evening cloak, and then kissed her until they were both out of breath.

'Twas most deliciously depraved, decided Gus, when he moved his lips away from her and she could think again, to be sprawled across a gentleman's lap; and she didn't care a bit if her cloak was tossed in a heap on the carriage floor, and her hair tumbled every which way. She didn't even care if the bodice of her gown had slid down around one shoulder, or that Conor had slipped his hand beneath her skirt to stroke her silk-clad ankle, which felt wonderfully fine.

She raised her hand to touch his lean cheek. "I thought you weren't worthy of me," she said.

"I'm not." He kissed her fingers. "But neither is Nigel."

"Nigel?" Startled, Gus sat up abruptly. Conor winced. "Why should you think I want to kiss *Nigel*?"

Clearly he had been foolish. Conor was so pleased that he drew her back down against his chest and saluted her eyebrow. "And Duke?" he inquired.

"It's Nit who wishes to kiss Duke, not me." Gus pressed her nose against his neck and inhaled his scent.

"I think you are attempting to distract me from gaming hells."

"Is it working?"

"Hmm?"

"Are you distracted?"

"Oh, yes," Gus breathed.

As was he. Rather too much so, for his hand had worked its way past her ankle and halfway up her calf. Reluctantly, Conor smoothed down her skirt. Gus would not wish to join his legion of mistresses.

Not that Conor would make her his mistress, whether she wanted it or not. He set her away from him and dropped a kiss on her nose.

Gus scowled at him. "Don't dare say you're not worthy of me again! It may be true—it probably *is* true—but if I don't mind it, why the devil should you?"

Conor picked up her cloak and wrapped it around her shoulders. "Because one of us must. It's no good arguing with me, sweeting. I'm returning you to Lady Syb."

TWENTY-ONE

A valise sat on the front doorstep. Viscount Daventry eyed it warily. The valise was very shabby, as if it had traveled a great distance under circumstances unimaginable to a gentleman like himself. Duke picked up the thing to give it a better look. Leather worn and stained with mysterious substances, and empty furthermore. What in Hades was such an article doing perched outside Lady Ysabella's front door? It had a distinctly unpleasant odor about it. Duke wrinkled his nose and held the valise at arm's length.

The door swung open before he could knock. Mortimer gazed upon Viscount Daventry hovering on the doorstep, clutching a battered valise, and wished Lady Syb might have warned him she was expecting another houseguest. The viscount must be in a prodigious pickle, judging from the condition of his bag. Master Nigel wouldn't like it if he were expected to share his valet. Bees would like it even less. Mortimer allowed himself a moment's hope that his archenemy might quit in a snit.

Unlikely that he would be so lucky. Perhaps he should quit himself. Definitely he *should*, considering that the condition of the household reflected on himself, but Mortimer could never abandon Lady Syb.

Why he couldn't, Mortimer wasn't certain, but there it was. "The family is in the drawing room. All the family, excepting Miss Nit. Including Master Pontius and Miss Helen, sir."

There was a most unbutlerlike note in Mortimer's voice. Duke glanced curiously at him. "That would be the pig and the hedgehog," Mortimer continued. "In general, Lady Ysabella does not approve of animals in the drawing room. However, she has relaxed her standards on this occasion. I fear her ladyship is not feeling quite the thing."

Nigel's voice drifted down the stairway. He appeared to be reading from a tract. " 'In the present era of vice and dissipation, how many females attend the card tables! What is the consequence? The effects are too clearly to be traced to the frequent *divorces* which have lately disgraced our country, and they are too visible in the shameful conduct of many ladies of fashion, since gambling becomes their chief amusement.' "

Duke wondered how much of Lady Syb's malaise might be attributed to the influence of her family. "Don't bother to announce me!" he said. Mortimer allowed himself the merest flicker of a last glance at the valise, then bowed himself away.

Duke followed Nigel's voice—"How many infamous villains have amassed immense estates, by taking advantage of unfortunate young men, who have been first seduced and then ruined by the gambling clubs!' "—and paused on the threshold of the drawing room. The family, or most of the family, was definitely at home. Gus and Cynthia sat at the cardtable, sharing a game of noddy and a plate of macaroons, Cyn occasionally interrupting her brother's sermonizing with comments about boggarts and brownies, Celtic Druids and blood sacrifice. Lady Syb was ensconced on a sofa, a shawl around her shoulders and spectacles perched upon her nose. In one hand she held a vinaigrette, and in the other a sheet of paper. A hedgehog was curled up in her lap. Her feet rested on a pig. The ladies resembled a garden of somewhat wilted posies, yellow and blue and green.

Nigel lounged in a chair near the fireplace. " 'Then came upon the nation the muddy flood of French emigrants, poured forth by the Great Revolution—a set of men, speaking generally, whose vices contaminated the very atmosphere—' " He glanced up and languidly waved a pamphlet as Duke walked into the room. "*Hints for a Reform, particularly of the Gaming Clubs, By a Member of Parliament.* I fetched it home for Gus."

"Stubble it, Nigel," said that lady. Cynthia muttered something about using silver to kill shape-shifters, and reached for a macaroon.

Pontius raised his head and blinked at the newcomer, whom he vaguely remembered, and associated vaguely with turnips. However, he felt much more strongly about the valise. Lady Syb's feet thudded to the floor as Pontius scrambled into a sitting position. She snatched up Helen before the hedgehog could tumble off her lap.

Gazing with fierce concentration at the valise, Pontius bounded up onto his dainty feet. Unaware that the source of the pig's interest was the valise and not himself, Viscount Daventry backed away. Pontius followed, swinging his snout from side to side.

Duke speeded up his pace. Pontius did likewise. The pair of them circled the room. While the audience observed that the viscount had a certain dash about him, it was generally conceded that the pig was more agile on his trotters. "It's the valise!" said Gus, in between chortles. "Pontius wants the valise."

Pontius was welcome to it. Duke dropped the wretched thing. The pig approached, sniffed, pushed at the valise with his nose, pawed it open, stuck his snout inside. After a lengthy inspection, he determined that the valise held neither food nor his mistress. With a plaintive grunt, he collapsed at Lady Syb's feet. Helen had been awakened by the tumult. The hedgehog sniffed and snuffled, then crawled up Lady Syb's arm to curl up on her shoulder and go back to sleep.

Lady Syb propped her feet back up on the pig. "One almost hesitates to ask, but—"

"How came you by the valise?" interrupted Nigel. "You see that I don't hesitate at all. If you've come to dote, you're too late. Nit has gone to the Park." He regarded the valise. "Unfortunately, Abby was persuaded to go along. What odds that this is Abby's bag?"

"Even I wouldn't take that bet." Gus shuffled the cards. "Is it as empty as it looks?"

Nigel picked up the valise, turned it upside down, and shook it. Nothing fell out, not even lint. "It was sitting on the doorstep," Duke explained.

"Interesting." Lady Syb tucked away her list of potential aspirants to her niece's hand before the viscount could recognize his own name, which she had tentatively crossed out. "Someone knows Abby is staying in the house."

"The whole world must know it," said Nigel. "The way you've been parading her about. Which might not have been the best of notions, if someone wishes her harm."

"Who would wish to harm Abby?" Cynthia looked up from her cards.

"Probably no one. Nigel is merely stirring the pot again." Lady Syb frowned. "Still, I wish I hadn't sent her off with Annette."

"You said at the time that you escaped by the skin of your teeth." Nigel turned confidingly to Viscount Daventry. "Aunt Syb's nerves couldn't stand the excitement of going out in public with Nit. We're keeping her company to make sure she don't start to convulse or drool. Or one of us doesn't! I've quite lost my own appetite."

Lady Syb shot her nephew a sharp look. "You can still be disinherited, Nigel. Come sit beside me, Duke. Does your presence here mean you have forgiven the abuse you've received at the hands of various members of my family?"

Gingerly, Duke skirted the snoozing pig and sat down on the sofa. If Lady Ysabella didn't feel her best, she looked far from her worst in her yellow muslin gown. The lace cap was absurd, of course, but charming. He watched her gracefully pluck the spectacles off her nose. "Your niece has flung herself at my feet and Almack's, and off a horse in Hyde Park. I'm afraid to think what she might do next."

Nigel looked up from the shabby valise. "No windows! That would be Gus. But first you must distract her from the tables. Look at the pile of buttons she has won."

There was indeed a handsome pile of buttons on the table in front of Gus, along with a fair scattering of cookie crumbs. "In the matter of skill and chance, the nature of cards is mixed, since the success of the player must depend as much on the chance of the deal as on his skill in playing the game. But even the chance of the deal may be influenced by the tricks of shuffling and cutting." She demonstrated. "Don't worry, I don't want you, Duke!"

Duke—who for the record had no intention of kissing Lady Augusta, not that he didn't like her, because he did; but if he ever thought about the matter, which he hadn't, he would have thought of her as having more sense than to wish to kiss a confirmed bachelor like himself—didn't know whether he was expected to be relieved, or go shoot himself. He looked at the hedgehog snoozing on Lady Ysabella's shoulder. "One cannot win with a losing hand," she said. "I repeat, you have forgiven us, Duke."

It was a summons from Lady Syb that had brought the viscount to this madhouse. Now he wondered if he might have done better to ignore it and risk offending her. "You, I would forgive anything," he said politely. "I am not so kindly disposed toward the rest of your family."

"Your feelings are still wounded because no one has ever given you the cut before," Lady Syb said soothingly. "You will recover from the slight. Indeed, it may do you some good. A gentleman such as yourself might gain an overinflated notion of his own importance with so many young ladies dangling after you in hope that you will reconsider the matter of a wife."

Duke studied his hostess. "Have I just been given a set-down?"

Lady Syb patted his arm. "Nothing of the sort. I find you irresistible myself. I meant merely that sometimes one must make allowances." She looked at the pig stretched out at her feet. "Sometimes one must make a great many of them."

The viscount and Lady Ysabella were engaged in conversation. Nigel was rapt on the valise. Cynthia was humming a somber tune beneath her breath. Gus knew the words to that tune, since Cyn had been humming it on and off since her arrival in Grosvenor Square.

> *"What will you leave your wife and child*
> *O my son tell me*
> *Sorrow and strife all of their life*
> *Is what they get from me, me, me*
> *Is what they get from me*
> *When will you ever come back here again*
> *O my son tell me*
> *When the sun and moon set in the sycamore tree*
> *And that will never be, be, be"*

She pushed aside her pile of buttons. "Do you think your husband won't come for you?"

Cynthia sighed. "I think that himself may be treating me to a dose of my own medicine. I would wish Duncan to the nether regions if I didn't miss him so much."

Gus propped her elbows on the table and rested her chin on her hands. "Men *are* the very devil, are they not?"

Though unaware that Gus considered Conor her own personal lighthouse, on whose jagged rocks she was doomed to smash herself to smithereens, Cynthia had a very good notion of how matters stood. "There is no better lover than a rake," she said, therefore. "All that experience. What woman in her right mind wouldn't rather have an artist in the matter of feminine seduction than a cow-handed *naïf?*"

Gus mulled over this question. Lady Syb and Viscount Daventry paused in their conversation. Nigel looked up from the valise. "*What?*" said Cynthia, irritably. "I merely said that I would rather marry a man who had been involved in various escapades and scandals than one who had lived like a monk."

Nigel looked ironic. "You did, sis, in case you have forgot."

Gus had been awake a great deal of the night thinking about rakehells and experience, and when that threatened to drive her lunatic, cardsharpers and gaming hells. "But what if he *keeps* philandering?" she asked.

"That's easy," Cynthia said gloomily. "Don't marry him."

Lady Ysabella looked away from the viscount. "This isn't like you, niece."

Cyn sighed. "I don't mean that Duncan is a philanderer. I think. I would hardly know, since he spends so much time with his blasted sheep. At least he *says* he is with his sheep. I suppose I should be grateful he hasn't brought them into the bedchamber. Or perhaps he has by now!"

Lady Syb and Viscount Daventry, both of whom had been married, paid little attention to this outburst. Gus stared. "I shouldn't be listening to this!" said Nigel, who had been eavesdropping shamelessly.

"Not *that* sort of attention!"His sister wrinkled her nose. "Although I have played second fiddle to an ewe. Nigel, never tell me that you are grown a prude. As I recall—"

"Never mind!" Nigel said hastily, and held up a hand. "I only meant that I didn't want to know that Duncan had been mistreating you, because if I *did* know it, then I would have to do something about it, and everyone knows how I feel about that!"

"I know a lovely recipe for baked sheep's head," said Lady Syb. "Nigel, give me that valise."

Nigel presented the bag with a flourish. Lady Syb inspected it with as much attention, and as little result, as he had done. "Perhaps the Abbess is an émigrée," mused Nigel. "Escaped from France with a fortune in jewels. A key player in some Royalist plot to see the Bourbons restored to the throne."

Both Lady Syb and Gus thought of a lady who *did* fit that description, and wondered where and how she was. "Meeting with a spymaster in Covent Garden?" inquired Lady Syb. "You outdo yourself, Nigel. In truth, Abby has become so much a part of the family that I doubt any of us care *who* she is, other than that she wishes to know."

Duke had followed the conversation with mild interest. "If she does have a family somewhere, they must be worried about her," he pointed out, after Lady Syb had explained the circumstances of her unexpected houseguest. "Perhaps were a notice to be inserted in the newspapers, someone might come forth."

"No doubt." Reluctantly Nigel abandoned the notion that Pontius might hold the secret to the Corsican's ultimate defeat. "Particularly if we hinted that money is involved."

Cynthia looked puzzled. "*Is* money involved? I thought—"

"No!" said Lady Syb. "No money. Not another word, Nigel, or I shall think you were on the wrong side of the hedge when brains were handed out. A newspaper notice seems so very vulgar. And to be truthful, I don't want to give Abby up!"

Gus looked at her buttons. It would be nice to be wanted, she thought. Or wanted by someone who wouldn't break her heart. For of course Conor would break her heart. Breaking hearts was what rakehells did, when they weren't frolicking with their game pullets and laced mutton, convenients and impures. Or being damnably noble and refusing to frolic with crabby spinsters like herself.

Silence descended upon the drawing room, broken only by pig snorts and hedgehog snores. Each of the occupants was lost in his or her own thoughts, none of which were particularly gay. "It occurs to me that everyone is very gloomy," remarked Nigel, at length. "I wonder why. Well, we know why Cyn is gloomy, but Gus won't tell."

Gus abandoned her cards. "You're not exactly a ray of sunshine yourself, Nigel. Perhaps Sir Edmond will loan you some of his leeches. I've never seen a more repellant waistcoat."

Nigel looked down at his waistcoat, which was a somewhat forceful combination of vermilion and lime green that suited his mood quite well. "What's wrong with my waistcoat?"

"It's ugly," said Gus, and bit into the last macaroon.

Cynthia wetted her forefinger, then picked up crumbs from the empty plate. "Loss of weight, drooping spirits, lack of interest in one's physical appearance, lowering looks, and a tendency to spiteful talk—He has all the symptoms, poor thing."

Nigel regarded his sister warily. Damned if she wasn't running a rig on him. Still, he couldn't help but ask. "Symptoms of *what*?"

Cyn wore a pitying expression. "*Amour*, my dearest brother. Moon madness. Cupid's dart."

TWENTY-TWO

As Nigel struggled with the notion that he might be lovesick—heaven knew he'd seen his sisters suffer that malady often enough that he should have recognized the symptoms, but he had never thought to apply the same yardstick to himself, and now that he did think to do so, he was appalled—his younger sister was struggling with Lord Ormesby's reins; or if not Lord Ormesby's reins, precisely, the reins of his team. Sweet goers, the steeds were, prime bits of blood; high-stepping, long-limbed thoroughbreds colored a lovely dappled gray. All four of them. Since Nit's papa agreed that a mere female lacked the strength necessary to control so many horses, she had never previously driven a team of four. Lord Ormesby had not grasped this fact. Abby had, and was wishing herself elsewhere.

In Nit's left hand she held the reins for the near leader and near wheeler; in her right the off leader, off wheeler, and the whip. Not that she was like to use the latter, pretty as it might be to see her flick the lash over the horses' heads. The beasts had already achieved more than sufficient speed. Nit was not accustomed to being perched in a seat so high one almost had to use a ladder to climb into it. Lord Ormesby's phaeton was very fine, painted and polished to a high degree, its predominant color a dusky rose. As was Lord Ormesby himself fine, in a matching jacket that unfortunately emphasized his tendency toward portliness.

Tolly was a generous man. Witness the readiness with which he'd handed her his reins. Unfortunately, Nit could not love him. Maybe she would never love anyone. She thought of Viscount Stanton, and how she had inadvertently insulted him; and despaired of ever becoming accustomed to town ways. Lord Ormesby was gazing at her with a besotted expression. It was very kind of him to let her tool the ribbons in the park, where all the world would see her, and be suitably impressed.

The world would be even more impressed were she seen to be capable of managing a team and conversing at the same time. Nit embarked upon a discussion of bascules and frogs and dorsal stripes, splayfoot and pigeon toes. When that elicited no response, she complimented Lord Ormesby on his phaeton. Tolly, who had added his own refinements to the vehicle, roused to speak with enthusiasm about linchpins and thoroughbraces and whippletrees.

Be strong and of good company; be not afraid, neither be thou dismayed; for the Lord thy God is with thee wheresoever thou goest. Abby hoped devoutly that "wheresoever" included her present circumstance. Whoever she was, and wherever she'd come from, Abby was certain she'd never ridden in a phaeton before. She wished she wasn't now. Phaetons were tall, well-sprung carriages, the front wheels smaller than the rear, raised considerably over the axle, offering no side protection to either driver or unhappy passengers. Such vehicles were known to corner well if driven by an expert, and to be dangerous if not, and as a result were popular with sporting gentlemen. In other words,

Abby was riding in a very tall carriage named after the son of Helios, whose only wish had been to drive the chariot that pulled the sun across the sky, and whose inability to hold the horses had led not only to his death, via a flash of lightning from the hand of Zeus himself, before he could set the world on fire, but also to the metamorphosis of his sisters, who had yoked the horses to the chariot, into poplar trees.

Abby scolded herself for being chicken-hearted. This chariot was not careening through the heavens, or along a crowded thoroughfare, but proceeding sedately through Hyde Park. Lord Ormesby's phaeton was a splendid vehicle, and even to Abby's inexperienced eye, his team was very fine. Alas, the reins of that fine team were in the hands of a shatterbrain, and Ormesby wasn't paying the least attention to his horses. His eyes were rapt on Nit's pretty face.

Had Abby the slightest notion she could handle the team, she would snatch up the reins herself. Unfortunately, she had not. Other tidbits of knowledge had presented themselves to her, however, since she had climbed aboard the phaeton, popping into her mind like a drowning man viewing various moments of his life. Her papa had been an avid gardener, fascinated especially by spiders, which he classified by the hairs on their bodies. He had also been a martyr to gout. Shipuah and Puah were two brave midwives who put their own lives at risk by defying the pharoah's law of death. Playing battledore and shuttlecock. Reading a pamphlet called *A Guide to Hell*. Which must surely have included in its pages a jaunt through Hyde Park with Nit's hands on the reins of a coach-and-four.

Abby was not alone in her misgivings. Any number of people had remarked upon the circumstance that

Miss Annette Slyte was tooling Ormesby's reins. Some remarks were salacious; others admiring; others observed that the young lady's *duenna* looked white as a ghost. Still others were appalled that Tolly was such a gudgeon as to allow a young woman the handling of his horseflesh.

Among the latter contingency was Sir Frances Braceborough, who paused midsentence to sputter and creak. Mr. Harcourt, witness to this queer reaction, turned in his saddle to stare. Not privileged to be a member of the Four-in-Hand Club, Mr. Harcourt was stricken with admiration. "Now that is something I like!" he said.

Sir Frances, and his chestnut gelding, were already in motion. Mr. Harcourt followed. Lord Ormesby had already stolen a march on him. He wouldn't permit Sir Frances to do likewise.

Nit was speaking knowledgeably of navicular disease when interrupted by Sir Frances, who was so overset by a closer view of the position of the young woman's hands on the reins—she had the ribbons threaded through the wrong fingers, the silly twit; furthermore, she wasn't paying the least bit of attention to where she was going, and if she didn't take care would shortly find herself in the Serpentine—that he inquired if Ormesby was a trifle bosky, otherwise why would he entrust his cattle to such a featherwit? Further comments of a similar nature followed, during which Lord Ormesby stared; and Abby grimaced; and Mr. Harcourt smugly watched his rival dig himself into a pit from which there would be no crawling out.

'Twas not the first time Nit had been ranted at; her papa was prone to such explosions of temper when one or more of his daughters did something he would have preferred they did not do, which occurred not infrequently; but her papa had never referred to her as "a rum business" or "a dunderhead." It was the word "cow-handed," however, that set up her hackles. "What *are* you blathering about?" she snapped.

Sir Frances stopped midrant, and just in the nick of time, for his next words would have been "veriest whipster," which would have definitely caused the young lady to take offense, for even if she wasn't a top-sawyer with four-in-hand, neither was she wholly unskilled. She had not held the reins up around her nose, for example, or squared her shoulders, or done anything else unforgivable.

Nit's fine eyes were narrowed, her elegant nostrils flared, her delicate chin jutted forward aggressively, and her pretty lips thinned. Lord Ormesby's skittish horses danced as her hands tightened on the reins. Sir Frances allowed that perhaps he *had* been a trifle force-ful in expressing his opinions. "Ahem! No need to fly into the boughs."

"There is every need!" retorted Nit, while Lord Ormesby watched her in besotted admiration— damned if she didn't look like an avenging fury, or was it a fate, one of those females in Greek mythology who tormented criminals and inflicted plagues—and Abby clutched at her seat. "Don't tell me not to put myself into a pucker, because I am already in one! And it is all your fault for being so fusty and interfering—yes, and insulting, too! Even if I *were* cow-handed, which I am *not*, Tolly has been kind enough to allow me to drive his team, and it is hardly any of your affair!"

Sir Frances was not prepared for so sharp a set-down from the young lady, who looked even more beautiful when in a temper; nor was he prepared to hear her refer to Ormesby by his nickname. "Insufferable!" he gasped.

Nit bared her perfect teeth at him. "Quite!"

Lord Ormesby was enjoying the exchange immensely, though he didn't understand the half of it, other than that Sir Frances had set up his lovely companion's back, and she had given him as pretty a facer as Tolly had ever seen. Tolly had never especially liked Braceborough, who had once referred to him, in his hearing, as a niddicock. Perhaps his understanding was not powerful, but Tolly wasn't the one gaping at Miss Slyte like a fish yanked out of water. "That's the dandy!" he said, and patted her knee.

A number of events occurred then, all at once, and even later no one could say which was to blame for the accident, even Conor Melchers, who appeared on the scene in time to witness everything. Sir Frances sputtered at the insult Nit had administered to his dignity, and reached out to shake a finger beneath her nose; Nit started when Lord Ormesby's hand descended on her knee, and jerked the reins; a group of ducks entered into a loud squabble on the banks of the Serpentine. Whatever factor, or combination of factors, set them off, the end result remained: Lord Ormesby's restless horses, who had been left standing about a great deal longer than they cared for, took offense. Off they went, at a spirited pace, sending pedestrians and riders scrambling to get out of their way.

Nit didn't panic, or screech, or drop the reins. Instead she set her teeth and pulled back on the leather for all she was worth. "Good girl!" said Tolly, as he hauled himself back up onto the seat, reached around her to take the reins into his own hands, and drew the horses to a stop. Nit closed her eyes and let out her breath. Then she opened them. "Oh! Where's Abby?" she cried.

* * *

Shortly thereafter, Mortimer opened the front door to find an assortment of people gathered outside. Conor Melchers was carrying an ashen Abby in his arms, while Nit hovered and wailed, and Lord Ormesby assured her over and over again that the accident hadn't been her fault. Sir Frances Braceborough trailed after them, muttering beneath his breath about hens coming home to roost. Mr. Harcourt brought up the rear, wringing water from his cravat, which had suffered grievously, along with the rest of him, when his startled horse had pitched him into the Serpentine.

Since Mr. Melchers was clearly the only sensible member of the group, Mortimer addressed him. "You will require someone to fetch Sir Edmond Jessop?" Conor nodded. "Lady Ysabella and Master Nigel are in the drawing room."

Lady Augusta and Cynthia had gone off to ponder their various dilemmas, the former rakehells and card-sharpers, the latter indifferent spouses and Scottish blackface sheep. Lady Syb, Nigel, and Duke were seated at the card table, intent on a game of loo. They glanced up when the door opened. Pontius squealed at the sight of his mistress and launched himself at Conor's knees. Lady Syb and Duke and Lord Ormesby between them restrained the pig. Nigel preferred to be on the sofa with Abby's head in his lap, all indignation at his sister's accusations forgotten at the sight of that pale and somewhat dirty face. He touched her forehead, which was cool. Hopefully, that was a good sign. As was the pulse beating in her temple. "What the devil happened?" he said.

Nit fell to her knees beside the sofa. "I didn't do it!" she wailed, over Pontius's squeals. "It wasn't my fault!"

"Do something with that damned pig!" demanded Conor, as he inspected Abby for signs of damage, in the process unwittingly causing Nigel to wish to damage *him*, as he manipulated arms and legs. His fingers moved into her curls, and paused to gently inspect a lump. "It's as I feared. She has hit her head again."

Cynthia appeared in the doorway, drawn by the uproar. Her gaze traveled over the various gentlemen, and ladies, and rested on Pontius. "Poor piggywig!" she said, and went to give him a hug. "*How* did Abby hit her head?"

There was a brief silence during which several people regarded each other guiltily. "It wasn't my fault!" Nit said stubbornly.

Duke folded his arms across his chest. "I can't do it!" he said to the room at large. "I can't do it even if the entire town thinks I've lost all my blunt."

Nit was briefly distracted from the sight of poor Abby lying so still and silent on the sofa. "Oh, your poor man! How did your fortune get away from you?" she asked.

Duke ground his teeth. "It didn't. It won't. *I* have more hair than sense. However, your brother threatened to tell the world I was a pauper if I didn't dote on you."

Nigel looked up from Abby, whose head felt surprisingly comfortable resting in his lap. "*Not* one of my better ideas, I admit it!" he said. "But—"

"*Dote?*" echoed Nit, indignantly. "You have a queer notion of what doting is, sir! Now I suppose you think I contrived to hurt poor Abby so I might see you, in which case you must be a bigger goosecap than even I am, because I didn't know you were here!" She glared at him. "Besides, your nose is crooked. I cannot marry a man with a crooked nose. Indeed, I have decided that some other one of my sisters must marry well, because it is entirely too much trouble. *I* shall retire to the country, and be an aunt!" So saying, she elevated her chin, crossed her arms beneath her bosom, and plopped down in a chair.

Sir Frances and Mr. Harcourt exchanged an embarrassed glance. Lord Ormesby, with unusual presence of mind, stated that he didn't wish to keep his horses standing too long, since they had experienced considerable excitement already this day, and if there was nothing he could do for the young lady, one need only send him word; however, at the moment he was clearly in the way and would therefore take his leave. Mr. Harcourt and Sir Frances echoed these sentiments, and left hard on his heels.

Nit sulked; Duke paced; Cynthia sat on the floor with her arms around the pig. Lady Syb stood up, having coaxed an agitated hedgehog out from beneath the couch. Conor, who was leaning over the back of the sofa, looked around the room and frowned, for Gus was conspicuously absent, which with all the uproar would indicate that she was nowhere in the house.

Nigel was watching Abby, and thinking of paralysis and apoplectic stupors and ruptures of the brain. With considerable relief, he saw her lashes flutter against her cheek. "You gave us all the shivers, Abbess. Welcome back." He paused, because there was only puzzlement in her brown eyes.

She blinked at him, and winced as he helped her to sit up. Then she looked bewildered at the anxious faces turned toward her. "What happened?" she whispered. "Where am I?"

TWENTY-THREE

Gus stared at the young gentleman whom she had last seen across a faro table at the Maison de Bonheur Willy looked much less cheerful now. His clothes were rumpled, as if he had slept in them, yet the dark circles beneath his eyes suggested he hadn't slept at all. "My father warned me about Captain Sharps who prey on young gudgeons fresh from the country!" he said, and then went on to call himself a crackbrained jackass, while clutching his brown hair in his hands as if he wished to pull it out. "I don't know whether to shoot Stafford or myself."

"You will do neither!" Gus said briskly, and took his arm to steer him around a donkey cart laden with firewood. "If you do not give up these dramatics, I shall be forced to box your ears."

Willy looked somber. "You sound like my mama. In truth I won't shoot Stafford, any more than I will tip him the double. To do either would be dishonorable. Not that there is anything honorable about that blackguard." He looked morosely at a broadsheet seller. "I thought I was fly to the time of day. Instead I'm a lobcock."

"Fiddle!" Gus took a firmer grip on Willy's arm, lest he decide to dart out in front of a carriage, for the street was busy and filled with all manner of pedestrians and vehicles. "You are hardly the first to get caught up in a cardsharper's snares. I know of one young man who was plundered in the course of a few years of all his family's wealth, and fled the country in fear of being thrown in gaol. Someone should have thrust Stafford's hand through with a fork a long time ago."

Willy blinked. What had forks to do with his dilemma? "You were acquainted with that young man?" he asked.

Gus looked up and down the busy street, anywhere but at her companion, and settled on studying the window of a chandler's shop. "He was my brother. You remind me of him in some ways."

Briefly, Willy was distracted. "And you still play? Forgive me for saying so, Lady Augusta, but ain't that beyond foolish? I mean, I came to warn you what Stafford was, and here it turns out you should already know."

Gus didn't care to contemplate her potential follies. She walked with her companion past the tantalizing aromas of pies and tarts issuing from a baker's shop. "I am *not*," she said, "quite so foolish as you may think. You may take my word on it. Now, how the blazes do you expect me to help you when you won't tell me what you've done?"

Lady Augusta wasn't responding to his warnings as he had thought she might; hadn't screeched or fainted or told him he had been a fool. Willy wondered if perhaps he was still a little cup-shot, which seemed unlikely, due to the energy and emotion he'd expended during the hours he'd passed cursing himself and pacing the floor. "I don't expect you to help me! I shall go home and confess that I am all to pieces, and take my medicine."

Willy was demonstrating a stubborn reluctance to explain the particulars of his downfall. "How much?" Gus demanded. He hesitated. She pinched his arm, and then strained to hear his muttered response above the noises of the street. Surely he had not said, "Four thousand pounds." She scowled at him. He muttered the words again.

Four thousand pounds! If she had thought even briefly that she might help him pay his shot, Gus abandoned that idea. "Your father will stand the nonsense?"

Willy looked even unhappier. "Papa dislikes scandal more than anything. He will not like the world to know that his eldest son is a sapskull."

"Stop that!" said Gus.

Willy scowled at her. "I *am* a sapskull. You haven't heard the rest."

Gus paused, arms akimbo. "You are *worse* than a sapskull if you don't let me help you out of this muddle. Now tell me the story without further circumlocution, if you please!"

Willy opened his mouth, then closed it; opened it again and the whole dreary tale came stumbling out, an all-too-familiar story of impatient creditors, bills that had to be paid. Stafford had provided the needed funds, on the condition that Willy play at *écarté* with a Frenchman, and substitute two decks of cards for those that should have been furnished by the *comte*. "It was a conspiracy," Willy concluded gloomily. "I ended up owing four thousand pounds. And then—I must have been drunk as a wheelbarrow!"

"What you are going to be is strangled," Gus informed him. "In less than a moment's time. And then *what*?"

A moment before she would not have thought such a thing possible, but Willy's expression was even more miserable. "They forced me to sign a letter saying I'd used substituted cards. The cost of redeeming *that* will be considerably more than four thousand pounds."

Gus stopped to stare at her companion. He was taller than she, a well-made young man of perhaps two-and-twenty with brown hair and a pleasant, open countenance which was currently shadowed with worry and fatigue. Precisely the sort of honest and gullible young man who made a perfect victim for the Jack Staffords of the world. "Where is this letter now?" she asked.

Willy shrugged. "In a chest in his rooms at the Mapleton, I imagine. At least I saw him put it there. What are you thinking, Lady Augusta? He'll hardly hand it back to me."

Willy was far too honorable a young man to be informed of her intentions. "What if he did?" asked Gus.

Clearly Lady Augusta hadn't grasped the seriousness of the situation. Willy clutched her hand. "He wouldn't. Don't you see—"

Gus watched a clown from Astley's drive by in a carriage as quaint as his costume, and counted to one hundred and ten. "You're not listening to me. What if there were no longer such a letter? What if you were no longer in debt?"

Willy contemplated that impossibly blissful notion. "I would never play again. I may be *green,* Lady Augusta, but I am not a fool. This is useless speculation! I must go home now and face my papa. He won't even ring a peal in my ears, he'll just be disappointed, and I

would far rather he prosed and preached at me! I just
wanted to warn you that further association with
Stafford will surely lead to your downfall."

Gus didn't care to contemplate downfalls at that moment. "Swear it," she demanded. "Swear that you will
never play again."

"On my grandfather's grave, I will never again gamble." Willy frowned. "Lady Augusta—"

"Never mind!" said Gus, before he could ask what
she meant to do, because he would try and stop her,
and she didn't feel like arguing. "Go home, Willy. Tell
your papa nothing. Pretend you never came to town."

He demonstrated the stubbornness for which gentlemen are noted. "But—"

Gus grasped his shoulders, turned him away from
her, and gave him a push. "I am going to talk to a gentleman called the Dimber Dabber. Trust me, Willy, and
go home!"

Thus it came about that the bustling Mapleton Hotel
unwittingly acquired an additional chambermaid; and
if the young woman didn't know how to clean marble
or wash windows, she did know how to make rose
water, and also that oil of roses and white wax and
spermaceti mixed together made an excellent remedy
for chapped lips. Not that she intended to get close
enough to Jack Stafford's lips to see if they were
chapped or not. She glanced up and down the corridor,
knocked, waited, and then slipped the picklock into the
door. A twitch, a twist, and the lock opened. Gus
slipped inside and closed the door behind her. Jack
Stafford's rooms were empty, as she had known they
would be. Gentlemen—or scoundrels pretending to be

gentlemen—would be abroad at this hour, seeking out credulous saplings upon whom to prey.

A lady could hardly visit a gentleman's hotel. An anonymous chambermaid might go anywhere she pleased. Therefore Gus wore a black dress and ample white apron. Her hair was tucked up under a starched cap, her complexion buried under several layers of rice powder, her eyes hidden behind thick spectacles. Jeremy had provided the costume, and the picklocks. Why she wished the items, he didn't want to know. This suited Gus fine, because she had no intention of explaining herself.

The Mapleton was located in Bond Street, a luxurious gentleman's establishment run by a refugee from the French Revolution, a one-time favorite of Louis the XVIII, whose cooking was superb. Jack Stafford didn't stint himself, Gus reflected as she walked around his suite. There was an anteroom with fireplace, a living room that opened by way of fine double doors into the bedroom, and a dressing room behind. The mahogany tester bed was large enough to hold several people, the tubs on the washing stand made of handsome porcelain, the large standing looking glass of the finest quality, as was the carpet on the floor.

But she was not here to change Mr. Stafford's linens, or supply his room with water, or clean his chamber pot, unless she emptied the latter over his head. A search of the quarters brought her an appreciation of his wardrobe—boots by Hoby, hats by Lock; coats by either, since she was no expert on gentlemen's fashions, Weston or Stultz; and furthermore the man owned what seemed an extraordinary number of cravats—but no nearer to a chest. Then she thought to look beneath the bed.

There it rested, amidst an army of dust bunnies that bore mute testimony to the lackadaisical efforts of the real chambermaid, who might appear at any moment and raise a ruckus at finding herself replaced.

Gus bent down and reached for the chest, which proved surprisingly heavy. She hauled it out from beneath the bed, then sank back on her heels. The picklocks didn't work, and time was running short. Gus carried the chest into the antechamber, grasped the fireplace poker, and gave the lid a good, hard smash. One smash, and then another. The wood cracked open. Gus stared at a rogue's treasure trove of letters and vowels and even jewelry. She picked up a deck of marked cards, touched the slight and almost imperceptible indentation that made a ridge or wave on the back of the ace, thereby announcing its presence, or absence, to a practiced eye.

Unthinkable, to save one of Stafford's victims and leave the others to their fates. Hastily, Gus built up the fire. She shredded Willy's confession, then dumped all the papers on the fire, along with the pieces of the wooden chest. Let Stafford think Cyn's mischievous boggarts had spirited away his ill-gotten gains. The jewels, she scooped up and thrust into her pocket. Perhaps Lady Syb could help her determine the rightful owners. She stood up and turned to leave, then gasped as her heart leapt straight up into her throat.

Jack Stafford stood in the doorway watching her. In his hand was a gun, and it was aimed at her chest. "Did you think the room too chill, my dear? I must question your choice of heating fuel." She stood rigid as he walked across the room toward her, reached out and yanked off the spectacles. His eyes narrowed. "I wondered what your game was, Lady Augusta. You have surprised me. Not many people have done that."

Not and lived to tell the tale, thought Gus. With considerably more courage than she felt, she thrust out her chin. "You will not harm Willy now. He is free of you."

Stafford grasped her wrist and dragged her toward him. "Perhaps he is, but you are not," he said. "You little fool."

TWENTY-FOUR

Dusk was darkening the street outside the windows of the Duke of Charnwood's elegant town house in Bedford Square. Candles already gleamed in the drawing room, glinted off rosewood tables and brocaded chairs, the pianoforte, an elegant fire screen, the bronzes on the cap of the chimneypiece.

The duchess was seated at the piano, idly depressing the keys. She wore a pretty dress of white piña cloth embellished with multicolored silk embroidery. The duke stood by the fireplace, frowning at the letter he held in his hand. It was a scene of peaceful domestic harmony, save for the great scarlet macaw that was chasing several black kittens around the chamber, while their mama perched on the back of a settee and watched the goings-on with a wary eye.

Impatiently, Elizabeth struck a minor chord. "I dislike this waiting. Are you sure he'll come?"

Before her husband could respond, Conor Melchers walked into the room. His gaze lit on the misty mountain vista that adorned one wall. "Does memory fail me, or did a hunting scene hang there last week?"

Justin contemplated the portrait. "Elizabeth dislikes looking at dead rabbits. Lady Syb keeps trying to give us Birdie's portrait, but to date we have managed to discourage her."

Conor glanced at the parrot, which was currently chasing one of the kittens around a piano leg. The mama cat, whose name was Minette, leapt down from her perch to rub against his boot. "What is of such grave importance that I must miss my dinner?" he asked.

Justin held out the letter. "I do not immediately perceive what you have to do with this matter, but Elizabeth insisted you would be interested."

Elizabeth swung around on the piano bench. "He is interested because he kissed Gus. There's no use denying it, Conor! Gus told me that you kissed her. I had the impression she liked it very much, though she *didn't* tell me that."

"Conor kissed *Gus*?" Justin raised his eyebrows. "One cannot begin to imagine why."

"Yes, one can," Elizabeth murmured. Her husband looked from their guest to her. She twinkled. Justin looked bemused.

He collected his wits, and frowned. "Are you telling me that Conor has been toying with Gus? I won't have it! He's a rakehell. And she's—"

"Touchy and difficult?" suggested Elizabeth. "At her last prayers? Don't scowl at me, Justin. No, and neither need you scowl at Conor! Must I remind you of what happened the last time you two quarreled?"

Both gentlemen had excellent memories. As one, they looked at the duchess to make certain she wasn't holding a gun.

Elizabeth rose from the piano bench. Justin growled as Conor eyed the neckline of her gown. "Stop that!" said the duchess. "We must put our heads together and determine how we are going to resolve this predicament."

Justin's expression didn't lighten. "*We*?"

Elizabeth's eyes sparkled. "Why would it not be *we*, pray tell? Gus is your cousin. I am your wife."

Conor didn't care to become embroiled in a marital squabble. He cleared his throat. "Forgive my lack of perception, but resolve *what* predicament?"

Justin transferred his glower from his wife to the letter in his hand. "Gus is being held for ransom. It's a very large ransom. Considerably larger than she's worth."

Surely Conor had not heard correctly. "Ransom? *Gus?*"

The duke snatched up the kitten that was trying to climb his boot and regarded it with disfavor. "Behave yourself, you wretched creature, or I shall feed you to Birdie as a treat. Yes, ransom. Gus has been compromised. Or she *will* be compromised if I don't buy Stafford off." Justin deposited the kitten onto the rug. "Elizabeth said you would wish to know. *I* find myself curious to know if my cousin has already been compromised."

Conor folded his arms across his chest. "Define 'compromised.'"

The duke wondered if he really wished to pursue this topic. The duchess picked up Minette, who immediately began to purr. "Maman says that a lady's reputation lies not in what she does, but in what she is thought to do. We all know that Maman is a stickler. Unfortunately, she is also sometimes right."

Justin dragged his mind away from recollection of the manner by which Elizabeth had made him purr just that morning. "As I recall, your maman told you that obedience is the indispensable virtue in a good wife."

Elizabeth wrinkled her nose. "I said *sometimes* she is right. The question is, where is Gus? You don't seem particularly concerned."

"Of course I'm concerned. She's my cousin." Justin sat down in a chair and stretched out his long legs. Another of the kittens promptly tried to climb his boot, and failed, leaving additional scratch marks in the fine leather. He regarded them with resignation. "Which is precisely the point. Stafford won't harm my cousin. He wouldn't dare. Because he knows that if he *did* harm her, I would see him hanged."

Elizabeth scooped up Birdie and sat the parrot on his shoulder. "Toplofty!" she remarked.

"Perhaps," said the duke, who didn't look at all toplofty with a parrot perched on his shoulder, checking his hair for lice. "However, rank does have its privileges, a fact well known to Stafford and his ilk."

"Ilk," Elizabeth repeated thoughtfully, as she lifted the mama cat from the back of the settee and dropped it in her husband's lap. "What a lovely word. Stafford and his ilk. It sounds like a particularly odious disease."

Conor had not come to Bedford Square to witness the Charnwood version of domestic bliss. "About Gus," he reminded them.

Justin regarded him without favor. "How did Gus meet Stafford? He is hardly welcome in the best drawing rooms."

Conor scooped up a kitten that was about to fall into a colorful japanned urn. "Lady Syb thought Gus would be less likely to tumble into a scrape if she was in my company. As a result, Gus encountered Stafford at the Maison de Bonheur."

"Let me understand this." Justin set aside cat and parrot, and rose from his chair. "You've not only been trifling with my cousin, you've also escorted her to gaming hells."

Conor eyed him warily. "I also made sure she knows how to spot a cheat."

Justin advanced. "Perhaps I shall cut out your liver and fry it. Yes, that sounds like a good idea."

"I've been nothing but honorable in regard to your cousin," Conor protested. At least he had tried to be honorable. And since it was his first attempt at nobility of character, Conor should surely be forgiven if he had slipped a little bit. "And as for livers, what makes you think I shan't fry yours?"

"Stop it, both of you!" Elizabeth stamped her foot, thus reminding the gentlemen of what happened when she flew off the hooks, and distracting Birdie from flirting with her reflection in a pier glass. "Biscuit?" the parrot inquired.

"No biscuit, but you may have a kitten if you can catch one." The duchess sat the macaw on the floor, then gazed sternly from her husband to their guest. "We are in a state of consternation, Conor, so you will forgive Justin for acting like a duke. And yes, Justin, for Conor to escort Gus to gaming hells was shockingly irregular, and I daresay she enjoyed it very much. Since there aren't a great many things your cousin does enjoy, you might try and be a little more tolerant. After all, Gus was well set out on the path she treads long before Lady Syb and Conor took a hand."

Things had come to a pretty pass when his wife gave him a rake-down. The duke regarded her without appreciation. The duchess smiled at him.

Elizabeth had a lovely smile. Justin touched her

cheek. Conor deemed it time for a distraction. "How is this ransom to be paid?"

"It's to be delivered to Stafford's rooms at the Mapleton, at which point Gus will be returned to the bosom of her fond family." Not sounding the least bit fond, Justin removed a pair of very lovely Manton dueling pistols from their brass-bound mahogany case. "One assumes he has her there, or is holding her nearby."

The duchess scooped up a kitten before Birdie could pounce on it. "Poor Gus! She must be terrified." Both gentlemen looked blankly at her. "Well, perhaps not terrified. Gus is hardly of a delicate sensibility. Still, she'll be overset by her ordeal, and will require a female's company."

The duke tucked away his pistols. "The Mapleton is a gentlemen's establishment. Ladies are not welcome there."

"Then I shan't be a lady!" retorted the duchess. "You will like that. Must I point out that Gus is apparently already present at this gentlemen's establishment? You can hardly whisk her out the front door without being seen, and therefore my help will be required. There's no need to scowl, Justin. I didn't take her to that place."

The duke shook his head at this example of female reasoning. "For all we know, Gus took herself there. Damned if I'm not tempted to let her lie in the bed she has made."

" 'Wherein you reprove another be unblamable yourself.' " While the duchess quoted her mama, Conor dragged his thoughts away, with immense effort, from lying with Gus in bed.

Justin conceded his poor choice of words. "Well, not lie in it exactly, but allow her time to reflect on her foolishness before I set out to the rescue. Of course I mean to rescue her. Stafford has already ruined her brother. He shan't be allowed to also ruin Gus. Nor do I intend to make him a present of my blunt." Suddenly, he smiled. "I've just realized that if Stafford plunges us into the scandal-broth, Elizabeth's mama will never speak to us again. Damned if I'm not tempted to do nothing at all."

The duchess swatted her husband, fondly. "Wretch!" she said.

It seemed to Conor that the Charnwoods were not taking Gus's predicament seriously enough. He was tempted to go rescue Gus himself. However, Gus's reputation would be in no better repair were she seen at the Mapleton with a man of his stamp. "And if Stafford *has* harmed her? Despite the fact that she's your cousin?" he asked.

Justin's smile faded. "Then I shall have his head."

"You may have his head *after* I am done with the rest of him." Conor plucked a kitten off his coatsleeve. "If he has laid a hand on her—"

"He must have laid a hand on her to take her captive," Elizabeth pointed out. "Goodness, Conor, now *you* are looking like a thundercloud. Why is that, do you think?"

"Excellent question." Justin narrowed his eyes at Conor. "If you don't want Gus, why do you care if Stafford has her or not?"

Conor was certain he'd never said he didn't want Gus. It would have been a lie. However, he didn't deem it prudent to explain his feelings to the duke, even if he *could* explain his feelings, which was questionable. "I'm a rakeshame, not a rotter," he said stiffly. "How long has it been since you received that note?"

Justin steepled his fingers. "You took your time getting here. I'd say it's been a good couple hours. Wouldn't you, Elizabeth?"

The duchess stroked Birdie's bright feathers. "At least," she mused. "Perhaps more."

"Damnation!" shouted Conor, with such force that the kittens ran for shelter, and the parrot squawked.

"I don't believe I've ever seen you in such a swivet," marveled Justin, when order was restored. "After all, it's only Gus."

"I'm *not* in a swivet," snarled Conor. "And you'd not be so bloody calm if Stafford had Elizabeth in his grasp."

"No, I wouldn't," Justin said thoughtfully. "But the case is a little different, don't you think?"

Conor looked at Justin and Elizabeth. They both returned his gaze. One looked sympathetic, the other very ducal. "Oh, hell," he said.

TWENTY-FIVE

Sir Edmond came to examine the patient, and pronounced her fit enough, if a little battered and bruised; and pointed out as well that he had said *gentle* exercise, which certainly did not include being pitched out of a carriage several stories high, and it would serve them all right if she *had* experienced a seizure of the brain. Since she had not, he saw no need for either poultice or leeches. If anyone was disposed to take his advice, not that he expected it, he suggested several days' bed rest. If his advice *wasn't* taken, he didn't want to hear about the consequences. In short, he washed his hands of all of them. So saying, he took his leave.

He would return, of course. The good doctor always did. Lady Syb looked about the blue-hung bedroom, where the various members of her household had gathered, except for the unaccountably absent Gus. One hoped Gus hadn't fallen into trouble. However, one could only deal with so many crises at one time. In addition to the family, Viscount Daventry was also present, though he would rather not have been, as were the hedgehog and the pig. Helen was snuggled in the curve of Abby's elbow, watching the goings-on with bright black eyes. Pontius was stretched out atop the coverlet next to his mistress, a position that had required the assistance of several stalwart footmen, and though Lady Ysabella hardly liked a pig in one of her best bedchambers, it had been the only way to shut the creature up, Abby having protested when Duke suggested slitting its throat.

Abby was worn out from her examination. She moved, and winced. Nigel bent to fluff her pillows, and thought she still looked confused. Who *wouldn't* be confused when presented with Nit wailing, and Lady Syb scolding, not to mention hedgehogs and pigs and all the rest. Still, she should have become accustomed to this madhouse by now. Nigel was very much afraid that Abby had remembered who she was, and forgotten who she'd been in the interim since then. In short, he was afraid she had forgotten him.

He supposed he could ask Abby what she remembered. She was clutching his hand, which might be construed as a hopeful sign. Although, were he to find himself abruptly amidst this lunacy, Nigel might clutch the nearest hand himself. "I have decided to give up my title!" announced Duke, as he edged toward the doorway where Lady Syb's abigail was hovering. "The eldest of my sons shall have it. I am going to become a monk. Take a vow of celibacy."

"A monk!" Nit stared. "I have never heard of such a thing."

"Of course you have. Monks and monasteries and haunted abbeys. Surely such drastic measures are not—" Cynthia broke off as a familiar bellow echoed down the hallway. Throckmorton was picked up as if she weighed no more than a feather and moved out of the doorway. A tall, red-haired, and very angry gentleman strode into the room and paused to glower at its various occupants. "Duncan. How nice that you could join us," Cynthia said coolly. He growled.

Nit brightened at sight of her brother-in-law, whom she thought very splendid in his leggings and kilt and linen shirt, even if his castle was drafty and his temperament dour. "*Is* your home decorated with the heads of your enemies? Cynthia said it was. She also said you would be very cross, and clearly you are. You have missed the excitement. My heart has been broken. Viscount Daventry is going into a nunnery. I have decided not to wed."

None of the several people in the bedchamber felt up to the task of explaining to Nit the difference between a monastery and a nunnery. Cynthia gazed upon her irritable and altogether wonderful husband, whose coppery hair was so bright it stole all other color from the room, and made her own golden curls, and Nit's and Lady Syb's and Nigel's, seem faded and dim. His eyes were green and bold as his Viking ancestors', his legs surely the finest in all the British Isles. A good thing all gentlemen didn't go about in kilts, for the sake of their ladies' presence of mind. "Um," she said.

Nit fluttered her eyelashes. If Cynthia didn't want her laird, perhaps he would settle for another of her sisters. A younger, prettier one. "I fell off my horse. But I didn't hurt myself. Cynthia called me a brat."

"You *are* a brat!" said Nigel, as his brother-in-law fixed Nit with a bright green stare. "Look here, Duncan, you ain't been philandering, have you? Because I don't have the least desire to face you over pistols at dawn." He ruminated. "Although I don't know that I have any choice after what Cyn said about having ewes in your bedchamber."

What nonsense was this? The black-hearted Mac-

Dougall of Dunally frowned at his wife. She was looking hagged, poor lass. Duncan was feeling a little
hagged himself, after so many nights of sleeping by
himself. Or trying to sleep. He said, "Were you so unhappy with me, lass?"

How she loved his Scottish burr. Still, he had said he
wouldn't live under the cat's paw, as if she were some
sort of *managing* female, which she wasn't, not really,
but if he'd wanted a milk-and-water miss, he should
have married one. Not that Cyn was unhappy, how
could the great addle-pate think such a thing? Had she
not slopped his hogs, and helped him shear his sheep?
Not to mention milking cows? Water kelpies were also
brought into the conversation, and her laird was given
to understand that it was an excellent circumstance for
him that there was no seaweed in his hair.

Duncan deduced from these disjointed utterances
that his wife had missed him. Och, he had missed her,
too. He stepped closer, and took her face gently in his
hands. Nit watched them. "I drove a phaeton," she volunteered. "And a team of four."

Nigel leaned against the bedpost. "You drove it so
well you tossed poor Abby on her head."

Nit's lower lip trembled. "It wasn't my fault! Anyone
would jerk the reins if Lord Ormesby put his hand
upon her knee."

A good brother would call out Ormesby for taking
such a liberty. "I'm going to pretend I didn't hear that,"
Nigel said.

Duncan smiled at Cynthia, who was mistily looking
up at him. "Did you leave me because you missed your
family, *acushla*? You need only hae been sayin' so."

Cyn sniffled. "You wouldn't listen to me."

Duncan brushed away an errant teardrop. "Am I nae listening to you now?"

As was everyone else, including Abby. "I believe," offered Nigel, "that you have not explained about the ewe."

Nit pouted all the harder. "I don't think you should fuss about an ewe when I saw Cyn kiss a pig!"

"Nit! Do try for a little conduct!" hissed Lady Syb.

Distracted, Duncan glanced at Pontius. "I cannae blame the lass for kissing such a grand fellow as himself. I'm thinkin' I've nae ever before seen a pig in bed."

"Och!" sighed Nigel. "Now we've given him ideas."

Maddening, the lot of them. Cynthia grasped her husband's sleeve and tugged. He looked at her with laughter in his eyes. She said, "What took you so long?"

Duncan ignored the indication that his wife knew he'd come to fetch her, because of course she'd known he would. Which he suspected was one reason for their collieshangie, a sort of testing of him, but he'd keep that notion to himself. "I'd a grand visit with your father. And your sisters and your stepmama. They were all verra curious as to why I dinnae know your whereabouts. Your father was full of good advice. He said—" Duncan glanced at Nit's wide eyes. "Never mind!"

Cynthia did not want to seem too easily forgiving. From somewhere, she dredged up a frown. "You should not have said those things to me, Duncan. I am *not* a managing female."

Certainly she was, but Duncan didn't mind being managed. He would explain the matter to her later. "Sometimes a man says more than he means."

"And sometimes a woman can be beyond foolish!" Entertaining as all this was, Lady Syb decided to move matters along. "Your wife has something to tell you, Douglas. And if she won't, I will."

Cynthia looked at her aunt and audience, then stood on tiptoes to whisper in her husband's ear. He clasped her shoulders and shook her. "A wee bairn? Are you sure?"

"I wanted to tell you, but you were only interested in sheep!" Cynthia burst into tears.

"My poor hinnie!" said Duncan, and swept her up into his arms as easily as if she were a bairn herself. Then he scowled. "Are you daft? Traveling that great distance in your state?" he roared.

Nit blinked in puzzlement. "Why is Duncan angry now? Maybe he doesn't realize that Cynthia was only pretending to be indifferent and moping about until we were all in the dumps. But still, she told us that—"

Perhaps instead of wine and water, she would resort to laudanum. "Your sister," interrupted Lady Syb, "is *enceinte.*"

"Oh." Duncan had stopped yelling, perhaps because Cynthia had flung her arms around his neck and was sniffling in his ear. "Please, what is *enceinte*?"

Lady Syb prayed for patience. "In a delicate condition. Increasing. In the family way." Nit looked no more enlightened. "You are going to have another niece or nephew upon whom to dote."

"Oh!" said Nit, but not in anticipation. "Dote" had made her think of Viscount Daventry. Douglas was doing to Cynthia exactly what Nit had wished Duke would do to her when she tumbled off her horse. Not to such a degree, perhaps—it didn't look especially comfortable to be squeezed in such a manner—but the general idea was the same.

She peered around the room. Duke was no longer present. "Where is Viscount Daventry?"

Had he any sense, Duke would be halfway to the

colonies. "Perhaps he went into the garden. Throck-morton will help you look for him." Lady Ysabella waited until her niece tripped blithely from the room. "Douglas, put down your wife. Yes, I know that you wish to bear her off to your castle, there to give her a scolding that she will not soon forget, but Abby is going to tell us something that Cynthia will wish to hear."

Duncan glanced quizzically at Cynthia. 'Twasn't scolding that he had in mind for his wife. She smiled damply at him. "I would like to stay, Duncan, please."

When Duncan was seated in the bedside chair, with Cynthia curled up in his lap, Lady Syb brought forth the battered valise. "This is yours, I think, my dear."

Abby touched the worn leather. Helen crawled down her arm to go exploring, black nose mightily a-twitch. "I am glad to have it back. It belonged to my papa."

"Did it contain anything of value?"

"I own nothing of value except Pontius." Abby looked at the people around her. "And my friends."

Lady Syb sat on the side of the bed opposite Nigel. "We are all your friends, my dear. Including Duncan. Now tell us everything!"

Abby touched the ring that hung around her neck, and glanced up at Nigel. "My papa was always ex-pected to take Holy Orders. He was a younger son. Since he had a private income, we lived in a fairly comfortable manner, in Penrith, although he suffered terribly from the gout. The doctor said it was due to the fine cellar that he kept. Papa also had a cavalier way with bishops, and was out of favor frequently. There were always rumors about indiscretions he'd commit-ted as a young man, before he entered the church. He shrugged them off, saying that providing he carried out his public duties, his private life was his own affair."

"In other words, the everyday tasks of the parish fell to you," Lady Syb said shrewdly, while Nigel contemplated the calluses on the hand he held, and wished that he might have Abby's head back in his lap.

"I didn't mind." Helen was attempting to climb out of the valise. Abby lifted her up and kissed her nose. "Indeed, I minded so little that I married a parson in my own turn. My husband was a different sort of person from Papa. He was very involved with the lives of his parishioners, and meticulous about visiting the sick, often changing their surgical dressings himself. Sir Edmond would have been dismayed." She set the hedgehog on the bed near Pontius. "Frances insisted on tending a sick villager and came down with smallpox himself, over two years ago. After the living passed on to his successor, I remained in the village until Pastor Rogers married, when it became apparent that my presence interfered with the villagers' acceptance of his bride." No need to wonder any longer why she knew so much about so many things.

"And so you came to London," Lady Syb said.

Abby nodded. "My brother Benjamin is a barrister with quarters in the Middle Temple. That is why Pontius and I were in Covent Garden. I meant our arrival to be a surprise. Since I didn't send word that I was coming, Benjie would have no way of knowing that I'd gone missing. He will be concerned he hasn't heard from me in some time."

"I shall send him word." Lady Syb got up from the bed. "We must suppose that someone knew we were making inquiries and became worried about the valise and therefore brought it back. Come along, Duncan,

Cynthia." She swept away from the room. Duncan rose from the chair, Cynthia still in his arms. Her head rested comfortably on his shoulder. He glanced at Nigel, and winked.

Nigel was left alone with Abby. He looked at her doubtfully. "You wouldn't expect a fellow to do such stuff, would you, Abbess? Spout romantic nonsense, and carry you about like a sack of wool? Although I expect Melchers would."

Abby gazed up at him. "What has Mr. Melchers to do with anything?"

"Then you *don't* remember," said Nigel. "I thought you must have lost your memory again with that second knock on the head."

Abby looked at his hand, which she still clasped. She had been fond of her husband, whom she had known from childhood, but theirs had been a relationship more friendly than passionate. Her feelings for Nigel were intriguingly different. *And they were both naked, the man and the woman, and were not ashamed.* "I remember everything. I'm sorry about Lady Augusta."

Nigel paused in counting the freckles on her adorably snub nose. "What about Gus?"

How warm his hand was. How beautifully formed. As was the rest of him. "Lady Augusta and Mr. Melchers. I know you have feelings for her," Abby said.

Nigel was puzzled by the conversation. "Of course I have feelings for Gus. I've known her forever. She might as well be—No, I take that back. She's not one of my sisters, thank God."

"Perhaps I was mistaken." Abby lowered her gaze to the coverlet. "It seemed to me that Lady Augusta and

Mr. Melchers are fond of one another. I thought you might mind."

Nigel was so startled that he sat down beside her on the bed. "Abbess, you've got the wrong sow by the ear. That is, they are, but I don't!"

At mention of a sow, Pontius opened one eye and looked interested. Seeing neither sow nor turnip, he rolled over and went back to sleep. Helen waddled across the coverlet and curled up between his front legs.

Abby raised her eyes to Nigel's face. "You don't?"

"No. I thought you did. Silk stockings, gaming hells? Remarkable! I thought Nit was the only female alive who didn't fancy Melchers, which is a good thing, because then she really would have gotten her heart broke."

Abby shook her head. "You are talking a great deal of nonsense."

Nigel regarded their entwined fingers. He didn't wish to have his heart broken either, but one had to take the chance. "The thing is, I think we'd deal well together, Abbess. You could enlighten me about female emancipation. I could work some of your more radical notions into speeches for the House." He raised her hand to his lips, and grinned. "We could explore the *Song of Songs*."

Abby touched his golden curls. With all her memories intact, she knew she'd never been happier in her life. "I don't think I have ever told you that I thought you were an angel when I first saw you sitting by my bed."

TWENTY-SIX

"This is most irregular," the porter said again, as he led the small party of visitors down the corridor. The porter was a pompous fellow, as well as very grand, in his coat with scarlet cuffs and collar and white buttons, scarlet waistcoat, velveteen breeches, and a hat with gold lace edging and a gold lace band. Fortunately, he was also venal, and most interested in adding to the sum he was setting aside for his old age, a fund greatly enhanced by the irregular goings-on at the Mapleton, such as this occasion was.

There were no flies on this porter, no indeed. He knew very well that the third "gentleman" was in fact a female, despite the breeches that she wore. A female moreover who appeared to be enjoying herself inordinately. Whatever was the world coming to when a gentleman couldn't be safe from females even in his lodgings? Not that Jack Stafford could be considered a gentleman. The porter sniffed as he reached out to place the key in the lock.

A hand shot out and grasped his wrist. "You may leave that to us," said the most impatient of the visitors, who was tall and muscular and dark-haired. A rakehell if ever the porter had seen one. A rakehell and a female were wishful of sneaking up on Jack Stafford. He looked forward to telling the tale downstairs.

The porter had no especial fondness for the occupant of this particular set of rooms, and looked forward to seeing mayhem enacted upon his person, at the very least. Still, a token protest was called for. "But—" he said.

The keys were plucked out of his hand and additional coins thrust at him. Demanded the other gentleman, "Go away!" The porter tested one coin, then another, with his teeth. His retirement fund was growing at a dandy rate. Satisfied, he left the visitors to enact whatever mischief they might.

As the porter walked down the hallway, Elizabeth pulled one of her husband's dueling pistols from her waistband. Conor flinched. "She knows how to use it. I taught her," said Justin, as he quietly inserted the key into the lock. Conor recalled the instance when the duchess and a pistol had scattered a herd of sheep. He glanced at her bosom. The duke snarled, "Concentrate!"

Conor could not help that he was a rakehell with a vivid memory of the occasion on which the duchess's lovely bosom had been put on public view. However, he had more urgent matters on his mind just now. "Ready." His own pistol drawn, Justin twisted the key.

The door swung silently open. Because the duke had his hands full trying to prevent the eager duchess from bursting into the room, waving her firearm enthusiastically about, Conor entered first, then stopped dead in his tracks.

"What is it?" Elizabeth stood on tiptoes in an attempt to see over Justin's shoulder. "Have we found Gus? Is she all right?"

Justin plucked the pistol from her hand lest she forget her lessons. "I am looking forward to determining that. Once Conor has moved out of the way!"

Conor stepped aside. Elizabeth ducked under her husband's arm and stepped into the room, then in her own turn stopped to stare.

Gus sat calmly on a sofa, rice powder plastered thick on her face, and a pair of very ugly spectacles perched on her patrician nose. In one hand she held a pistol, in the other a brandy glass. At her feet lay Jack Stafford, trussed up with a number of cravats, a poker-sized lump on his head, and an expression of intense anger on what could be seen of his face.

The black gown and starched apron were hideous, the cap tipsily askew. "A chambermaid! How very clever!" enthused Elizabeth. "No one would ever guess who you are. It appears we are too late to rescue you. Is that Mr. Stafford's gun?"

Gus nodded. "It has taken immense willpower not to shoot him. I reminded myself that your mama would not approve."

"No, she wouldn't! That was very good of you." The duchess squinted at the pistol. "English, is it? Made by Twigg?"

Gus studied the gentleman's pocket pistol, with its embossed dark wood grain. "Personally, I prefer an American pistol. Although firearms made by Gunney are also very nice. And of course there is the incomparable Mr. Manton. You will have seen Justin's dueling pistols."

"I have even fired them." Elizabeth sat down beside Gus on the sofa. "Justin is teaching me about such things. Firearms should be unloaded when not actually in use. Always keep the muzzle pointed in a safe direction. Don't aim at anything you don't wish to kill."

Gus pointed the pistol at her prisoner. "Justin has in his collection an Italian three-cannon pistol manufactured by Lorenzoni in 1680. It is particularly fine."

Elizabeth looked thoughtful. "Yes, but I believe I prefer the German axe-pistol from the seventeenth century."

The gentlemen regarded one another. Murmured Justin, "She's also partial to the French boarding cutlass with sidelock pistol." Mr. Stafford writhed and struggled and muttered unintelligibly behind the cravats knotted around his mouth.

"More profanity!" Gus sighed and set down her brandy glass to pick up the fireplace poker that leaned against the sofa. Mr. Stafford mumbled all the louder and struggled against his knots. Gus poked him ungently with the poker and he flopped over sideways.

"I take it he didn't hurt you," Justin said.

"He wanted to, but I had the poker in my hand. One assumes he thought I'd be easily overcome because I'm a mere female." Gus looked at her cousin. "I suppose now you'll say I've been foolish indeed."

Justin studied his cousin's costume, and tried hard not to smile. "I am more likely to say that Stafford was very foolish to underestimate you. But then he couldn't know that you spent your younger years playing Knights of the Round Table with Connor and Nigel and me."

"How splendid!" breathed the duchess. "Which knight were you, Gus?"

"She alternated between Morgan le Fay and Sir Gawain," said Conor. "As I recall, she especially enjoyed chopping off the head of the Green Knight. That is a splendid display of knots you've used there, Gus. I see a reef knot and a square knot and a constructor's knot. Ah, and a Bolyn."

Gus gestured with the poker. "And a Turkshead. I'm especially proud of that one. It's not easily accomplished when the person one is tying it around refuses to hold still."

All eyes moved to Mr. Stafford, who was trying to wriggle snakelike toward the door. "I think not," said Conor, and rested a booted foot upon the cardsharper's neck.

Gus could not look at Conor. Sitting watch over Jack Stafford had afforded her ample time to contemplate her numerous shortcomings. "I'm glad to see all of you," she repeated, and brandished the poker at Stafford, who abruptly stopped squirming and turned even more pale. "I couldn't decide what to do with him."

Elizabeth brightened. Perhaps she had not been permitted to dispatch the villain with her pistol, or play Knights of the Round Table, but the day was not yet done. "Sir Charles owns a shipping line," she said, referring to her steppapa. "Among other things. Perhaps Mr. Stafford—I assume this is Mr. Stafford? He looks like a Captain Sharp. Not that I have ever known one personally! Maman would never permit such a thing. I think we probably should not let her know that I have met one now. Sir Charles is quite a different matter. I'm sure he would be pleased to arrange for Mr. Stafford to enjoy a voyage to some exotic clime. Van Dieman's Land, perhaps. New South Wales."

"Botany Bay," suggested Conor. Mr. Stafford responded to the mention of these penal colonies with writhing worthy of a Vauxhall acrobat.

Justin smiled. "Botany Bay it is! How fortunate it is

that I have two footmen and a carriage waiting outside.
We shall escort Mr. Stafford to Sir Charles's ship." He
looked thoughtfully around the room. "Wrapped up, I
believe, in that nice Aubusson rug!" His wife clapped
her hands, and he smiled at her. "Are you enjoying
your adventure, Elizabeth?"

"Excellently!" said the duchess. "Maman would be
appalled."

Elizabeth had a lifetime of good behavior to overcome. As did Justin himself. "I believe, my darling,
that you must accompany us to the docks. Maman
would definitely not approve of that." He turned to
Conor. "I assume you're up to the challenge of getting
Gus out of this place with her reputation intact." Mr.
Stafford was thumping and straining and grimacing as
if he wished to be heard. "If nothing else, there are
other rugs."

Conor had been standing with his boot pressed
firmly down on Stafford's neck, alert lest the man
make a last-ditch effort at escape. Not that the
scoundrel was likely to get far before he was tripped up
by his own linen. "You may trust me," he said.

Justin looked from Conor to his cousin, who suddenly found the fireplace poker of great interest. "I
doubt that very much. However, be it on your head."

The footmen were called, the rug taken up, a furi-
ously reluctant cardsharper trussed up like a
missionary for the cannibals' pot. When the rug was
seen to wildly bounce about, Lady Augusta applied her
fireplace poker in the general vicinity of Mr. Stafford's
head. The rug went limp. The footmen hefted it up on
their shoulders and carried it away. The duchess followed, determined not to miss a moment's excitement.
The duke paused in the doorway. "I will speak with

you later, cousin!" he said sternly, and tossed Conor the key before he closed the door.

Gus watched Conor turn the key in the look. He looked especially Luciferish tonight, with his dark hair tousled, and his lazy eyes intent.

Perhaps he would turn her over his knee at last. Or throw her down on that large bed in the next room, and have his wicked way with her. More likely, he would do the honorable thing and take her home to Lady Syb. "I confess that I was frightened, just a little bit. But even more, I wanted to expose Stafford as a cheat. Your mother wasn't really a gambler, was she?" Gus said.

"No." Conor walked toward her. "We must add lying to my list of sins. My mother died of a putrid sore throat when I was but a year old. I was worried about what trouble you might get into, and therefore attempted to spin a cautionary tale."

Gus had been trying hard to get into trouble, but her companion stubbornly refused to cooperate. She frowned at him. "Don't even think about apologizing! In case you hadn't noticed, I still have Stafford's pistol in my hand."

So she had, and a maidservant's cap upon her head. It was an absurdly charming combination. Conor sat down beside her on the sofa. "I don't recall that I've ever before seduced a female wearing spectacles," he mused.

Gus scowled all the harder. "Don't make game of me!" she snapped.

Conor frowned in genuine puzzlement. "Why would I do that?"

Because she was a respectable cross-tempered spinster. Because he was the most wonderfully wicked man to ever walk the earth. "Why did you take me to gaming hells and introduce me to Jeremy?" Gus countered. "Not because Lady Syb asked you to, I think. You seldom do other than you please."

A gent might be damnably bubbled, if he ain't looking sharp. Conor was well and truly bubbled, and he found he didn't mind one bit. He plucked the silly spectacles off Gus's nose, and tossed them aside. "I didn't do other than I pleased."

Her fine eyebrows drew together as Gus struggled to make sense of this notion. Indeed, with Conor's body so close to hers it was difficult to make sense of anything at all.

Conor was relieved to see her put down the pistol. "I am an angry woman," she said, as if wishing to convince him. "Difficult. On the shelf."

"You are a darling." Conor reached up and discarded her cap. "And I am depraved beyond redemption, because I want you desperately even though I know I should not."

Gus tried to concentrate her thoughts, a task made even more difficult by the fact that Conor had brushed his lips over her knuckles, her fingertips, and was even now pressing a kiss into the palm of her bare hand. "What about all those other females?"

Conor paused to brush the hair back from her face. Her very stubborn, skeptical, and beloved face. He felt unusually awkward, his vast experience with the ladies useless now, for none of that experience had been with Gus. Or very little of it. A matter which he meant to quickly rectify. "I admit that I have kissed a great many females," he whispered, his breath warm against her ear. "Although I didn't realize it at the time, I was only practicing." A quick movement of his hand, and her apron followed her bonnet to the floor.

Gus drew back to look at him. There was a hint of doubt in his dark eyes, an unsure expression on his face. Could it be her lighthouse was also mizzy-mazed? She touched her fingers to the silver-streaked hair that had tumbled onto his forehead. "You said you didn't want to kiss me anymore."

Conor gave her a smile so sweet her heart almost stopped beating. "I never said such a crack-brained thing," he said, and drew her closer to him. "And if I did, I lied. I only refused to kiss you because I was trying to be noble. Unselfish. Allowing my conscience full rein. I must confess, sweeting, I didn't like it much."

Noble? Conor? What a horrid thought. "A fig for your conscience!" gasped Gus as his lips moved along the curve of her cheek to the corner of her mouth. "I would much rather you were bad."

Conor smiled against her lips. "I'm glad to hear it, my darling. For I'm certain that I've never seduced a chambermaid."

TWENTY-SEVEN

All the world was at Lady Ysabella's house, or at least that portion of the world that had been invited, which included several hundred of her closest friends. Prinny put in an appearance, and Brummel, and Alvanley, and Nit talked for quite a half hour with the Duke of Bedford about the conformation of various breeds of horses, thoroughbreds and Osdenburgs and Lippizaners, and what best to do for a swollen forelock. Since no one had told her Bedford was not married, and since Nit had spoken quite knowledgeably about the Andalusan mare he had just had brought from Spain, the duke was left with the impression that Miss Annette Slyte was a pretty-behaved and sensible young girl.

Lady Russell, whose own eyes had been opened on that matter, remarked to Lady Ysabella somewhat spitefully that it was a pity she hadn't gotten her niece off. Lady Syb, who knew more than anyone else in London about Lady Russell's history, including the fact that she had once been known as the Amazing Fennella, merely smiled and said it was early days yet, and she had every hope Annette might yet make a good match. At the suggestion that further favors might be required of her, Lady Russell went off in search of refreshments stronger than lemonade or orgeat.

An orchestra played in the background. Refreshments were set out in an adjoining room. In yet another chamber, the Dimber Dabber demonstrated various methods of cheating at cards to anyone who was interested, as a great many people were, and spoke at length of the maturity of the chances, and theories of probability. "The probabilities of throwing depend on the numbers of ways the totals can be made up by the dice," he said, as he watched Lady Augusta pass by on the arm of Conor Melchers, and wondered if it was for the sake of that worldly gentleman that she had dressed up like a chambermaid.

This evening's revels were in celebration of Mr. Nigel Slyte having gotten himself betrothed to Miss Abby Shaw, and Mr. Slyte had attired himself nattily in blue coat and pantaloons of stockinet strapped over varnished black shoes. His stockings were striped, as was his waistcoat, in a dazzling array of rainbow hues; his cravat arranged in the intricate Trone d'Amour. Miss Shaw was very prettily dressed in orange-striped and spotted silk; and if she was not quite so splendid as her fiancé, he told her, consider the male and female peacock. Since he also frequently quoted to her from the Song of Songs—hair like flocks of goats, temples like the halves of a pomegranate, bosom like two fawns—her cheeks were often flushed. Abby's brother Benjamin had been invited to the festivities, but, although he was delighted to hear of her good fortune, and sent her his best wishes, he had been prevented from attending by a case he was preparing to argue in court. Abby was relieved. She didn't think Benjie would care to hear her referred to as a palm tree, and her breasts its fruit.

The Duke and Duchess of Charnwood were currently the target of Nigel's profusions. "There is no doubt that we shall be happy as pigs in clover. 'At her feet he bowed, he fell, he lay down; at her feet he bowed, he fell.' In case you're wondering about our pig, he and Helen are in the kitchen, being regaled by the staff with earthworms and cauliflower and, at last report, a damson tart. Perhaps Cook may yet lose her temper, and chase him into the ballroom, where our Abbess will engage him in a country dance."

"Humbug," Abby said fondly. "Sir Edmond said I was only to have gentle exercise." Recollection of certain exercise undertaken with her fiancé, during which he had managed to count a great number of her freckles, caused her to turn pinker still.

Nigel touched one rosy cheek. "Will you miss your parsonage, oh my pearl of great price? We can organize a bell-ringing group, if you like. Or you could boil up a batch of soap. If you insist, I will read to you from the *Book of Common Prayer*."

He was looking at her with mild apprehension. Abby smiled at him. Life on earth might be unimportant, but she anticipated that it would also be most agreeable. " 'Slay me with flagons,' " she murmured, " 'comfort me with apples, for I am sick with love.' "

The laird of Dunally was present, also, with his lady. Duncan was not a poor man, for all he was frugal, and liked to have a hand in the running of things. Since he found himself in London, he decided he might as well enjoy the sights. So he had, both in public and in private, to his wife's great delight. Duncan wore conventional evening dress for the occasion, Cynthia not wishing her husband's magnificent legs to be put on such public view.

The laird was talking about sheep just now, specifically the outstanding mothering and milking qualities of Scottie ewes. And dinnae Cyn look bonnie in that silk dress made up in the MacDougall tartan, with twisted satin trim on her sleeves and hem, his great-great-great-grandmother's emerald and gold necklace hung around her throat? He pulled her to him and kissed her nose.

Lady Ratchett did not approve. Elizabeth's mama did not approve of Scotsmen in general, and kissing in public was simply not done. Or *shouldn't* be done, even if her own daughter was frequently guilty of that sin. Nor did Lady Ratchett approve of the various portions of her person that Elizabeth was displaying in a shocking dress of sea green sarcenet which clung so closely to her curves that her petticoats surely must have been dampened. A licentious style of dress was of certainty a token of like laxity in manners and conduct. It was all Charnwood's fault.

At Lady Ratchett's side, her husband was not half so critical. Sir Charles had been happy to indulge his stepdaughter by shipping off a certain parcel to Botany Bay. Now he was looking forward to meeting the Charnwood kittens. Lady Ratchett disliked felines. Sir Charles thought he might bring home two.

Lady Syb swooped down upon them. She was stunning in lilac silk and a great many diamonds, and carried a fan of pierced horn leaves. Lady Ratchett clucked disapprovingly at the sight of Conor Melchers.

"Conor and Augusta are going to make a match of it," Syb said.

Lady Ratchett knew Mr. Melchers' reputation. All London—nay, all England—must know Mr. Melchers' shocking reputation. "But he is a rakehell!"

"And Augusta is a gambler," countered Lady Syb. "They should do very well."

Whether Mr. Melchers and Lady Augusta would do well together was a question that was also occupying the Lord of Charnwood, for Conor had just asked Justin for his cousin's hand. "As well as the rest of her," Conor added, with a rakish twinkle. "In case there was any doubt."

Justin glanced at his cousin, who was speaking with Elizabeth. Gus wore a dress of white crinkled silk spotted with white satin, the bodice made of faux black velvet, with black silk roses and leaves forming two large bands around the hem. Her hair was drawn up in a double chignon that ended in ringlets. She looked not the least bit cross tonight, but smug as a cat who'd licked the cream pot dry.

Compromised wasn't the half of it, thought Justin. Not that he cared to know the details. Still, he couldn't throw her to the wolves. Or wolf. "How do you mean to keep her away from the tables?" he inquired.

Never had Conor looked more irresistibly wicked. "I shall introduce her to the pleasures of strip piquet."

The orchestra played merrily. People strolled, and chatted, and danced. Nit thought she must be the only person in this entire gay crowd who wasn't having a good time. (In truth, she wasn't, but Annette had managed to avoid Lady Ratchett thus far.) Lord Ormesby seemed unable to say anything other than that he was relieved no real harm had resulted from the mishap with his team, and had stumbled all over himself attempting to tell Abby he was glad she was all right; while Sir Frances muttered at equal length about how only a dunderhead would let a female take the reins.

Lord Ormesby reached the limits of his tolerance. "And only a jackass would keep harping on the subject!" he snapped.

Mr. Harcourt set down his wineglass to applaud. "Oh, I say!" The gentlemen then went on to discuss the points of a filly up for sale at Tattersall's.

Maybe Nit would go into a monastery. Or sink into a decline. Being an aunt was all very well and good, but aunts didn't get to cuddle gentlemen. And if her spirits hadn't been already blighted, what must her brother do but warn her against becoming an astonishment, a proverb, and a byword. Chastisement by scorpions was also mentioned.

As Nit was wondering how scorpions might chastise a person, a stir swept through the rooms. Nit craned her neck to see Viscount Daventry make an entrance. He was not alone. A curly headed and freshly scrubbed child clung to each hand.

The boys looked rebellious. The viscount looked harassed. "The tutor quit, the nursery maid is in hysterics, and the entire kitchen staff is on the verge of rebellion," said Lady Syb, as she materialized at Nit's elbow. "I knew Duke wouldn't wish to miss our little celebration, so I suggested he allow his household to settle while he brought the twins to us."

Nit's pretty mouth dropped open as she watched the viscount's progress through the crowded room. She was hardly unaccustomed to children, having younger siblings of her own. None of her siblings were so ill-behaved as to bite hands that reached out to pat them, however, or kick at anyone within reach. Unbeknownst to her, Nit was in agreement with Lady Ratchett, who claimed that young people should be seen and not heard, except in the case of Viscount Daventry, whose young people should be locked away somewhere until they reached a civilized age. "They will be handsome when they grow up," said Lady Syb. "Like their papa but without the crooked nose."

True enough that the noses beneath the identical mops of auburn curls were straight. Straight noses, however, were not nearly enough to recommend such *enfants terrible*. "I don't believe," said Nit, "that I wish to see them until then."

"If you marry the viscount, you will have to see them," Lady Syb pointed out, as one of the twins deliberately tripped a servant carrying a refreshment tray. "Several times a day. You will be their mama, and thereby expected to become very closely acquainted indeed. Oversee their lessons, and their deportment, play games with them, and read them bedtime stories, and heaven knows what else. The viscount believes in a hands-on style of parenting." Hands on the brats' posteriors might be helpful, thought Nit, as one of the boys stepped on a lady's lace ruffle, and looked proud to hear it tear.

"How good of you to bring your sons, Duke!" said Lady Syb. "My niece has expressed a desire to meet them. Amos, Evan, make your bow to Miss Annette Slyte."

Neither child obeyed. "Don't want to!" said one, while the other enlarged upon that sentiment by adding the words "fubsy-faced female."

Fubsy-faced, indeed! Nit looked down her little nose at the monsters, who she thought must be about seven years of age.

The viscount released one young hellion long enough to bend over Nit's hand. "I regret that you have decided we would not suit," he murmured.

Nit didn't believe she had said precisely that. Her memory being what it was, perhaps she had. Not that she cared to quibble. One of the twins—Amos, she thought—developed a fascination with a nearby ostrich feather, and the viscount released her to grab his offspring by the scruff of the neck. "Pray excuse me!" stammered Nit, and fled.

Several people had been privy to this little scene. "That was damned clever," said Nigel. How did you persuade the poppets to do their very worst?"

"As a rule they don't need persuading," admitted the viscount. His offspring fidgeted. "However, in this instance, I told them they might meet a pig."

"Wheesht! What a pair of fearsome nackets!" said Duncan with admiration, Scotsmen not being prone to regard innate bloodthirst with as much dismay as their more civilized counterparts. "Come away now, and we'll take you to the grand fellow." Awed into unusual compliance by this copper-headed giant who managed to look half savage even in evening dress, the boys allowed themselves to be led off. Cynthia was heard suggesting that they might like to play Knights of the Round Table. A scuffle resulted; both wanted to be king. Cyn pointed out that King Arthur had been slain in battle. Both boys promptly demanded to be the one who slew him. They were quarrelling as they left the room.

Duke removed Lady Syb's champagne glass from her hand, and drank it dry. The viscount looked uncharacteristically disheveled tonight, his clothing slightly rumpled, as was his auburn hair.

He met her amused glance. "All this because I don't know how to dote," he said.

"My dear Duke." Lady Syb tucked her arm through his. "It is never too late to learn."

Nit passed through the refreshment room. At least maybe in a monastery she might wear a color other than white. Not that Nit wasn't grateful to Aunt Syb for this pretty dress with its embroidered leaf border, because of course she was. She only wished that she might dunk it, and the rest of her wardrobe, into a vat of brightly colored dye. But then she could grow weary of that color also, would she not?

It was all a puzzle. Nit wandered up to Lady Augusta, who was talking to a gentleman she didn't know. Mr. Melchers stood to one side with the Duke and Duchess of Charnwood. They seemed to be discussing marriage settlements. Mr. Melchers didn't want one. The duke insisted. The duchess seemed more interested in piquet.

"I hit him over the head with a fireplace poker," said Gus. "And tied him up with his cravats. Then my cousin bundled him up in a carpet and took him to the docks." The rest of the experience, including how Conor had soundly seduced her and then smuggled her out of the Mapleton wrapped in nothing but a blanket, she didn't think her visitor needed to hear.

"My father wished me to tell you that we are forever in your debt, and he didn't know the half of it." Willy glanced around the crowded chambers. "I'm sorry to interrupt. I've just come back to town."

"No one is in my debt. I did what I did as much for myself as for you." Gus felt a presence at her elbow, and turned to see Nit regarding Willy with interest. At the sight of her, he looked stunned.

Nit eyed him up and down. She saw a well-made man in his early twenties, brown-haired and hazel-eyed, with a face not handsome but pleasant all the same. Above all, he looked *comfortable.* "I am Annette Slyte," she said. "My family calls me Nit, because I am a featherhead."

Willy collected himself sufficiently to clasp the hand that she extended to him, and raised it to his lips. "You are beautiful, Miss Slyte." He blushed. "Pray forgive my forwardness. I shouldn't have said that."

"Whyever not?" Nit's mood was improving by the moment. "I don't suppose, sir, that you are a duke or an earl? If I am to marry, and not enter a monastery—and the more I think of it, the less I like the notion; but I'm not sure either that I wish to be an aunt; not that I have a choice because Cynthia is increasing, and my eldest sister already has a large number of children—I must have a title, alas."

Willy regarded her with bedazzled fascination. "Why is that?"

"Tiaras," Gus interjected, before Nit could further muddy the waters. "Younger sisters. The usual sort of thing. Annette, allow me to introduce you to William Drakelow, Marquess of Chilcote. His papa is the Duke of Eldroth."

Nit's eyes widened. She giggled enchantingly. "I've made a cake of myself again."

"Yes," said Gus.

"No," protested Willy, in the same moment. "I'm

pleased to have a title, Miss Annette, if that's what you require."

Nit tilted her golden head to one side. "A title is not *all* that I require, alas. I don't suppose that you have a great deal of wealth."

Willy didn't even blink. "My family does."

Titled, wealthy, *and* comfortable. Nit beamed at him. "Do you have horses? Would you let me drive your team?"

"I have many horses," said Willy. "And you may drive any or all of them, in whatever configuration you wish."

"Jupiter!" Nit dimpled. "You must come and meet Aunt Syb."

ABOUT THE AUTHOR

Maggie MacKeever lives in Los Angeles. She's currently working on her next Zebra Regency romance, which will be published in November 2004. Maggie loves to hear from readers and you may write to her c/o Zebra Books. Please include a self-addressed stamped envelope if you wish a response.

BOOK YOUR PLACE ON OUR WEBSITE
AND MAKE THE
READING CONNECTION!

We've created a customized website just for our very special readers, where you can get the inside scoop on everything that's going on with Zebra, Pinnacle and Kensington books.

When you come online, you'll have the exciting opportunity to:

- View covers of upcoming books
- Read sample chapters
- Learn about our future publishing schedule (listed by publication month *and author*)
- Find out when your favorite authors will be visiting a city near you
- Search for and order backlist books from our online catalog
- Check out author bios and background information
- Send e-mail to your favorite authors
- Meet the Kensington staff online
- Join us in weekly chats with authors, readers and other guests
- Get writing guidelines
- AND MUCH MORE!

Visit our website at
http://www.kensingtonbooks.com

More Regency Romance
From Zebra

Embrace the Romance of
Shannon Drake

__Knight Triumphant
    0-8217-6928-6 $6.99US/$9.99CAN

__Seize the Dawn
    0-8217-6773-9 $6.99US/$8.99CAN

__Come the Morning
    0-8217-6471-3 $6.99US/$8.99CAN

__Conquer the Night
    0-8217-6639-2 $6.99US/$8.99CAN

__Blue Heaven, Black Night
    0-8217-5982-5 $6.50US/$8.00CAN

__The King's Pleasure
    0-8217-5857-8 $6.50US/$8.00CAN

Available Wherever Books Are Sold!

Visit our website at **www.kensingtonbooks.com**.